About the Author

In the mid nineteen seventies Jennifer (Jen) Green saw a gravestone and became a writer. Born in Hampshire at the start of a second world war, she is one of the six children. After a basic secondary education she worked for Boots the Chemist before joining the Women's Royal Naval Service attached to the Fleet Air Arm. On leaving the service her career progressed through mechanical engineering into senior posts in university and arts administration in London. This was followed by a move into executive management at the Family Planning Association which helped shape her humorous approach to life.

Three years later she discovered the gravestone of Mary Morgan a sixteen-year-old servant girl hanged in 1805 for murder. Obsessed with her plight, Jen left the Home Counties for the Welsh Border, and set about researching the awful tale. Later she became a freelance reporter and feature writer eventually leaving the day job to concentrate on writing full time. Her first book *The Morning of Her Day* published in 1987 and a second edition in 1990. It was later optioned by Scott Free and a screenplay developed. Jen continues to research and write, her last published novel *What Ever Happened to Trixie Skryme* is based on the life of the most dangerous and unscrupulous adventuress Scotland Yard had ever set out to capture in the early 20th century,
Jen currently lives in Leominster, North Herefordshire and if she ever gets the time can be found at the cinema, watching cricket, writing poetry and exercising her sense of humour with her chums.

DEDICATED TO
JOAN TINGEY-ROBERTS
"MY BEST FRIEND IN ALL THE WORLD"
FOR OVER 50 YEARS

AND IN MEMORY OF MY BROTHER
ARTHUR GREEN

JANUARY 1932 – MAY 2015

Jennifer Green

A Small Nuclear Fallout

Betty B

Best wishes.

Jennifer Green

12/3/2017

Austin Macauley
PUBLISHERS LTD.

A CIP catalogue record for this title is available from the British Library.

ISBN 9781786127082 (Paperback)
ISBN 9781786127099 (Hardback)
ISBN 9781786127105 (E-Book)

www.austinmacauley.com

First Published (2016)
Austin Macauley Publishers Ltd.
25 Canada Square
Canary Wharf
London
E14 5LQ

Cover artwork - "Spanish House" by Pauline Vincent. Villafranca 2007.

This is a work of fiction. Names and places are entirely fictional, any resonance to real characters is coincidental.

Much Thanks to

Sarah Boston
Jennie Braithwaite
Anita Corbin – O'Grady
Johnny, Penny and Sam Green
Peter Logan
Sue Newbould.
Gill Tew.
For their continuing support, friendship and laughter.
Special thanks to
Pauline Vincent
for just being there.
The One Stop Print Shop & Computer Knowledge
Leominster
For their practical help.

'Dory'
The cat who sits on the mouse
mat as I write.

Finally
We must never forget the courage of the women of
Greenham Common.

Chapter One

The marble, chrome and glass architecture at Barcelona Airport's central concourse reflected far more arrivals than accounted for. Armed, half-threatening, police officers watched over the small groups of travellers as they passed through the exits to the rows of taxis and buses lined up outside the main concourse. It had been a good flight from Bristol; Go-Fly had lived up to expectations; fast, efficient and just five minutes over scheduled arrival time. Outside the heat came as a sudden shock to the late autumn chill the two English women had left behind and they wearily coped with their baggage on the way to the adjacent railway station.

Destined for Villafranca, some 50 kilometres away, connections had to be checked and meeting points arranged and the station cafeteria provided the ideal place to take a breather and check out travel details. Clean and simple it offered the Spanish equivalent of York ham baps, and, more important, much needed coffee after the water only flight recommended to ward off headline hitting deep vein thrombosis warnings.

Dee Donnington knew her way around Barcelona. She occasionally flew to the city to watch AFC Barcelona play soccer. A keen football fan since late childhood, Dee was a long-standing Tottenham Hotspur supporter and despite the ups and downs of his soccer career, she still rated Terry Venables the best ever.

Happily refreshed, Janet, the more practical of the two friends, made the phone calls and sent Dee to sort out the platform for the Villafranca connection. Boarding was not easy; their heavy bags needed lifting up a few steps and with a big effort they just about managed to climb on board.

Settling into their seats they kept a watching eye on the luggage stacked nearby noting each station until they reached Barcelona Santa. Another muscle-pulling struggle down onto the platform did little to improve their stiff and creaking bones but after a short wait the Villafranca train arrived.

Much to their relief, a kindly Spanish mother with six strong teenagers in tow, helped hoist the bags on board and it was a pleasure just to sit and look out of the wide windows to watch the graffiti decorated Barcelona suburbs disappear into stunning the Cataluña countryside. Dee was particularly delighted to see it was vineyards and vineries most of the way, and champagne quality at that.

"I always fancied myself as a bit of a 'Champagne Charlene' in my dotage, Jan. How about you?" she asked.

"Can't say I gave it much thought, dotage or not. Diabetes and alcohol mean more hours on wasted peeing, but I'm prepared to give it a go if you are" she replied with a grin. "Anyway, we're supposed to be here for Angela and help her sort her Spanish inheritance, not boozing on the grape."

Dee nodded. "I still can't get over it. Who'd have thought Daphne Oxbridge harboured a Spanish lover for all these years and I have been wondering what else we might turn up at their rural hideaway. It's no wonder she greeted us with 'Viva Espana' whenever she returned from her Continental adventures," Dee added, her raucous laughter catching the other passengers off guard.

The clickety-clack of the wheels and the warm sunlight streaming through the windows encouraged a comforting drowsiness, despite the air-conditioned carriage and within minutes they had both nodded off.

Janet Bodmin, Dee Donnington and Angela Anderson-Shelta first met in Mid-Wales. Jan, keen to continue with her research into the myths and rumours of the Welsh Border, had rented a small cottage in the border town of Lugworth-upon-Usk.

Caught up in and enjoying her new way of life, she decided to go for broke; chucking in her Home Counties life style and comfortable income, she pitched her metaphorical tent and stayed put.

The weeks became months; the months became years and in time Jan was quietly welcomed into the strange little community, eventually becoming one of them. It wasn't long before she was persuaded to stand for the Mid-Border District Council, taking the vacant seat unopposed and it was her local Government connections which brought about her long and committed friendship with Dee, who, by then was a 'half way up the ladder' broadcast journalist with BBC Wales. The third link in the friendship was Angela Anderson–Shelta, faithful but exasperated wife of the Chief Executive of the Mid-Border District Council.

When they first met, the three women were awaiting the anticipated mid-life crises; they never came, except for Dee. Working freelance on a small town parochial weekly in South Shropshire she crossed the ambitious News Editor, menopausal mad Felicity Carp, and told her to get a life. She didn't but Dee did and she soon rose to the top like the cream on a bottle of full milk.

Together again for an unscheduled autumn break, twenty years had flashed by since they first hooked up with each other and much water had flowed under the bridge. Each had, for whatever reason, moved on, but despite promising to ease their increasingly busy lives, they had bonded enough to always stay in touch and usually met up half a dozen or so times a year for a bit of a beano. It was a friendship that made space to flourish, and it did. Watered regularly by good memories and mutual encouragement it was a spirited, warm and caring union of three very different lives. The unexpected get together in Spain came after Angela had tossed an unexplained bouncer into their close friendship.

Casually mentioning that the lover of her late Aunt Daphne, who had died almost 4 years before at the ripe old age of 83, had left Angela the 17th century Spanish love nest they had shared for almost 40 years she needed to meet with the executors in Villafranca. It had been specifically left to Angela and any female heirs and shocked to hear that her dotty old Aunt had a longstanding lover, she talked it over with her two friends rather than her estranged partner. Still married but living a separate and contented life from her husband, Anthony, out of courtesy to the deceased, she dropped everything and drove to Spain to meet the family lawyer. At the time Jan and Dee had offered to travel with her but she declined, believing that it was important she meet the aristocrat Spanish family for the first time by herself.

She had no idea of the content of the inheritance and throughout the drive across Europe she pondered on what it might be? She knew it was some sort of dwelling; a small cottage perhaps or maybe a converted vinery, but whatever it was; it had brought a new dimension to Daphne and her seemingly eccentric and sheltered life. Above all else, Angela knew her much loved godmother would have wished her to pay last respects. Deciding to make it a worthwhile trip, she ignored her husband's suggestion that she was 'a bloody fool' for attempting it by road instead of flying' she chose the endless motorways through France and Southern Spain. From the moment she left Plymouth for the long drive through France into Spain she tried to recall a little clue or hint that might hold the key to her Aunt's love affair.

After connecting with the N240 to Tarragona where she made a second overnight stop, she took the N340 coastal road to Sitges and cut inland to Villafranca.

She had arranged to meet Senor Jose de Cabolet, the familia el abogado (family lawyer) at his stylishly refurbished offices in the town square; he was on his feet and bowing from the waist the moment she entered the room. Greeting her warmly but with due respect, he offered no explanation for the unexpected inheritance or even hinted as to what it might be. Inviting her to be seated he called for his assistant advocate Senor Garcia.

"Necesito una fotocopia de esto" (I need a photo copy of this) he ordered and in a flash it was done. Briefly scanning the document which had been transcribed into English, he handed it to Angela. She read it calmly and carefully her heart beat increasing with each paragraph and when she had finished, she looked quizzically at Senor Cabot. He nodded back with a wry smile.

"My Aunt's lover was the Senora Consuela de la Barca of Castellvi?" she questioned.

"Si Senora," he replied. "Por Favor La familia esperar usted at the Castilla," and he left the room, leaving his English speaking assistant to fully explain that the Senora's family were waiting for her at the

Castle to show her the premises. Escorting her across the square to her hotel, Senor Cabot instructed her to "Please find your way there within the hour's drive and be assured all is well. Your Aunta very fine woman for the Senora," he said with a grin. A hint of the effeminate gave enough of the game away for Angela to paint the full picture for herself.

The drive through Cava country caused more of a rumble than a stir among the grape pickers; the shiny metallic silver grey car threw up a flurry of dust as Angela skirted the rows of vines waiting to be relieved of an abundance of grapes. Across the ripe fields she could see a magnificent castle on the hillside and muttered;

"Heaven knows, Aunt Daphers, just what you've been up to all these years but it's going to be fun finding out. Just wait until Dee and Janet see this – par favor."

Eight weeks had passed since Angela finally took over the unbelievable and beautiful house on the Baca Castellvi estate. Everyone on the estate had been very co-operative during the legalities insisting she was now one of the 'famili' and she was made to feel most welcome. Nevertheless the first visit had been nerve-racking, so many cousins, aunts and children of all ages and for a childless, only child it was overwhelming and or a while she was left alone to settle in and make her own mark on the place and eventually show it off to her friends. Indebted to Janet and Dee for finding the time to visit, she was waiting for them at Villafranca station on the platform below the footbridge. They had both known Daphne for some years and she was fond of them both; they were equally fond of her. Like Angela they too were amazed by the revelations of a secret liaison and with the help of a splendid wine cellar and some good memories, Angela hoped to lift the lid on a Pandora's Box that once was the real Daphne Oxbridge.

Some ten years in age stretched between the three of them; Dee Donnington the youngest of the trio. She had not yet retired and was still Katie Adie-ing it on national television, although she was more inclined these days to drop the travelling and opt for her own news show. However, despite the September 11 atrocity in New York and the news coverage which accompanied such awful tragedy, especially the possibility of war, she put friendship first and took leave to be with her friends. Dee was particularly close to fun-loving Janet Bodmin, now turned sixty. She had taken early retirement from the day job in the Home Counties eight years ago but was busier than ever writing and researching local history, and doing the rounds on the after dinner speaking circuit. With a bit of planning she had managed to rearrange her schedules and travel to Spain with Dee. The three friends knew that, for each other, they would be 'off at the drop of a hat' and to hell with the consequences.

Angela watched her friends stagger across the footbridge and laughed up at them.

"I'll get the bath chair oiled next time, there's an old wicker one up at the house." she said. "For God's sake, what have you got in those bags?"

"Memories old girl and a couple of bottles of Chivas Regal" Dee yelled back. "They tell me it's what the expats drink to loosen the tongue and watch the sun go down. Pretty good I'd say for recalling old times and you can skip the bath chair routine if you don't mind."

Carefully lowering her much-used battered pigskin travel bag – Lilywhites of course – onto the last step, Dee wrapped her arms around Angela and kissed her heartily on the mouth.

"None of this continental air kissing nonsense for us, right Janet?" she called back.

Janet smiled warmly and said, "Really lovely to be with you, Angie," and kissed her with matching enthusiasm.

Angela was made up to think that this time, it was not a flying visit and they were staying for a week or two; she also knew Dee was keen to see Barcelona play in a European championship match. Greetings over and done with, they carried the luggage between them and loaded up the car. Angela made sure she handled Dee's bag very carefully.

"Better get this safely home if it's got the Chivas on board. We can have a spot of lunch in town before driving to the house."

Café de la Rambla, quiet at siesta time, was almost empty and provided the perfect place for a light lunch and couple of hours catch up. They were well into the second bottle of Torres Vina Sol when Dee, having consumed most of it, got down to the nitty gritty.

"We know what it is, where it is and how old it is – the cottage I mean, but how about the low down on the lover. Who was she and what are the in-laws like, pav favor?"

"Cut it out, Dee," Janet said. "I told you, Angie; she's been at the Spanish lessons ever since she heard the news, splashing out on cappuccinos, and spluttering ole, gracias and beunas nochas on the mobile for the last five bloody weeks."

"Let's get her home before she starts on the waiter with come on you Spurs, el Tel for Spanish ambassador."

"Best we should, before she does something we, not she, will regret," Janet replied. "Thanks for the lunch,

Ange. Come on, Dee; let's see what good old Daphne has been up to all these years."

Dee hauled herself up to her full five feet-ten. "Who's driving, dear heart, me or you?"

"Don't even think about it, Dee," Angela challenged. "This is my car, my roads, and for now, my country and after eight weeks I now know the quick way to my home."

That said Dee winked at the attractive waitress, pressed a large tip into her surprisingly soft hands and stood up.

Angela drove steadily as she manoeuvred her way through the Vilafranca traffic watched by an admiring Janet. "You've certainly mastered the left hand drive. Is it tricky?"

"At first yes, the left hand gets a bit confused to begin with but I have driven on the continent before, when Tony would let me without doing his 'Jesus Christ, the edge woman, you're too close to the bloody edge!' There were times I wanted the passenger door to fly open and drop him out."

"Still a pain in the arse then is he?" Dee muttered from the back seat, "I thought the widow Tremlett would have sorted him out by now."

"Oh she has, Dee," Angela replied. "He spends most of his time with her these days, she's all but moved in to the Rectory since the Hugh debacle."

"Heart attack wasn't it?" Dee asked.

"Not surprised are you, Dee? After all it was your mob drove him to it with all that 'the sixth man Russian spy stuff' someone raked up to sell newspapers," Janet reminded her.

"Not my lot, Jan, tabloids not TV. I was invited to comment on 'Newsnight', declined though, bit too close to home. Not too keen on being cross-examined by the lovely Jeremy – Paxman, not Vine, he's a bit of a sweetie. I could go for him if I wasn't batting for the other side. Mind you, bit of a shocker for poor old Ruth when she found out; still she finally got Anthony off your back."

Angela smiled. "Yes and eventually onto his, she was a bit of a goer I believe. Fair play though I'm still rather fond of the old goat and distance can be a good thing. He loves his golf and the Lodge, and she fronts up well on Ladies' Nights, but he would never give up the Old Rectory for love nor money. As for me I'm far happier back home in Hampshire where I grew up. Money isn't a problem and I paid off Tony's mortgage before I finally left. He's got a damn good pension to live on and Ruth to do for him."

"In more ways than one," Dee announced, "What say you, Janet?"

"I sometimes see him in Hereford in the Green Dragon having lunch with his old local Government cronies. He hasn't changed much. Still asks me 'if you're going to Greenham Common do give my best to the wife' and laughs himself silly. For all his faults you can't help liking the man."

Dee suddenly shot up. "But what a bloody shambles he made of that defence exercise back in the eighties. Talk about fallout, it was the biggest cock-up in Welsh political history and you Cllr Ms Bodmin, was on the Council which gave him bloody carte blanche."

"And you set the cat among the pigeons trying to bluff your way into a news story," Jan retorted. "All because of a bit of pillow chat with the doctor's daughter from the Welsh Office. As for you Mrs Anderson-Shelta, you got yourself involved, too!"

"Don't remind me, Jan. I was the bored wife of the Chief Executive with a dotty Aunt, who insisted on camping out at Greenham Common with us just when Anthony's defence exercise was about to kick off."

"It was more nuclear farce than nuclear defence, Jan," Dee said. "It was you who got herself elected to his Council in the first place."

"Yes! I know and I will never be allowed to forget it. I was there at the beginning, middle and end of the bedlam caused by your husband's chaotic attempt at nuclear law and disorder. One day Lugworth will be carved on my headstone, just like Elizabeth the First at Calais. Whenever I pass the District Council Offices

I shudder at the thought of what happened in that dark gloomy Chamber.

"It was the early eighties," Dee said. "Government cash to build underground nuclear fallout shelters was up for grabs, defence exercises came with the package and most local authorities took advantage. Despite Lugworth being a small District Council the MP pulled a good few strings and your ex managed to swing a pot of gold, so to speak. Like barn conversions these exercises were happening in rural areas across the country."

Angela shrugged her shoulders. "True enough, but Lugworth was more an off the cuff pantomime without a director rather than a well-rehearsed stage show. Still it did happen and we live to tell the tale.

Chapter Two

At the turn of the nineteen-eighties the Council Chamber of the Mid Border District Council was large, airy and predominately masculine. Light oak panels reached to a point halfway up the walls and above these, including the ceiling, the decorative plaster work washed in a variety of soft pastel coloured emulsion paint. Originally chosen to promote quiet meditation during the regular periods of boredom during Council meetings, today it appeared faded and well-aged. Not unlike most of the sitting Councillors. Hanging from the picture rails in strict date order, the dust-covered portraits of past Chairmen of Council watched over the meetings. Some were painted oils on canvas, others photographs in sepia, black and white and Kodak colour. Every smug pose told beaten contenders, "I made it, you didn't."

At the front of the room on an elevated platform furnished with a heavy, carved oak table and matching chair sat the current Chairman, Councillor Thomas, Tomo to his friends at the Welsh Club. Ranked in order of precedence alongside him the Council officers, a motley crew of part academic, part 'I did it my way,' former grammar school boys smiled a smile of anticipation. They shared three things in common; the Lodge, the golf club and a collective obsession to become the next Chief Executive Officer of the Mid Border District Council; an achievement the present, comfortably placed, sitting tenant, would stonewall to the bitter end, and they knew it.

Anthony Anderson-Shelta was well established in post and smoother than a baby's bum. Welsh by birth right and ancestry but very much English in all else, he oozed charm like an uncontrollable tube of toothpaste whenever the occasion required it. He was local Government through and through; it was embedded like the letters running through a stick of Rhyl rock. However, he took his civic duties very seriously often recording his finer moments in office with greater detail than any university archivist could ever document. At dinner parties he had total recall to the point of utter boredom. His televised endeavours as Returning Officer on election night when he almost succeeded at being the first in the UK to announce the result, was a dead cert to sour not only the cream, but also the entire evening. Politically, his leanings bent so far to the right it had been rumoured among the local and national press that he was once seen at the Cenotaph in Whitehall on Remembrance Sunday adjusting his poppy in the shine on the Gucci shoes worn by his friend Crispin Davenport-Jones, Conservative Member of Parliament for the Mid-Border and Usk Valley constituency. However, today, on what was to become the usual non-momentous event in the life of the Mid Border District Council, the Chairman, Chief Executive, and departmental officers came face to face with the elected members. It was taken as read that all they needed to know was that anything relating to matters farming, land deals and EEC grants went through on the nod and places on Quangos were usually dished out like sweets at pre-meeting drink sessions in the Chairman's hospitality room. They, too, usually went through on a second nod, but when it came to matters important to the community, like setting the rate, housing the homeless, parks and cemeteries, estimates and budgets it was a different matter. These were matters for officers to decide not the elected members and undemocratic as they may be, these arrangements suited everyone nicely. The only word ever to cause an officer of the Council a problem was expenses; not theirs they were competently and speedily dealt with but those handed out to the members. Items on the agenda such as attendance allowance, travelling, car mileage and subsistence guaranteed the most dull of mind to break into bloom like a belated daffodil suddenly realising that spring was almost over and it was about to miss out on Mother's Day. But today was different.

Meetings of full Council took place in a horseshoe arrangement with members seated in official order of merit generally based upon golf handicap, sheep sales figures or longest political career. There was no party split, all but three of the serving members were predominately male 'Independents' divided up into three categories; elderly well off farmers, retired high ranking ex-service officers and those 'in trade.' Each and every one unconditionally committed in the first instance to getting the best for themselves and then for the small rural communities they served. Of the three women Councillors one had little to say and voted as directed by her male associates, another was middle-aged widow, strictly chapel, and a working farmer who actually cared for her community; and then there was Janet Bodmin! A newcomer to the Council, she had taken the by-election at Lugworth-upon-Usk unopposed some eight months previous. Janet Bodmin's strong personality harboured a broad feminist overview which committed her to rocking the Council's boat now and again and in the eyes of the local press, in particular the Border and Usk Valley

Express, she was decidedly newsworthy and well worth a 'listen'. Silently respected by the hardened local hacks eager for the Chairman to 'wrap up' the agenda before closing time, she was worth a drink or two from out of pocket expenses.

At the top table Anthony Anderson-Shelta was in close conversation with Mrs Ruth Tremlett, his minute secretary; she was also the Chief Executive's personal assistant, private secretary and informer grade one. Ruth was in her forties, her rampant sexuality hidden under the stylish clothes for the fuller figure 'run-up' for her by a clever little woman up the valley. For some years she had been dallying in a yet to be consummated romantic liaison with her Chief while her husband, a Naval Commander on attachment to the Foreign Office, worked overseas. Occasionally she allowed a hint of her ample cleavage to catch the eye of the Chairman as she leaned across the table to retrieve her rubber. However, this morning it was to prove too much for him. Her elevated bosom brushed his arm and he went weak at the knees, his stifled coughing allowing him to escape from the chamber for a quick breather and a stiff drink in his hospitality room. The decision did not go unnoticed by the Chief Executive who cast a raised eyebrow towards his paramour. She smiled back in a compensatory manner which offered him the promise of an evening later that week. Official and daily papers rustled expectantly as the possibility of the meeting coming to an early close. Sensing the meeting was over, at the back of the room the local reporters and the odd freelance stringer pocketed their note books and pens and arranged to meet up in "The Lazy Poacher" for a swift pint and a spot of lunch, expenses permitting. The anticipation of a pint of good Welsh ale slipping down the throat was already having a heady effect on the press gallery as they muttered over the latest rumours concerning infidelity among the officer ranks of the Town Hall personnel, Housing Officer excluded. He was already sailing close to the wind with offers of new fire places in exchange for a bit on the side with the economically depressed single mothers living on the Council's poorer housing estates.

During the idle gossip Dee (Debra) Donnington, the ambitious journalist from the local radio station and occasional contributor on television's 'Mid-Wales on Air,' had slipped out of her seat and left the chamber; it was her turn to get the first round in. The others were about to join her when the Chairman, face flushed not from embarrassment, but from the quick breather he'd taken earlier, returned to his chair. Looking around the room he pointedly studied the sea of faces and unexpectedly stood up; it was a rare moment for press and public alike. The rustle of papers and idle chit chat suddenly ceased; Tomo Thomas had never been known to stand and address his colleagues before.

He was a once-sat-down, he stayed sat down man, excepting of course for the Welsh national anthem which, sobriety permitting, he managed to rise for the occasion. Puffing out his ample chest and adjusting his horn rimmed spectacles he addressed the meeting in the sonorous tones of a Welsh Baptist lay preacher in full flow preparing to raise Lazarus from the dead at the umpteenth attempt.

"Well that concludes the meeting proper, gentlemen." He hadn't yet adjusted, despite ten years of trying, to cope with the lady members, as he liked to call them. "Oh ... err ... and ladies. Now is there any other business before we come to a special item the Chief Executive wishes to preamble upon?"

Heavy eyelids popped open and agendas studied intently; the press corps looked at each other quizzically, sighed and withdrew their note books from deep jacket pockets. The seasoned reporter from the Usk Courier leaned back to address his opposite number from the County Express seated behind him.

"Bad sign this, Johnno, must be something in the wind if he is on his toes then."

"As long as he doesn't go on till closing time," Johnno replied without moving his lips.

Ignoring the comment, the Chairman carried on regardless. "Thank you, gentlemen, err and ladies. Right then, it's over to you Mr Anderson-Shelta."

The Chief Executive rose from his seat with the exaggerated ease of a man with something up his sleeve. He was tall and imposing which may have been the reason he was accepted for national service at the Mons Officer Cadet School in Aldershot. He had tried hard to find an occupation that would exempt him from national service intruding into his well-planned career but accountancy didn't qualify. Nevertheless he enjoyed the social standing that officer status gave him and revelled in a uniform that enhanced his good looks, particularly the 'mess undress' worn on special occasions. When recommended, he eagerly took up the six-year commission with the Army Education Corps because it also provided a place at college to continue his studies in public accounting and management.

Anthony made the most of his time in the army, even taking private elocution lessons with a well-qualified woman in nearby Farnborough Park. This had two major benefits for the young officer; his part hidden Welsh accent was brushed away without regret and at the same time he met his future wife Angela, the only daughter of Brigadier Dudley Plunkett-Brown of the Parachute

Division Royal Horse Artillery. Held in great affection by his men, the Brigadier, 'Plunk' to his troopers, was expecting promotion to higher office; his extraordinary feat during the invasion of Suez in 1956 had been 'mentioned in dispatches' and in the London Gazette. However, in some quarters the Military Cross he was later awarded was considered over the top by one or two paper-pushing Generals. After completing his national service with distinction, Anthony had, society wise, struck gold and his father-in-law to be was much impressed by the young officer who relentlessly pursued his only daughter. His eventual marriage to Angela Plunkett-Brown augured well for his future prospects and his career was set fair. Today as he stood to address the meeting, Ruth Tremlett looked him up and down with the eye of one who knew the body almost as well as the man. She found him very stimulating on two levels; the first was quite simply a sexual challenge once she could persuade him to stop the foreplay and get on with it. The other was a little more complicated. Anthony was her chance to reach out for promotions beyond her wildest dreams, perhaps even to thinking about turning her thoughts to Westminster and standing for the Mid Border and Usk seat. But at this precise moment she had but one item on her mind, the bombshell, if she dared call it that, her beloved Chief was about to drop upon the peaceful calm of the Mid Border district. His slightly breathless "thank you, Chairman" brought her back to reality and a glow of excitement flushed across her cleavage as her beloved prepared for the fray. Anderson-Shelta met the moment head on. Clearing his throat he casually leaned upon the table lectern and addressed the gathering. His voice gave no hint of what was to come; he needed no notes and knew that he had the rapt attention of the entire chamber.

"Ladies and gentlemen, this will take some time and may spill over into the afternoon session." He paused and waited for the expected groans from press, public and the restless Councillors before continuing. "But I have consulted standing orders and established that lunch can be claimed plus the full afternoon attendance allowance if needs be."

The broad smiles on the faces of the 'on the make' members of Council immediately eased the tense atmosphere until Councillor Ms Janet Bodmin broke the moment. It was all the reporters needed to sit up and take notice that fireworks were on the cards. Anthony sat down beside a smiling Mrs Tremett.

"Chairman," she said, "Is it proper that full attendance allowance should be paid regardless of the time spent on this additional item and not, I might add, on the current agenda? We are still one hour from the end of the official morning session."

Much to the delight of the smirking Council officers and the constantly flushing Mrs Tremlett, shouts of 'sit down, let's get on with it' echoed around the chamber forcing the Chairman to intervene and Janet sat down.

"Mrs Bodkin, I'm sure…"

Janet was on her feet again, "It's Ms Chairman, pronounced Mizzz. I know it is a new word for you to conjure with, but do we have to go through all this at every Council meeting?" Throwing her hands heavenwards she looked round and appealed, tongue in cheek, to her supporters.

Tomo Thomas smiled weakly. "My apologies Mizzzz Bodkin."

Still on her feet, Janet cut him off again and for the umpteenth time in her short political career informed him sharply. "It's Bodmin, as in Bodmin Moor, not Bodkin as in needle." and sat down.

Bored by all the confusion and knowing he was well hidden from view by the table, Anthony fondled his secretary's knee and whispered to her.

"These single ladies really don't know what they are missing do they, Mrs Tremlett?"

She smiled at him secretly before realising they were being watched by Bill Jones, longest serving member and Father of the Council. Blushing, Ruth caught his saucy wink and whispered to her careless lover.

"I think they are waiting for you, Anthony."

Pulling himself together, he stood up once more and adjusted his jacket. "Ah yes, now where were we?"

Bill Jones casually brought the situation down to earth and addressed the Chair.

"Mr. Chairman, when the Chief Executive has finished playing with his 'err … thoughts, could I propose further business rather than wasting time discussing the nomenclature of the delightful lady member from Lugworth?"

Janet audibly sighed at the chauvinistic comment, but let it go. She looked across to the press benches for silent support from Dee Donnington but was surprised to see that she had left the room. Her thoughts were interrupted by the syrupy tones of the Chief Executive eager to show his superior knowledge of local Government procedures.

"Certainly, Chairman," he said with a condescending air. "First, the ruling concerning payment is permissible under standing orders, copies of which can be seen in my office. Secondly, owing to the sensitive nature of the special item I am about to disclose, may I recommend that the rest of this meeting be held in camera."

The mouth-open silence was starkly interrupted by Councillor Ned Tonkin farting in his sleep, a sound usually hidden by the verbal patter of Council business.

"So it's him that's been letting 'em go all these years then," the anonymous voice from the back of the hall muttered. Amused at the comment the officers tried hard to choke back their laughter; Ruth Tremlett hid her smile behind the pale lemon handkerchief she had brought to her nose a few seconds earlier.

Totally thrown by the announcement, it was plain to see that Chairman Thomas, despite his long political career, had never heard the phrase before, leaving him and many of the members confused that after twenty-two years of service as a local Councillor, it had been a mistake to stand for election in the first place. The thought left him thinking that the meeting of the Mid Border District Council on 21st April 1982 would be etched on his mind forever. The knees that had, until now, served him well, weakened as he struggled to stand up again and he wished for a second glance at Mrs. Tremlett's heaving bosom, a sight he knew would give him the stimulation he needed to stay up! But he was out of luck. By now it was well hidden by her chubby arms as she continued to stifle her amusement behind the lemon handkerchief. Every inch the professional, Anderson-Shelta controlled himself. Not an ounce of emotion escaped from behind his spectacled face as he willed his Chairman to finally cock it up once and for all. And he did. With the knuckles on his sixty two year old fingers turning white Tomo Thomas gripped the arms of his chair and hauled himself to his feet, his fluttering Welsh heart giving notice that if he couldn't get out of this one he was a goner in more ways than one. Relying on his strong Welsh vocals he nervously addressed the meeting.

"Right oh then, to the cinema it is."

Janet Bodmin was almost hysterical as she verbally challenged the announcement. "What? Go to where?"

The Chairman hesitated before making his reply. The wicket was going to be even stickier as he tried to hide his fears in a bold and firm approach. Encouraged by a rush of alcohol infused blood to the brain, he gripped his hand-carved gavel and confidently rose to the challenge.

"I now close the meeting and we shall reconvene at the Picture Palace across the road."

He brought the gavel down with such a wild blow he might well have crushed the soft, manicured hands of the Chief Executive but for his secretary who, in her excitement, accidently brushed the top of his inner thigh. The speed with which his hands moved to protect his crotch beat the falling gavel by a millionth of a second. Adjusting himself via his pocket, Anthony watched in amazement as the inept Chairman of Council pushed past him and made for the swing doors leading to his ante room. He was immediately followed by half the Council; those left behind were either crippled or asleep; officers, press and bemused members of the public stayed put.

On the raised platform the Council officials collapsed like a row of dominoes as they let loose the laughter they had been holding back for a mite too long. With the top half of their suited torsos partly across each other it was the first public showing of a united front that the press had ever seen from this or any other local Council. The hilarious moment prompted a chain reaction of unsuppressed giggling from the press and public galleries which gave Ruth Tremlett the opportunity to grasp the hand of her executive lover in an auspicious display of dignified joy. The recipient of her unexpected show of warmth and affection remained passive until he was able to reach into his trouser pocket for his handkerchief or something!

Exasperated, Janet Bodmin pleaded with those who were left in the Chamber.

"Someone call them back for heaven's sake or we will be here all night as well as all day."

Her prompt announcement brought an instant response from the Chief Executive who demanded. "Mrs Tremlett please order them back."

Overcome by events Ruth almost forgot where she was.

"Certainly darli—" but she managed to stop herself in time. "I'll catch them at the pedestrian crossing."

As she hurried out of the chamber, her chunky Cuban heeled shoes clattered like a determined flamenco dancer as she crossed the mosaic tiled foyer leading to the main lobby.

Bill Jones could no longer contain himself. The former Captain of the Welsh Schools XV was building up to an extravagance of inherited emotion that would soon render him uncontrollable. Whatever the stupidity of the occasion Bill's rhetoric was well worth waiting for and Janet relished the moment even though her journalist buddy Dee was, as usual, absent when something or someone was about to explode.

"Bloody hell, Janet, I've seen it all now. What the hell is he up to?" Bill said and turned towards the amused faces of the officers on the top table.

"This is no laughing matter, Chief Executive, and you can tell your grinning monkeys to take the smile of their collective faces if they want overtime."

Janet looked around muttering. "Dee Donnington where are you? You should be here to capture this." Looking upwards in mock despair, she appealed to the pastel nodules on the ceiling for an answer to her hopeless question. The reply was instant. Swing doors crashing, Dee bounded into the chamber and by-passing her colleagues fell into the empty space alongside her friend.

"For God's sake, Jan. What's going on? It's like a frenetic version of one man and his dog out there. The whole lot of 'em are dashing over the pedestrian crossing like hysterical sheep. Old man Lewis is out of control, shouting to puzzled pedestrians, anybody for the back stalls? Ben Neal is running after them like a border collie on pot. Have they all gone bananas, gaga, or something Jan? I told you it wouldn't be long before this Council became a classic example of group nervous breakdown."

While Dee rambled on, Janet tried to clear her own head. Rational thinking was needed but she was overwhelmed by a sudden attack of crazed laughter and needed to calm down before explaining.

"It all happened when Anderson-Shelta recommended that the rest of the meeting be held in camera."

"He what!" exclaimed Dee, "In camera, a meeting of the Mid Border Council held in camera. He's gone all bloody pompous again and such a bloody know all. How did Tomo cope with that? The poor old buffer wouldn't have a clue."

"He didn't," Janet replied.

"He had no idea that 'meeting in camera' meant clearing the chamber of press and public before discussing a matter of a secret or delicate nature so he took a stab at it and adjourned the meeting to the cinema. I tell you, Dee, it's hard to believe that people elect our Councillors to public office in good faith. My God, they haven't got a clue about what goes on behind these doors."

"You exclude yourself of course." Dee threw back her head and laughed loud enough unwittingly to attract the attentions of her colleagues in the press gallery.

Johnno Johnson, hack of the first order, called across to her.

"Come on, Dee, what's happening out there? Give us the low down. You've been up to something?"

"Wait and see, you impatient old leek, I'm talking to Councillor Bodmin and then I'll be over. Just sit on it for a bit longer, there's a good chap."

Dee ignored the one-fingered gesture he threw in her direction, the one he reserved for English supporters when the Welsh scored at Cardiff Arms Park, and carried on talking to Janet, but this time she lowered her voice.

"I'll tell you what I heard out there when that lot gets back from the pictures. All I can say is – Janet Bodmin, prepare to meet thy doom. The true meaning of shock horror is about to be revealed to Mid Wales." Pausing for breath, she glanced towards the swing doors.

"Listen, it's the dulcet tones of the lovely Mrs Tremlett yelling like the whipper in at the Boxing Day hunt."

Sensing that Dee knew something she didn't, Janet whispered.

"Cut the crap, Dee Donnington, and tell me what the big secret is. You've picked up something and you're keeping quiet. I thought we were comrades in arms."

"I live in hopes, darling," she replied flirtatiously. "But we have to play this one low key if you follow my drift."

Janet followed her drift all right and quizzed her further. "You're at it again aren't you, Dee? Is it the doctor's daughter from Llandaff? If I remember correctly she works at the Welsh Office doesn't she? I bet she's in the frame somewhere."

Dee looked around before replying.

"Look, Jan, I'm not exactly sure what, but something big is in the wind."

"And that's why you're covering a boring old Council meeting here instead of your Cardiff patch." Jan suggested, "I wondered why you were stepping out of your class."

Casting an eye towards the press she added. "You've tipped one or two of that lot off haven't you? You really are a bit of a rogue."

Dee smiled the engaging smile that she always kept back for her closest friends. She wanted to hold onto her latest secret for just a little while longer, the lovely girl from the Welsh Office was a corker of a secret too so she changed tack.

"I knew there was something in the pipe line when I saw Davenport-Jones slip in to the Chairman's room when I went out earlier. He was a bit flushed, had a few from the look of him, but you know as well as I do that he only shows his twitty Tory face at a district Council meeting when it's just before a general election. We both know that's not on the cards and he knows something we don't!"

"And where does the doctor's daughter from LLandaff come into the picture?" Janet asked.

"You mean Gill? I thought you might bring her up again. Well, at a pleasing moment after a particularly delicious night out, she just happened to mention that a directive from Whitehall had arrived at the Welsh Office."

"About what?" Janet enquired.

"Something about testing the emergency services in case of a nuclear attack. I really don't know much more than that. It was a casual conversation during an informal moment."

Dee was a little bit too nonchalant as she stretched and made a move to go back and join her colleagues. Janet couldn't resist a bit of teasing.

"Pillow talk again, Dee? My! You do get about, darling."

With a swift turn of the head Dee winked at her old friend. "Don't I ever, dear heart? You know my routine, darling, try it sometime!"

Flicking back her well cut fair hair she sauntered over to her associates stopping for a brief word with the housing officer on the way; ignoring the demands of her peers to open up, she called out "Be with you in a second, chaps, I need some advice on fire places." Winking at her colleagues she politely asked the housing officer: "Any idea where I could get a nice fireplace, David?" Without waiting for an answer she strolled back to her rightful place in the press box. Janet already knew the answer; it was common knowledge that the housing officer had a habit of offering new fireplaces with central heating back boilers to single mothers in return for an afternoon of pleasuring on his rounds.

Dee loved being 'one the boys'. She was a joy to her intimates and a pain in the arse to those who were not. Her fellow scribblers had ambivalent feelings about her; these depended on whether they respected her talent, resented her competitiveness or fancied her women. To the casual observer she was tall, elegant and gifted with a personality and sense of humour that hid an intelligent and sharp mind. Her background was definitely upper middle class.

Born in Rawalpindi, her father, a Major in the Royal Engineers attached to the Indian army, was later transferred to the Colonial Office to assist with partition. Dee's arrival was delightfully unexpected; her mother's fertility had been in doubt after the difficult earlier birth of Dee's older brother and she was much loved by her parents. Educated by an English governess until she was eight years old the family returned to England and resettled in Wimbledon where she attended a private prep school. This provided her with a good basic education, scholarship preparation and a solid grounding in the social graces. As expected she won a place at an Independent Girls Public School in South West London before going on to Sussex University to read English and political history. Trying out various careers from teaching to commerce, finally at the age of twenty-eight she opted for journalism. It was a good move; her hunches began to pay off and her reputation for digging out a good story grew in a career that fluctuated between broadcast and broadsheet news. Based in Cardiff where she free-lanced for the BBC and a few nationals, she was in Lugworth on a duty call. Her now widowed mother had moved out of London to be near her Brecon based daughter and this, coupled with her increasing fondness for rural Wales had encouraged her to stay put for a while. The occasional tip-off from her girl friend at the Welsh Office made the area newsworthy and she liked to follow up leads and sit in at interesting local meetings. What little information she had on a possible Central Government defence exercise in Mid-Bordershire had more than just twitched her inquisitive nose and she was itching to get on with it.

Chapter Three

The commotion outside brought the Council chamber sharply to heel. The bored officers stopped doodling and swiftly tore off the top sheets of the pads on their local authority clipboards; that is, with the exception of Dick Dobie the Planning Officer. He had somehow managed to get his Welsh Cricket Association tie caught up in the mechanism of his brand new, state of the art flip chart. It had become entangled around a small oily cog and he had spent some time trying to get it out. At one point he almost strangled himself when Hobson, the Environmental Health Officer, tried to help by pulling one end. This caused the knot to slip and Dobie turned puce; it could have been nasty had not the Chief Executive leaned across and cut him free with his readily available pocket nail scissors. Dobie was still trying to get his breath back when the swing doors burst open, but it didn't seem to bother Ned Tonkin who had slept throughout the entire incident. He opened half an eye and for a brief moment surveyed the scene like a heavy lidded tortoise and then dropped off again. It was left to the intrepid Mrs Tremlett to herd the delinquent Councillors back into the room; Ruth's cry of achievement would have brought back the Apollo shuttle from the moon.

"I have them Mr Chairman, every man jack of them," she yelled.

"Mr Chairman is behind you, Mrs Tremlett," the Chief Executive advised her, "Perhaps you would care to propel him and your good self in the direction of this table."

His sardonic smile did not go unnoticed and Janet Bodmin could not resist a caustic comment.

"Chief Executive," she said in her most sarcastic manner. "May I take this opportunity on behalf of those who have been left alone in this holy chamber to welcome back the lost tribes of Snowdon."

Anthony responded with just a hint of humour. "Thank you, Ms Bodmin. I'm sure it will be very much appreciated especially from the only admitted socialist on this Council who knows what it must feel like to be out in the wilderness for so long."

Joining in the laughter echoing around the chamber she nodded in admiration to the Chief Executive. She had not seen the witty side of his nature and perhaps believed he wasn't so bad after all. After some positive encouragement from the Chair, members settled into their rightful places and Tomo Thomas took to the floor again.

"Now what's to do Mr Chief Executive, what's going on?"

Anthony slipped into his 'I know it all' mode and grasping control of the meeting again announced.

"Chairman and members, if I may, I shall spend a moment or two running through Council procedure for eventualities such as this."

Frustrated by the delays, Bill Jones threw his hands in the air.

"Run through the bloody farm yard if you like, Chief Executive, but for God's sake let's get on with it. I've got a business to run."

"I intend to, sir, if you will let me," Anthony replied but was stopped in his tracks by a timid voice addressing the Chair. Councillor Mrs Ida Williams was on her fluid filled feet.

"Just a small point of order, if you please, Mr Chairman. May I?"

Anderson-Shelta sat down with a sigh. Janet turned to speak to Dee.

"Here we go again. It's a small matter of the language, Chairman..." Janet mimicked and Dee laughed.

As always Ida Williams addressed the meeting in the singsong tones of a Sunday School Superintendent.

"It's a matter of the language, Mr Chairman, my chapel upbringing, see. It cuts through me to hear blasphemy in this Chamber. Could Councillor Jones please leave the swearing for his friends at the Labour Club?"

As she sat down Bill Jones bowed low.

"My respects, dear lady, I will try to accommodate your feelings but if we can't move this meeting along I cannot guarantee what I might say. Please accept my apologies in advance Ida.

"Offering her his prize-winning smile he sat down and waited for the Chief Executive to once more make his presence felt.

"May I continue, Chairman?"

Slowly wilting under the pressure Tomo Thomas muttered his agreement. He was beginning to feel his age and it showed; he badly needed another quick breather in his office but Anthony ignored him.

"When one holds a meeting in camera it is to exclude from the proceedings all those who do not officially represent the people of the Mid Border district, members of the press, the general public and uninvited representatives from business and public bodies. They are specifically excluded from all matters of a secret or confidential nature, by law."

Pausing only to allow the murmur of approval to catch on before the punch line, he added. "It does not mean ladies and gentlemen that we all retire to the local picture palace."

The officers collectively sniggered as Tomo Thomas, keen to capitalise on the Chief Executive's words, pushed his chair over the back edge of the rostrum as he stood up to speak. The clatter brought sleeping Ned Tonkin back into the meeting breaking his wildest dream yet. Embarrassed by the commotion he had caused, the Chairman went on the attack.

"Ah, that's it is it? Right, I know the procedure now. Clear the public gallery. Usher, remove the press!"

"Hell fire!" said Bill Jones. "He thinks he's on the bloody bench now. Sorry, Ida."

A voice from the press benches called out "All ashore who's going ashore" as he left the room with his pals.

Amid all the noise and chaos it was hard for Janet to contain herself. Ted Evans the member from Nantywyln got it about right when he leaned over and said.

"Appointing Chairmen on a head count of sheep instead of a secret ballot is wrong you know Miss. It seems the more sheep yer got, the more chance yer got of getting in. What with lambing starting four weeks before the elections all these bloody farmers are inducing labour well before they be due. 'Tis wicked Miss."

"Arr! And it don't produce a better Chairman," muttered Ned Tonkin without lifting his head from his chest.

The room was soon emptied of its unwanted citizens and for a brief moment Janet let her head fall and closed her eyes in an effort to blot it all out. Her quiet meditation was blown out of the window by the booming voice of the Chairman, who having achieved what he thought was the impossible, wanted to get on to the 'good bit' while he was on top. Once more he tried to clarify the situation.

"Chief Executive, advise us of what is so important that only those gathered in the room can hear about it?"

Janet Bodmin remained head in hands.

"Are you still with us Miss Bodkin?" he asked and she slowly lifted her head and glowered at him.

"It's Bodmin. Oh God! Never mind, let's get on for heaven's sake or we will be claiming 'sleeping in' allowance if this goes on much longer."

"Ned already is," Bill Jones said, "I suppose that's all he gets these days."

Patiently waiting for the banter to stop, Anthony prompted.

"Ladies and gentlemen may I remind you time is short and we must move on. However, before I disclose the contents of this highly secret communication from Central Government, via the Welsh Office of course, I should like to recommend that we invite our Member of Parliament …"

He held the pause just a little too long and Bill Jones couldn't resist another go.

"Your true blue friend and mine…"

Anderson-Shelta ignored him and carried on "Crispin Davenport-Jones, our much respected Member of Parliament, into these proceedings. It is of course only my recommendation and is for you to approve. I do, however, think it would, in this instance be advisable."

Janet Bodmin was on her feet in a flash.

"Does this mean another adjournment while we await his arrival from London or does he just happen to be in the Chairman's hospitality suite knocking back the rate-payers gin and tonic?"

The Chairman was again taken by surprise and it was beginning to dawn on him that he had been deliberately left in the dark. He immediately went into 'I've got a big chip on my shoulder' mode, staggered to his feet and let fly at the Chief Executive.

"Sir, just who the hell gave you carte-blanche to invite anyone into to my office to drink at leisure? If anyone is going to knock back the rate payer's gin and tonic it's me, not the Member of Parliament."

Ida Williams blushed and leapt to her feet again.

"Language, Chairman. Now what is all this about gin and tonic? I hope my rate payers are not being asked to foot the bill for this so called hospitality?" Confronting the treasurer she asked him. "Might we have a breakdown of the cost of alcoholic drink for the Chairman's parlour?"

Smug Arthur Yorkshire had waited for this moment for a long time. His normally dour, expressionless face lit up as he answered the question.

"I shall have them ready for the next 'Ways and Means' committee, Madam," his weasel-like features breaking into a rare smile as he sat down and whispered to the housing officer. "I've been waiting for the chance to get at these bastards and now I've got 'em by the short and curlies. Thank you, Mrs Ida Williams, thank you very much indeed."

The housing officer laughed." Good one, Arthur, it's time to show who's got the real balls on this Council and it's not the pack of village idiots out front."

Bill Jones had the bit between his teeth.

"For God's sake, Chairman, get on with it. We're supposed to be discussing nuclear bloody warfare, not do we want 'Jack-the-Lad' from Westminster shoving his

Tory oar in. Let's take a vote now and get this show on the road or he will have knocked back the Chairman's booze allowance in one go."

He waited for the wave of fury that always encouraged the purple vein at Anderson-Shelta's temple to swell up and pulsate rapidly. Anthony knew he had over-stepped the mark by keeping the Chairman out of important decisions and the fact that Bill Jones had somehow got wind of the plans irked him. Before he had time to regain the advantage, Tomo blew his final fuse. Unable to lift himself from his chair, he emitted a chesty wheeze which suddenly caught in his throat. Flashing his eyes towards Bill Jones and the Chief Executive, the unexpected change of key in his voice shocked the silent Council chamber.

"Nuclear warfare! Who said anything about nuclear warfare?" Beside himself with rage he turned on the Chief Executive in a manner that caused Ruth Tremlett to tremble.

"Once and for all, Anderson-Shelta, what the hell is going on? I'm the Chairman of this Council and know bugger all about this meeting. I've been shut out and I want to know why."

Anthony kept his professional composure when all about were losing theirs. "Because, sir, it is top secret."

"If it was so bloody top secret and I apologise for the language, Mrs Williams, then how the hell did Bill Jones know about it?"

Anderson-Shelta was ready for the question.

"I was coming to that, Chairman – perhaps, Councillor Jones you can tell us just how, where and when you picked up such top secret information?"

Relishing the moment Bill Jones made the most of getting to his feet. Pausing for longer than usual he announced, "In the gentlemen's urinals. I heard all about it in the gents."

The look of amazement around the chamber said it all until Ned Tonkin woke up again and said it for them. "What has it got to do with the gents bog?"

Formality cast to the wind, Janet Bodmin addressed the Chair whilst remaining seated.

"What on earth has nuclear warfare got to do with the gentlemen's lavatories, Bill?" she quietly asked.

Thrusting his hands deep into the pockets of his poacher-style tweed jacket the genial, long standing Councillor set about blowing the whistle on matters secret.

"Patience, dear lady, I'm coming to that. I'm sure you all know by now that the gentlemen's urinals are adjacent to the female office staff powder room. Well, friends, earlier this week I was at a planning committee meeting and during the session went for a pee." Ignoring the gasp of disapproval from Ida he went on, "Lo and behold, above the sound of rushing waters I heard the sweet tones of the good and faithful Mrs. Tremlett, personal assistant and, for want of a better word, confidante of our Chief Executive."

Pink with embarrassment, Ruth Tremlett fiddled with the buttons on her beige blouse and waited silently for Bill Jones to unravel his story.

"The dear lady, unaware that she was being overheard, was engaged in close and secret conversation with Miss Axe from accounts." Smiling mischievously at Arthur Yorkshire the Treasurer he added. "I do hope she won't be up for the chop, Arthur." Chuckling at his own joke Bill quickly moved on. "However, little did they know, that on the other side of the wall, with his good ear cocked and tuned in, was my good self, William Idris Jones, listening to every word of their top level conversation. Agog at gossip of a possible nuclear attack, I forgot where I was, turned away rather too quickly and found myself pissing over a well-polished pair of hand-stitched shoes standing slightly apart in the next stall. I put two and two together and made ten for Downing Street and in a flash knew something was up."

Pausing to wait for those Councillors suddenly lifted out of their complacency to come down to earth, and for the Chief Executive to control his giveaway facial twist, "And that, Mr. Chairman, is how they passed the bad news from Gwent to Usk."

Bill was best known for his sometimes witty comments that, to be fair, more often than not drifted over most heads in the Chamber but it didn't take long for the penny to drop. Chief Executive and Personal Assistant stood up together locked in shared shock; the atmosphere was electric as the two custodians of the state secret verbally jostled. Ruth Tremlett, as ever, got in first, her words a staccato of indignation.

"Mr Chairman ... Anthony, this is despicable. Councillors listening in to one's private conversations through a lavatory wall is not only ungentlemanly, it is conduct unbecoming a public servant. It is too awful for words and I shall have to resign." Pointing directly at Bill Jones she suggested. "That man should be banned from Council, he really should."

The sleeping Ned Tonkin once again came to life. "Band! Who the devil called out the town band? I never sanction money for a band function unless it's a Masonic do and that's a different matter."

"Well, you wouldn't be far wrong with this lot, Ned," Bill said. "Anyway, it's not the town band we're on about."

"No it is not," Ruth replied. "Councillor Jones should apologise at once or I won't answer for my actions. I do have an *English* lawyer you know."

Realising that his beloved Ruth was losing control Anthony tried to calm the situation before she said something highly embarrassing for both of them. Quickly interrupting her before she reached full throttle, he tried to calm her down.

"Mrs Tremlett, Ruth, don't be hasty now. Sit down while I sort this out."

His officers smirking in anticipation of things to come, he gently eased her back into her chair. Leaving his usual cockiness aside he quietly asked, "Now, Councillor Jones, what else have you gleaned whilst at the urinal?"

"Enough to wipe the smile off their faces I can tell you," he said, pointing an accusing finger at the top table; the Housing Officer paled as he slid slowly down into his chair.

Ned Tonkin well awake by now and moreover raring to go; all thoughts of sleep brushed aside, he amazed his colleagues when in a rare moment in his political life he actually proposed some action leaving them in some awe."

"Go on, boyo have ago," Ben prompted, and he did.

Staggering to his feet he pleaded. "Mr Chairman, if we don't get on with the business it won't be a late lunch we'll be claiming for, it will be more like an early supper. I move for a vote on whether or not Jones-the-Member should be allowed to sit in on this meeting at all."

At this point Ned did something even more extraordinary; he offered an opinion. "It's my feeling gents – and ladies, that if we are to come under nuclear attack from the Red Army then our MP should put his blue rowing cap on his pretty boy head and front up with the rest of us."

It was enough to set Tomo off gain. Waiting until Mrs Tremlett dried her eyes with her useful lemon hanky she moodily dragged the Chief Executive's hidden hand from her knee; he once again took control and called for a seconder for the proposal. Ida Williams cautiously raised her hand.

"Right then. Hands up all those in favour of inviting the Member of Parliament into the meeting."

Everyone except Janet Bodmin and Bill Jones voted for the proposition and the Chairman, attempting to show his authority, announced with some relief, "Motion carried. Now can we get back on track please? Over to you Chief Executive, invite him in."

"You had better get him in quick, otherwise he'll be halfway through the gin bottle by now and it's your expense account," Ned announced to much laughter and sat down.

Delighted with the vote Anthony was up and off the podium in a trice. "A pleasure Mr Chairman," and left the chamber, swing doors crashing behind him.

Much to the concern of Ruth, the mutterings of discontent increased in his absence and she called upon the other officers for support but they ignored her pleas. Leaning across Dick Dobie, Arthur Yorkshire broke the silence and spoke to a colleague.

"He'll be briefing Davenport-Jones by now, telling him what to say and when to keep his parliamentary mouth shut."

"And so would I be if I were in his shoes," the legal officer advised, "That idiot could drop us all in it if he's had too much to drink. Let's hope the Chief gets a grip on him, otherwise it's chaos all round."

The swing doors crashed open again. In the presence of his Member of Parliament Anthony was, as usual, walking backwards and almost bowing as he escorted Crispin Davenport-Jones into the Council chamber.

"He hasn't been knighted yet, Anthony," Bill Jones said in a voice loud enough to be heard; the Chief Executive straightened up so quickly he almost slipped a disc.

To hide his embarrassment he insisted that the Vice-Chairman should vacate his seat and let the Member of Parliament down. It was at this point Janet did her Wynford Vaughan-Thomas impression and described the scene to her fellow Councillors. Adopting the reverent tones of the late BBC commentator she announced.

"Enter stage left The Honourable Crispin Davenport-Jones, Tory Twit of the year and twice winner of the 'I've put my foot in it with the PM nine times since Christmas' award.' Mr Davenport-Jones is an expert in the study of 'I'm learning to be Welsh' just in case the PM gives me the Welsh Office, hence my double barrelled surname."

Bill Jones, keen to get in on the fun and games carried on with the jesting.

"How can you say such things, Ms Bodmin? What was it Sir Thomas More said? Come on girl, you're the literary genius."

She responded instantly, "It profits a man nothing to sell his soul for his country, but for Wales ..."

"Exactly," said Bill, "Just look at him. Where do they find them?"

Ned Tonkin was getting fed up with the banter. Turning to his pal, the Vice-Chairman of Council he said, "For pity's sake George, give him your seat or we'll never get home this side of Lady Day."

George Blunt churlishly walked across to the front bench. As he sat down alongside his colleagues he was applauded for his unwillingness to offer his seat to his Member of Parliament.

Chapter Four

Crispin Davenport-Jones, 'Jones the Member' to those who had no personal insight into the finer points of his manly bearings, was in his mid-forties, although he looked younger. Educated at a variety of good public schools, he never quite made it academically despite having been to a rather fine college near Aberdeen which specialised in cramming for university entrance exams. However, with a push from the family purse he was accepted at a strapped for cash University in the West of England and managed a second in anthropology. After university his father bought him a directorship in a friend's business where he muddled through until Conservative Central Office, with the help of another considerable sum of money from the family banking business, found him a difficult by-election seat in Wales. To the amazement of everyone, including himself, he won the seat and from then on kept it safe for his leader and party.

Crispin had the good looks of the English upper class coupled with a slight tendency towards the effeminate highlighted by his very fair hair, blue eyes and a pale skin which, on occasions, hinted at a maidenly blush. Bodily he was in very good shape due perhaps to the many hours he spent in the House of Commons gymnasium during the late night sittings held to sanction the "Prevention of Terrorism Act."

Lately though he had given up late night exercising due to an unfortunate incident whilst running through a personal training schedule. It was during the early hours of the morning when the division bell had unexpectedly sounded and in an effort to reach the voting lobby he collided with a radical lady member from the Opposition Party in the swing doors leading from the fitness suite. Trapping his lower regions in her chest expander, it was said by close friends and companions that for some time he suffered withdrawal symptoms of the worst kind and flatly refused to go into the gymnasium again. The Chief Whip believed it was a deliberate attempt by the opposition to stop him from casting his vote. Nevertheless, his political career progressed quickly and he held the Mid-Border and Usk seat at the 1979 general election with an increased majority.

Despite being unmarried, his prospects improved as he sold his soul to the party cause in exchange for early promotions. He also worshipped his Prime Minister and she had a soft spot for him, too, although some of his colleagues felt that it was down to the gin and golf day trips with her husband that found him in the inner sanctum at Downing Street. Crispin was very much a snob well positioned among the Sloane Ranger set. He owned a large, fashionable apartment in Eaton Mews left to him by his godmother, the late Dame Hildegarde De Boche, Founder and Director, until her demise at the splendid age of ninety two, of the Ballet Galavante.

He also had the use of a substantial sea front apartment overlooking Cardigan Bay which doubled-up as a constituency office but his pride and joy was the three storey Edwardian villa at Borth on the Cambrian coast. It backed onto the beach where he was able to launch his classic, wooden-hulled sailing boat 'Nut Cracker Two.' His partner Dunky, a promising young actor from the Prince of Wales Company of Shakespearian Players shared the house when he wasn't on tour or doing a stint at Stratford. However this was not common knowledge in the constituency. Borth became his playground and during the long summer recesses, his endless house and beach parties attracted a select few from the London literati, some often sailing across Cardigan Bay from Newquay Marina where they kept their own boats.

Sartorially Crispin preferred tweed jackets, slacks and flat caps from Aquascutum in his constituency, dark blue Saville Row suits in London and Lilywhite sportswear by the sea although it was rumoured that his favourite 'off duty' casual wear was kept in the closet. His one constant formal accessory, a conservative blue tie given to him one Christmas by the Prime Minister and whenever the occasion required it, he wore a fresh flower in the buttonhole of his jacket. Sometimes, just for the hell of it, he sported a badge claiming, 'I like being blue;' this had caused much comment in the satirical magazines.

Crispin's father, Lord Davenport of Collingwood End, a popular market town in North Wiltshire is a retired merchant banker and some years ago, he received a Life Peerage for his services to the 'think tank.' Currently living in the South of France with his second wife and former mistress of twenty-five years standing, he is writing his memoirs. The co-habiting Lady Davenport, a former J Arthur Rank starlet, had received much critical acclaim for her performances on the silver screen, one of which attracted an Oscar nomination. On the other hand, she was not Crispin's cup of tea and definitely not the goods; in his opinion his glamorous stepmother bordered on the common. Encouraged by an excess of expensive champagne she was known to throw herself at trendy young filmmakers during the annual BAFTA awards and invite then to join her for the Cannes Film Festival.

Since the divorce, Crispin had had little to do with his father preferring to be with his natural mother. The Dowager Lady Davenport lived in her ancestral home in Sussex, a rather fine Georgian house handed down to her through her mother's line. Her income, inherited from both parents, was substantial in its own right, but over the years, thanks to sound investments made for her by her former husband, it had increased annually into a small fortune.

Lady Davenport adored her son. She constantly indulged him with large donations which allowed him to avoid the pitfalls of unsuitable directorships and seek out prestigious rather than lucrative companies to represent in the House of Commons. Fully aware of his sexuality she adored the amusing company of his boyfriends often entertaining them in her box at the Royal Opera House. A gifted contralto, she had a promising singing career before her marriage but was swept off her feet by the merchant banker and never took it up again. Occasionally she was invited to sing at charitable functions and was once offered a substantial donation to a well-known Children's Hospital if she could sing 'Rule Britannia' at the Last Night of the Proms. It never came off.

A very good friend of Covent Garden, she once raised a considerable sum for the redevelopment fund by singing with Hinge & Bracket at a Friend's Gala Supper. The event raised £100.000 for the Opera School.

Crispin's Welsh constituency was ideal and suited him well. The friendship he shared with the Chief Executive of the largest district Council in the Principality was both useful and productive. But today, seated before the full Council, his nerve was beginning to fail; his bladder was restless and his bowl irritable as he worried about how he was going to survive the next hour or so. Very much aware of the criticism and rumour that filtered through local party headquarters it was fortunate that the majority of members on the District Council had no real opinions on his capabilities. Nonetheless, during the last year or so he was beginning to realise that his political nous was virtually nil and that he was hanging on to his once safe seat by his fingernails. This he believed was due to the recent influx of the 'converted barn brigade' keen on flexing a few muscles in the local political scene, having an unsettling effect on party morale.

Liberal minded and Home Counties tarnished, the new trendy invaders were a pain in the backside and Crispin knew that one more major cock up could finish him off politically.

It was well known that Anderson-Shelta had a bit of a thing about his MP. It kept him in good stead with the voters but Crispin knew that it was a friendship built more upon the possibility that he could swing a knighthood Anthony's way. Facing up to his present situation what Crispin needed now was a little more Dutch courage and the calm and guiding hand of the Chief Executive to see him through the next half hour or so. He also needed a chance to show his better side to his supporters on the Council and not stick his well-heeled foot in the mire again.

The demanding voice of Tomo Thomas brought him back to earth, "Right then one and all, shall we get on?"

Before Anthony was able to reply, Councillor Mrs Williams beat him to it.

"Before we start Chairman, I must formally insist that you exercise a far stronger control over the rude, and sometimes blasphemous, language we have heard at today's meeting."

She sat down with such a flourish of indignation that Crispin saw it as an invitation to improve his standing.

"Quite right, dear lady. We in 'The Campaign against Life's Filth' are right with you on this. It is the downfall of society I'm worried about, it has to start somewhere and I believe—"

He didn't get the chance to finish before Ted Evans, who never had much to say except "mine's a pint of brown, Chairman," thumped the table with the huge clamped fist of a man who had spent most of his working life in forestry.

"With respect Mr Chairman, I'm not here to listen to the Member of Parliament's views on sex, prostitution or bad language. Let him leave that to his evenings in Soho. If we don't push it, it will be closing time."

To make his point he took a small leather flask from the pocket of his shooting jacket and drank the contents all in one go.

Looking a shade weary, the Chief Executive attempted to retake the initiative. Leering at Bill Jones he pompously declared.

"Onward ever onward, ladies and gentlemen. This is a serious matter and concerns us all. I shall now unveil the great secret that hitherto has only been available to those who have the use of the gentlemen's lavatories."

Pausing for effect he took a deep breath and continued.

"I have here a directive from Central Government passed onto us from the Welsh Office."

Janet leaned across Bill and muttered out loud,

"I suppose they need something to do in Cardiff apart from trying to justify their large salaries."

Itching to bring matters to a head Anthony grumbled. "If I might continue, Councillor Bodmin, this is no time for idle chitchat." Pointing to the large file before him on the table he solemnly announced.

"The communication states, in the usual Government jargon, details of an important plan which, in some part may need to be simplified for some of you. My officers are of course, fully conversant with Government procedure, as is Mr Davenport-Jones. Those of you unable to grasp the situation can see me afterwards."

Crispin looked decidedly uncomfortable as the Chief Executive continued his briefing.

"Central Government has selected our Council to be the leaders in the field of civil defence and community service and I, on your behalf, have accepted their challenge and their faith in us to carry it out to the letter."

He looked around for approval but most faces remained blank, except for Janet Bodmin who sarcastically asked.

"And what challenge would that be, Chief Executive. What have you let us in for this time?"

It was all Anderson-Shelta needed and he was ready with the answer, an answer he knew would cause uproar in the chamber. Taking another deep breath he whispered to the admiring Mrs Tremlett.

"In for a penny in for a pound, Ruth, that's what I say. Let us hear the socialist view on this and then we can get on with it."

She gave him her most salacious smile and replied.

"Most definitely Anthony so pull back the cock and let 'em have both barrels."

She almost called out in orgasmic joy at the wild look that crossed her beloved's face. Looking about him to make sure Ruth had not been overheard, he saw from the tension in the facial nerves of his officers that her voice had carried. Studying his box file long enough to get a grip on himself, he cleared his throat for the third time, wiped his damp brow with the handkerchief his wife always ensured was in his pocket for such emergencies and delivered his bomb shell.

"The Minister of State for Defence has decreed that the Mid-Border District Council will carry out a nuclear defence exercise within its boundaries. It is scheduled for a late summer weekend – date yet to be announced – and is expected to last for a period of three days and two nights. The Chief Executive of said Council, my good self, will be in charge for the duration of the exercise and will be designated 'Controller of Emergency Fallout Services'. Pausing long enough to allow his secretary's smug smile of 'I told you so' aimed at the management team, to sink in; he verbally kneed them in the groin.

"Annual leave for all officers and employees of the said Council will be suspended for two weeks before and one week after the exercise period."

Taking out diaries to compare notes, it was obvious from their shared expressions of shock that this part of the directive had been deliberately kept from them. But the punch line was yet to come and Anthony relished the moment.

"Lugworth-upon-Usk has been designated the area of most devastation. Further communications will be processed through the Welsh Office on a need to know basis. The letter is signed J. J. Jenkington, Minister of State for Defence (Wales)."

With the secret out in the open Anderson-Shelta believed his initial worries were over and he could now devote all his time and energy to getting his 'nuclear show' on the road. His brief moment of mental and physical relaxation was instantly shattered by the sight of 'honest' Ben Neal, long standing representative of Lugworth-Upon-Usk, staggering to his sixty nine year old feet, his normally ruddy face surpassing itself as he blurted out his feelings.

"I protest, Mr Chairman. We are always being devastated in Lugworth and my constituents won't hold with it any more. Last year it was the fir tree bug that unfortunately escaped from some quarantine station in Scotland, and where did it choose to settle down?"

"Lugworth," Janet said in solidarity with her joint Councillor.

"Yes, Ms Bodmin, Lugworth and our forestry has not been the same since. Christmas celebrations were ruined when every other branch or twig snapped the moment a decoration was hung from it."

"Yes, Councillor Neal," the Chairman interrupted. "We do realise that you've had it a bit hard in Lugworth this last year or two, but you see …"

Ignoring his Chairman and his blood pressure at bursting point Ben Neal persisted.

"And don't forget how the so called flood avoidance scheme went wrong and our most architecturally interesting 'Cobblers Street' was flooded for the first time in its history and it's halfway up a hill. Yet despite all that went before, are you seriously suggesting that we could be blown up by a nuclear bomb? Good God, man, what next for Lugworth?"

Before his colleagues could offer a few words of sympathy he collapsed into a state of sheer panic and unholy fear. Tomo Thomas tried to help him come to terms with the situation. "Steady on, Ben, old chap. It's not as bad as all that, it's not for real."

"Not from where you sit, it isn't, Chairman, but I don't trust him," he said pointedly looking at the Chief Executive.

One or two of the other Councillors were also uneasy with the situation including Janet who, as the junior representative from Lugworth, attempted to offer her idiotic senior colleague some support.

"It's alright, Ben, it really is. They call it war games and it does have some real value for some people, if only to show the emergency services in a good light."

Ben Neal relaxed just a little and allowed Janet to put a kindly arm around his shoulder and ease him back into his seat. Using the short break to gain control of the meeting again, it was obvious that Tomo was unsure of his ground as he tried to sort the situation out.

"We must not get too carried away by all this scary talk of warfare and bombs. Nothing has been said about bombing Lugworth, Ben, at least I don't think there's any chance of that is there, Chief Executive?"

The questioning tone in the Chairman's voice was a sure sign that he still hadn't got a clue so the Chief Executive needed to think on his feet to take the heat out of a developing and difficult situation. In an effort to convey her support Ruth quietly but efficiently gripped Anthony's thigh as he stretched his legs. He stood up far too quickly and flushed as he spoke.

"Of course not, Councillor Neal, bombs will not be allowed to fall on Lugworth, I shall personally attend to it. It's not real, just a practice exercise in case the odd nuclear weapon falls on the West Midlands. During the cold war defence was a priority all over the country and Central Government believes if it did happen today, the effects of radiation fallout could soon reach the Welsh border." Pausing for some sort of reaction, he added.

"Therefore, we, the Mid Border District Council, would be first line of defence for the Mid Wales area and it is our statutory duty to ensure our emergency and voluntary services have to be assessed as to their ability to cope."

Agog at the news, Janet Bodmin challenged.

"What emergency services? The United Kingdom hardly has any emergency services, let alone Lugworth. Do they realise Offa's Dyke runs from Chepstow to Prestatyn, about 170 miles as the crow flies, and we are expected to provide cover. This whole plan strikes me as another glorious Tory farce to justify keeping the defence spending down and antagonise the ban the bomb brigade. Never mind Lugworth, the Tin Lady at Westminster will be looking for some little island to invade next."

Janet surprised everyone, including herself with the intensity of her attack. General agreement circled the room and her colleagues, more out of self-preservation than anything else, took a much closer interest in what was being planned for Lugworth. The anonymous voice from the back benches mischievously summed it up.

"Even if I lived on Anglesey I'd be keeping my bloody head down these days, in case a bomb or two is off target.".''

Genuine dissent was in the air. Crispin fiddled with his old school tie, the officials sensed it, too, and mentally made ready for the verbal punch-up that was surely on the cards.

A cloud of uncertainty fell on the meeting as members took stock of the unexpected and serious situation. Pale faces identified the brave from the not so brave and it was soon obvious to Bill and Janet that the confusion in the ranks was reaching farcical proportions. Ever ready to make mischief, Bill toyed with the rising blood pressure of his confused colleagues and realising that Anderson-Shelta was showing signs of nervous irritation, he decided the time was right to chuck another spanner into the works. Trying his hardest to keep a straight face he fired off his next salvo from an upright position.

"Chairman," he said, "I must ask you what assurances have we that the good fairy of Downing Street won't press the button and discharge a nuclear warhead into our area?"

He managed not to smile as he turned and winked at Janet but she failed to respond knowing that any movement of her facial features would declare her uncontrollable. She was already aware that the Chief Executive was about to explode and the tightly suppressed laughter she had been holding back was causing her a problem. The sight of Ruth Tremlett gripping her paramour's left buttock in a desperate attempt to stem his rising emotions was not helping the situation. Her kindly act had quite the opposite effect on her boss who, struck by a rush of blood to his brain, shot to his feet and let rip.

"Good heavens, man, do you really believe that our Prime Minister would for one moment send rockets flashing across the Midlands with the sole intention of blasting Lugworth to oblivion?"

He tried to ease the situation with a little humour.

"Gracious me, Councillor Jones, are you implying that we're up for some nuclear fireworks? It's not Guy Fawkes Night, Mr Chairman – or is it?"

His half laugh didn't fool anyone and he looked around for support but all he could see was a concerned Ruth biting her bottom lip. His management team kept their heads down, hoping the union motto, 'Ring the bell now, Jack, I'm on the bus', would see them through to the end of the meeting.

Meanwhile, Davenport-Jones gazed at his shiny Gucci pumps choosing to adopt his usual policy 'See nothing, hear nothing and do nothing unless the party PR machine is hanging onto your coat tails'.

Sensing he was on his own, Anthony knew when to pass the buck; his composure contained, he off loaded the question and with the skill of a Barry John, lobbed it into the path of the Member of Parliament who was about to score another own goal.

"What do you think, Mr Davenport-Jones?" Anthony asked politely. "Will she do it?"

Badly shaken by the turn of events Crispin needed every sentence of the Central Office training manual he could muster. Fully expecting the whole business of the nuclear exercise to go through on the nod, by now he expected be in the Border Arms Hotel celebrating with a bottle of his favourite bubbly accepting praise for a mission accomplished. Sweating profusely he knew it was too late to back out; wilting at a greater rate than the fresh flower in his buttonhole. It was time to front up and face the music. He was in trouble from the word go.

"What! Christ, no. Sorry, Mrs ... err ... Williams. Gosh! Of course not, Anthony, mm I mean, Chief Executive. Well, at least I don't think she will."

Still fiddling with his favourite tie he wrapped it around his thumb and tried his utmost to bring some sense into his words. Wide eyed he tried again.

"Look at it this way. I mean she's got nothing against Wales, well except 'Super Ted' on Channel Four but that's understandable. She thinks it's about Ted Heath. Nothing nasty about the Prime Minister; stubborn, yes I'll grant you that but blast Wales that's highly unlikely, what!"

Trying to assess the effect his words were having on the meeting, he carefully unwound his tie from his thumb. The silence said it all. For the first time in its ignominious history members and officers of the Mid-

Border District Council were collectively gob-smacked. Just about every pair of eyes had been opened in more ways than one. Janet and Bill were staggered by the stumbling rhetoric of the man they called MP and despite the rumours of his ineptitude currently being bandied about the Welsh Marches, it was still hard to believe his panic-stricken performance. The entire Council waited for him to do something utterly stupid and he did; encouraged by the gin circulating in his blood stream, Crispin had a bright idea!

"OK, everyone," he said. "I've got it. I'll just nip out and give Central Office a bell. They will know what is happening, I'll use the phone in your parlour if I may Mr Chairman."

That said he leapt over the oak table and landed with the acrobatic skill of a Russian Cossack dancer at the feet of a half hysterical Ida Williams. Wobbling in front of her he steadied himself and made a hasty retreat helped on his way by the unexpected swing of the right hand door which caught him square on his well-dressed bum projecting him into the outer vestibule. The silence was disturbed only by the squeak from the big brass hinges on the doors as they closed behind him.

Chapter Five

The breathing space was a godsend for the bewildered Councillors. Tense limbs were stretched to the limit, a spluttered cough or two hid embarrassment and all eyes were gradually focused on Anthony. His demeanour said it all.

"What a wanker," he muttered. "There goes my Knighthood."

His devoted secretary knew what he was thinking without a word being spoken. Nodding knowingly she tried a moment of secret comforting and reaching for the pencil sharpener she once again exposed her moist, ample cleavage for his personal perusal which, among other things, brought a light flush to his unusually pale cheeks. Grinning from ear to ear, Bill Jones informed the Chairman that, "If you don't take control of this meeting Tomo you should call 'end of business' and send everyone home."

Responding with uncharacteristic gusto, Tomo yelled.

"Order, gents, order. We must press on. Chief Executive kindly sort this mess out once and for all. If we don't get away before milkin,' this lot will sound like a pack of hysterical women."

Janet Bodmin was on her feet in a flash. "Really, Chairman, I resent that. It's the men who are hysterical; look at Councillor Neal, he's in a state of near collapse.

As for the others, see for yourself, white as sheets and scared half to death at the thought of valuable grazing going up in nuclear smoke and no EEC compensation. It's ridiculous! The whole damn lot of you are pathetic."

Tomo Thomas had just about reached the end of his tether. A woman addressing a Council in such a way was beyond the pale and he sharply reprimanded the Junior Councillor from Lugworth.

"That's enough, Councillor Bodmin, any more of that sort of behaviour and I shall be forced to bar you from this chamber."

Keener than usual to stick his oar in, Ned Tonkin muttered "Pompous bloody fool."

Not only because he favoured Janet Bodmin's viewpoint, for years he had an eye on the Chairmanship for himself. After all, it was obvious to everyone that Tomo was making a pig's ear of everything and the press were there to see and hear him do it.

Struggling to make up lost ground Anderson-Shelta brought a touch of local Government gloss to the proceedings and casually asked the chairman to qualify his last statement for the minutes.

"Would the Chair confirm your proposed ban on Councillor Bodmin for the minutes please. Matters of this importance must be clarified, am I not right, Mrs. Tremlett?"

"You are indeed, Mr Chief Executive," Ruth instantly replied, delighted that her man had once more gained the upper hand.

"How would you like it worded, Chairman?" Perhaps it would be better if you repeat the charge and I can write it down verbatim."

"I don't know about verbatim Mrs Tremlett but I'll give it a go," Tomo confidently replied. Addressing Janet, he pompously announced,

"Councillor Bodmin, for the record and not withstanding verbatim, I must warn you that if you persist with your unruly behaviour I shall have you removed from the meeting."

Janet glowered at him and in a voice clearly suggesting try it you bastard, just try it.

"Under normal circumstances Chairman, it would be a pleasure, particularly as for once you have got my name right. However, may I assure the Chair that at times like this I would rather be in the Chamber of Horrors instead of this one. Have you got that, Mrs Tremlett, or shall I spell it out and then leave?"

Officers and press were enjoying every moment of the personal attack and longed to provoke the situation but it was taken out of their nasty little hands by the anonymous commentator on the back benches.

"That's it Jan old girl, give him the works. He knows he hasn't got the power to bar you from Council, verbatim or otherwise."

Councillor Mrs Williams stood up too quickly; her high blood pressure forcing her to sway a little before she spoke.

"All this bickering between the Chairman and the floor is very petty. We have serious matters to discuss and I am anxious to get back to the farm. Could we move on please?"

Councillor Evans, normally the silent type at meetings, was mentally working out the rate for lamb at the next sales at Brecon but today he unexpectedly jumped into the fray.

"The good lady is correct, Chairman, it is a bit of a nonsense all this. You'll soon have us believing the Government is going to bomb Wales; come on, pull yourself together, man. As for the Nancy-boy who has just done a runner, what the hell does he know about

Welsh affairs – other than sexual? You can bet your last buck that he only came to the meeting to make sure he and his fancy friends get a place in our bunker. Now let's get this nuclear show on the road, I need be home for the milkin'."

Keen to get on with it Bill Jones muttered, "Well said boyo. Over to you, Mr Chairman."

But Tomo refused to let it go. "He can't go saying things like that about our MP. It's not bloody on, Bill, its slander, that's what it is."

He turned to the legal officer for confirmation but he shrugged his shoulders in the non-committal way of a solicitor who knew that there was nothing in it for him. Bill Jones also knew he was on solid ground and made his next point very clear.

"But you ordered a closed session, Chairman, so what's been said cannot be challenged. That's why young 'Rumpole of the Dyke' over there is keeping a low profile. I don't suppose he's ever done slander before and why we got him on the cheap."

Still studying for the final part of his law exam the three times failed trainee solicitor looked as if he might weep. His colleagues kept quiet, aware that they could be next if the meeting went on much longer. Continuing his rant Bill Jones reminded.

"I've been against the press being excluded from this meeting all along but that's the way you wanted it. Now can we get on and sanction the motion for special powers, get things moving and confirm the Chief Executive as overall Commander."

"Why him and how come you know so much about it?" Tomo asked peevishly.

"Because I've read standing orders, that's why, Boyo, and if you brushed up on them yourself it would do us all a bit of good. They also recommend that the person appointed should be of sound mind and body, but after today's fiasco I'm beginning to have grave doubts."

"Hear, hear," Janet cried out in mock joy. Enjoying her support, Bill Jones triumphantly pointed to the top table.

"As for the rest of you up there, the so called Management Team, let me remind you that you are paid employees of this Council and will do as requested and it's no good looking affronted. You know full well that under those same standing orders you can expect substantial discretionary payments to cover the long hours involved in the organisation of this event and a committee will be appointed to oversee day to day expenses. If he can pull himself together for long enough, the senior Councillor for Lugworth is automatically elected Chairman."

Ben Neal, already shaken by events, looked flustered until Bill reminded him of the perks to go with it.

"To help Councillor Neal and others to decide whether or not to volunteer, I had better point out that the an emergency committee would command all the attendance and subsistence allowances on offer plus travelling expenses to and from Lugworth for up to six months. So, folks, every one of you stands to make a bit of extra pocket money out of this mad scheme."

Slumping back into his seat Bill waited for the response, he wasn't disappointed. It was quite obvious from their efforts to control their expressions of glee the collective gut reaction of full Council was to yell "count me in, Chairman," but discretion being the better part of an unexpected expenses claim, they kept quiet. By now totally bewildered, Tomo tried to clear his head.

"Very impressive, Councillor Jones, but surely it's up to me to announce or confirm any such arrangements, after all am I not the Chairman of this Council?"

Addressing the Chief Executive he added, "What have you to say on this, Anderson-Shelta, is Councillor Jones out of order on this one or not?"

Anthony always did have the knack of knowing when he was onto a winner and this was it.

"I'm afraid, Chairman, the matter is entirely out of my hands. Let me explain. When the directive from the Welsh Office was delivered, this particular issue became the province of the appointed Central Co-ordinator. Rules and regulations for defence exercises are no longer under the direct control of local Government; they are now a matter for central Government under a local commander, my good self, and the nominated central co-ordinator. I trust this clarifies the situation?"

Tomo was not yet defeated. "I suppose so but surely the Chairman of Council would automatically assume that role?"

"I'm afraid not, Councillor Thomas. The appointment is made from the rank and file members of Council. As I said before, it is out of my hands."

Deflated and realising he was on borrowed time, the ball was no longer in Tomo's court. On cue Ned Tonkin was ready with the final blow.

"Having got that little problem out of the way, I propose that Councillor Jones be appointed Central Co-ordinator for the Nuclear Defence Exercise at Lugworth."

Before it could be seconded, Bill Jones announced.

"I already am the co-ordinator. It was all arranged two years ago in anticipation of such an event. Perhaps the Chief Executive can remind us of the meeting that confirmed my appointment."

Anthony was smiling again.

"Indeed, Councillor Jones, I am most keen to clear the matter up," Gathering his thoughts he carefully explained, "At the special meeting of full Council convened to rubber stamp the Ministry's contingency plans for just this kind of directive, Councillor Jones was indeed confirmed Central Coordinator."

"Now we're getting somewhere," Janet said with a sigh of relief." Can we now persuade my Lugworth colleague to comment on this proposed committee and then perhaps we can all go home."

Ben Neal looked blank for a moment before despairing grumbling. "Lugworth will not like this at all, not at all. Whatever will the Town Council say? Is it going to cost us votes and some cases money?"

His concern was, in a way, justified. It was common knowledge throughout the district that Lugworth was not keen on what they termed 'uncalled for interference from that bureaucratic lot up the valley', their own Councillors always having to bear the brunt of it. Fairly new to the post, Janet was more accepting of the situation. However, it was well know that long serving Ben Neal was not adverse to the occasional perquisite from local traders and businessmen and liked to keep his back pocket arrangements under wraps; he was on the defensive when it came to officer interference. Aware of his dilemma, the timely intrusion of District Treasurer, Arthur Yorkshire, helped smooth the way of progress; with the contempt of an unfrocked Bishop, he suggested.

"Might I might butt in, Chairman? I believe I can throw a little light or two on the situation and hopefully ease the obvious worries of the good Councillor from Lugworth."

Pausing for effect he added, "I am sure that when he realises just how much Government money is available for the community hosting the defence exercise I'm sure he, and the Lugworth community will respond with great enthusiasm."

Affronted by the suggestion that he was swayed by monetary gain, Ben responded.

"If you are insinuating that I and my committed Council team at Lugworth may be motivated by pledges of cash from Central Government, I shall be obliged to protest at the highest level." Pausing briefly to consider the prospect of receiving additional grants he questioned. "For the record of course Mr Treasurer, just how much is involved?"

"Believe me Councillor Neal, a considerable sum; much more than your Council has ever handled before. I am of course available to act as your locum Treasurer."

Quick to catch on Janet nudged Bill. "Here we go, again, it's jobs for the boys and there is nothing we can do about it."

In an effort to flex a little of his imagined political muscle, Tomo Thomas tried to get in on the act.

"May we assume, Chief Executive that you have fully approved the roles and duties of your officers?"

"Of course, Chairman. By anticipating this meeting the District Management Team have already pencilled in extra staffing arrangements."

"Too bloody right they have, boyo. Let's make sure the lads are alright for extra payments. You've got to hand it to the man, Janet, he's got it all worked out. "Bill said. "I honestly don't know what we are doing here. Like the man said, it really is out of our hands now."

Catching his comments, Tomo butted in. "You said something, Councillor Jones?"

"I was saying to Councillor Bodmin how impressed we are with advanced plans so far," he replied with a wicked grin, forcing Ned Tonkin to have another jab at his rival for high office.

"Does that mean Chairman that the officers knew about this Welsh Office thing before we did. I thought it was supposed to be top secret?"

"Didn't we all, Councillor Tonkin. I've been kept as much in the dark about this as you have."

Looking long and hard at Anthony he warned. "I think you had better answer him Chief Executive. Did all the officers know before full Council did?"

Anthony responded with his usual political slant.

"My officers share my trust and of course each one knew about the plan."

The smug smiles from the top table team would have lit up Blackpool even though one or two were more of a leer at Ruth Tremlett as she adjusted her bra strap to a more comfortable position.

"Well that's just fine, Chairman. The entire district will know by now, assuming of course that your team up there are still knocking off their secretaries." Bill supposed.

The mood of the meeting changed the moment hints of 'sexual peccadillos' slipped into the agenda.

"Make your point, Bill," Ned Tonkin said. "Shut up or front up and say what yer mean."

"I intend to, Ned, loud and ruddy clear. By now secretaries will have told the tea lady who keen on gossip will have passed the news to the cleaners and the refuse collectors. The secrets of the staff toilets will be all over town by now. My God! What a cock-up," Bill replied throwing up his arms in despair.

"Nice turn of phrase under the circumstances," Janet said with a chuckle wishing Dee was around to record it all.

The officers were shocked at the unexpected disclosures and it showed; the innuendo aimed at them was a little bit too close for comfort and they began to bicker among themselves. However, Dick Dobie, the planning officer, had nothing to fear from such allegations; it was a departmental joke that the only thing that he could erect in any reasonable time was a bus shelter. It was common knowledge at the staff Christian Fellowship Group that sex, as far as conjugal rights were concerned, was a no go area. The sexual exploits of his colleagues pained him and they teased him unmercifully about his own unconfirmed escapades floating the corridors of local power that he was up for it if and when offered. Upset by the schoolboy behaviour of his colleagues he often toyed with the thought of blowing the whistle on the lot of them but he never had the guts to do it. However, from time to time, he mischievously hinted at their own philandering and today, with the heat on, he unwisely decided that it was time to give the fire a poke. In a stage whisper mixed with a little too much humour he went for the housing officer.

"I don't fancy your chances, Gordon, if your little game gets out."

"What little game is that, old boy?" Gordon Kempton asked anxiously.

"You know the one, old boy; one good turn for the housing officer and six points up the latest housing list for the ladies who come across."

Dick nudged him with his elbow and grinned at the others but being a bit short on common-sense he hadn't bargained for a public counter attack.

"Steady on, Dick, you're not entirely in the clear you know?" Gordon replied, winking at his pals. "All those improved erections you've been boasting about at site meetings. What little typing pool lovely has been on the end of those … Dickie boy?"

Dick Dobie looked so sick that Ruth Tremlett felt obliged to pass him a mint Imperial. Embarrassed, he tried to settle back in his seat but he looked a sorry sight as he played with his wedding ring. It didn't help at all when Arthur Yorkshire belatedly advised him, "If you want to start a dog fight, Dick, you don't pick on the Red Baron."

Meanwhile, the Chairman, having missed out on the social track records of the officials was desperately trying to maintain a sense of decorum in the chamber.

"Ladies and gentlemen simmer down, best we keep this under the covers for a while, at least until the defence plans are finalised," Pausing briefly while he worked out his next move he suggested,

"Now, Chief Executive, all you need do is to circulate the procedures to the proposed committee members as soon as possible and convene a meeting between the Lugworth Town Council, the Central Committee the Local Group Commander and Bobs yer uncle."

Mighty pleased with himself for having, against all odds, sorted the problem out, he sat down, ogled Ruth's breasts and waited for the applause.

"Just like that! Really, Chairman, you have no idea of what is involved. With respect your little list is just the tip of a very big iceberg, sir. There's plenty of work to be done, I can assure you of that," Anthony replied.

"Well get on and bloody do it then" Bill Jones said." Get your secretary off her back and onto her typewriter and only then will the smooth wheels of local Government start turning again."

Shocked to the core, Ida Williams blew her Methodist top.

"This really is the end Mr Jones, we are on the slippery slope to bawdiness. Closed session or not members of this Council are verging on the crudest behaviour. I have never heard such goings on. What would my dear Henry say if he were alive to hear this today? It is shocking, quite shocking."

Bill, overcome with laughter, challenged.

"My dear Ida, if your Henry was with us now he would be laughing his tartan socks off. He knew full well what this lot was up to and given half a chance he'd have been at it with 'em."

Bursting into tears Ida sat down and relying on her chapel teachings to turn the other cheek she quietly hummed her late husband's favourite hymn, 'Will your Anchor Hold in the Storms of Life.' He had been Captain of the Boys Brigade at the local Chapel and slightly out of tune, they bravely played it as he was lowered into his final resting place on the hillside above the village. The Chairman was not so godly in his response.

"Order, order. This is disgraceful, bloody disgraceful," and rapped the gavel up and down with such ferocity that it caused his water decanter to tremble and spill over. Brushing away Mrs. Tremett's loan of her lemon handkerchief, he tried to stem the water with his papers but it crept to the edge of the table and dripped onto the trousers of his Sunday suit.

"Apologies, ladies and gents, it won't happen again I can assure you. This whole episode has got me down, it really has, but whatever happens the press must be kept at bay until matters are under control. One little paragraph in the 'Courier' and the balloon will go up, and we can't have the public in a state of panic, can we?"

"Far better than a nuclear missile, not when we are panicking like hell already. That will never do, Chairman," Janet proposed with a touch of sarcasm.

"Just who is panicking, Councillor Bodmin? Not me, I'm the Chairman and I have control of the situation.

Now if we can get back to business perhaps the Chief Executive will outline the programme of events and then we can call it a day."

"Programme of events, it's a nuclear exercise not the village fete," Bill sighed.

Battle fatigue was a gross underestimate for the way Anthony was feeling as he wearily faced his increasingly hostile Council.

"To ensure we are all moving in the right direction, may I remind you that the arrangements for the exercise, although not yet in full detail, will be as laid down in the minutes of the special meeting held two years ago? For those of you who may have disposed of the ones circulated at the time, copies are available from the ever reliable Mrs Tremlett"

Peering over his designer spectacles he continued,

"It is the recommendation of Central Government, through the Welsh Office of course, that the code name for the exercise should be Operation Fall Out."

"Judging from today's performance, a very appropriate name it is too," Janet Bodmin replied, raising her arms to acknowledge the applause and laughter from her colleagues. Anthony was not amused and turned sharply to Ruth,

"I hope you are making a note of all this bickering and backbiting, Mrs Tremlett," he said, his voice beginning to show the strain he was under. Paramour or not Ruth was not going to be bullied; she knew her place and her responsibilities and was going to have her say.

"Of course I am, Mr Anderson-Shelta, that is what I'm paid to do is it not? The ratepayers expect their money's worth you know." The lead in her pencil snapped under pressure of controlling her feelings.

Bill Jones instantly picked up the tension between the two and was in on the act like a shot.

"Well, if I may say so, dear lady, they have certainly got their money's worth from you today. That dainty wrist of yours has been flying like the wind in your endeavours to keep up with the spoken word." His backhanded compliments out of the way, he carried on regardless.

"Now, if I may Chief Executive, let me remind everyone that if this minefield of extra marital activity ever got out, we are all finished? As for you lot up there sitting comfortably at the top table it will be the end of your index linked, inflation proof pensions and you will all be joining Norman Tebbit's 'biking for jobs brigade' looking for work. So beware, boyos, the slippery slope is nigh."

Every face, with the exception of Mrs Tremlett's, was looking pig sick. As the reality of the situation suddenly dawned, the sullen-faced officers shifted uncomfortably on their well-padded chairs until the Environmental Health Officer could take no more. Wheezing hysterically and watched with little sympathy by his colleagues he dashed from the room. Unperturbed by the cowardly display from his officers and eager to get on with matters before the golf course club house closed, Anthony continued to explain the rudiments of central and local Government planning.

"As I was saying, in the interests of security and brevity, 'Operation Fallout' has, for the time being, been shortened to 'Operation F.O.' Ignoring the grins that flickered across one or two faces, Anthony continued with what was becoming a Headmaster's address on Speech Day at the local Grammar School.

"In due course Lugworth Town Council will be issued with an official communiqué and it will be up to them to convene a special meeting of the community. In accordance with standing orders, Defence of the Nation clause 42 Welsh Valleys. Appendix B, paragraph 29.

"All emergency and security services must be ordered to attend this meeting and Councillor's Neal, Thomas and myself will meet with Councillor Jones to make the appointments to the special powers committee. Are you with me so far? If so I will get onto bunker space."

"I'm with you, Chief Executive," Janet responded wearily. "But half this lot are still in the fourth form, the only bunker space that interests them is the bar at the nineteenth hole."

Anthony's temper was shortening by the minute.

"Thank you, Ms Bodmin, please do not interrupt again. Time is at a premium and I have other details to attend to. Now, as I was saying, allocation of space in the bunker would normally be left to the co-ordinating committee although it is fair to say that priority must be given to senior officers of Council and as I am the only one, that means me. This will also include my family if they happen to be in the area of attack and my friends."

Beaming at Ruth she smiled back secure in the knowledge that she was as well placed in the bunker as she was in his affections. For the rest, badly shaken by the news that there was to be no place of safety for them or their kin was one thing but hearing it was to be open house underground for Anderson-Shelta, his retinue and his paramour was just about the last straw.

"Well, I'll be damned," Ned Tonkin said. "That just about takes the bloody biscuit. This is a rum do, Janet, a rum do."

"Too right, Ned, he's taking this nuclear family idea a bit too far. The barefaced cheek of the man," she loudly acclaimed.

Ben Neal was quick to scotch the idea. "It's not women, children and paramours first, it's emergency leaders and co-ordinators and it's down to me, as Chair of the Town Council, as to who goes where."

Absorbing the banter Anthony pushed ahead without further ado and invited questions.

The response was instant. Questions were bowled at him from all corners of the chamber and he fended them off with the skill of a young David Gower taking on the might of the West Indian bowlers without a safety helmet. Admiration shone from Mrs Tremlett; her beloved Anthony had again come up trumps in a very sticky situation.

Silent for far too long and realising he was rapidly losing ground, Tomo Thomas wiped his sweating brow and dived into the fray again, without thinking. Aware that the Chairman was already in the mire up to his knees, Anthony listened patiently and waited for him to rekindle the discord in the ranks.

"Let me say now, ladies and gents, this is not a ruddy raffle; every man-jack of us on this Council must have a fair a chance of a billet in the bunker. Rest assured, each case will be taken on its merits and not on the Chief Executive's say-so and social listings. I've still got some pull you know," Tomo insisted.

Slumping back into his chair, the Chief Executive inwardly sighed. All the advantage he had gained went down the pan the moment his Chairman opened his mouth. Despite his vast experience, he had never known such civil unrest even though he had worked for some petty administrations. He awaited the outcome of yet another verbal wrangle.

"A bunker is the last thing that this Council needs at the moment," Councillor Evans acknowledged. "By the time you lot have decided on available space and who gets it they'll have dropped the bloody bomb."

"I still think it should be calculated on the number of sheep per head of family," Ned Tonkin, the largest sheep breeder in the Mid Border area suggested.

"Order, gentlemen, order," the Chairman yelled. "Everyone will be taken into consideration. There will be little compromise on what I have had to say so best we leave it now and let the Chief Executive and his team tie up all the loose ends."

"You know what that will mean, Janet old girl, FO to the lot of us," Bill suggested.

Ida Williams blanched! Gathering up her papers she screeched.

"Really, Mr Jones, this is the end. I cannot remain in this decadent Council Chamber any longer. My apologies Mr Chairman, but I resign," and she swept out of the chamber.

"Oh no, not another by election, the ratepayers won't like it I can tell you. Well, I think that concludes this extraordinary meeting. It has wreaked havoc upon our emotions perhaps we should retire to my office for liquid refreshment."

"And what will the ratepayers have to say about that, Chairman?" asked Janet.

"Well, what I meant to say was …"

Before he could explain the swing doors burst open and a breathless Dee Donnington staggered into the room. Shocked at the sudden intrusion into a closed session, Anthony, hoping for an acceptable explanation, silently stared at her. The unwanted intrusion was kicked aside without apology. Dee composed herself and stood defiant in the empty press gallery.

Obliged to speak the Chairman asked: "Young woman, what on earth are you doing in here? This is a closed meeting and we are holding it in camera, the press must withdraw."

It was plain to Janet that her friend was clearly in a state of agitation, something had upset her and it showed in her flushed features. Before she could ask her, Dee, unable to control her anger, demanded.

"How dare you exclude the press from something as important as this? The public have a right to be told what is happening. Nuclear bombs in the Welsh Borders! This is hold the front-page stuff. You can't kill this story, I won't let you."

The game was up for Anderson-Shelta. It was clear from her ranting that she had somehow become party to the detailed defence plans and she was about to blow the meeting and his reputation with it to smithereens. Unless he could stop her blowing the whistle all would be revealed in print on the front page of the Western Mail and dropped through ninety percent of the letter boxes in the Principality before he had time to clear his walnut desk. His first reaction was to let the situation take its own course and see how the Chairman handled her before bringing his own powers of office into force.

Tomo Thomas was ready for his version of 'Call my Bluff', the one the management team called the heavy metal version of 'Give Us a Clue.' Sweating profusely he leaned across Ruth Tremlett in a vain attempt to grasp some help from his Chief Executive. To avoid his challenging body odour she waved her useful yellow handkerchief and he backed away. His blood pressure already at boiling point, he yelled at the invading journalist.

"What on earth are you on about, young lady? There is nothing untoward going on I can assure you; we have simply been discussing one or two items additional to the agenda. Now, I suggest you re-join your colleagues in the press room and I will bring the meeting to a close and adjourn for a late lunch."

Defiant, Dee stood her ground; framed in the doorway, hands on hips, she looked every bit a latter day Christina Pankhurst.

"Nothing going on and you lot closeted in here like a conclave of Cardinals waiting for the white smoke. Come on, chaps, I'm not stupid, I know you're discussing nuclear defence."

"She's right, Chairman, she definitely isn't stupid," Janet Bodmin said calmly. "I suggest we come clean otherwise it will be curtains as far as security goes."

A little more calm and with Janet backing her up, Dee tried to appeal to his better judgement.

"Look, Tomo, I do know what's been happening in here, come on, you know and I know what the real agenda is. Share it with us for God's sake."

Anderson-Shelta wasn't quite fast enough to stop Ned Tonkin shouting his mouth off and finally giving the game away.

"Look here, Miss," he said. "Who tipped you off, Councillor Williams? She's not long since left the meeting."

Dee shrugged her shoulders and ignored him.

"Okay then, it's the Environmental Health Officer? It must have been him. The gutless idiot, he couldn't take it."

"No, not him either. He passed me, wheezing so much that he couldn't get a word out. Anyway I never disclose my sources."

"Come on, Dee," urged Bill Jones. "Best out with it. You've got us over a barrel and we'll have to give you the story if only to keep it in the camp. Come on; tell us who let the rocket off its launcher?"

"If I tell you, can I have the exclusive?"

The Chief Executive paused and thought carefully before answering.

"Within the confines of standing orders, I think that might be possible Ms Donnington but you to will have to abide by the rules and play the game."

"And what rules are they Mr Anderson-Shelta," she asked him politely.

"Nothing and I mean nothing must be released without prior agreement from the co-ordinating committee. Do you agree Councillor Jones?"

"Fine by me, Chief Executive, subject to Ms. Donnington confirming her source, we have to know that. Also she must not go all around the Wrekin to tell us."

Taking her time, Dee strolled across the room, mounted the rostrum and perched herself on the edge of the oak table. She waited a moment or two and winked at Janet before dropping her own bomb.

"Fair enough, Bill. If everyone is sitting comfortably, then I'll begin," she mimicked. "When you asked us to withdraw from the meeting Chairman, Phil Bennett from the Express and Star, decided to call it a day and go for a swift pint with the others. I wanted to hang around in case there was an announcement of some sort so I went for a coffee from the vending machine."

Pausing to pour a glass of water from the Chairman's carafe, she took a sip and continued with her tale. "After a while, I felt a bit useless so I studied the notice board and then went for a pee. I used the female cloakroom by the main entrance, the one used by the secretarial staff. I was combing my hair when I heard some chap ranting and raving in the gents next door."

Janet Bodmin started laughing. "De`ja`vu, Bill," she said. "This is where you came in."

The penny was slowly dropping; Anthony lowered his head into his well-manicured hands and pleaded with his maker not to let this nightmare go on any longer. Not even the sensual touch of his live out lover could stem the black cloud hovering over him; Dee's excited voice brought him back to reality.

"Shall I continue, Mr Chairman?"

"Continue! Good God, is there more to come? I don't think I can cope with anymore."

"Not much more, Chairman," she said. "As I was saying, there I was in the ladies toilet and over the sound of water splashing against the adjoining wall some half cut, upper class twit was ranting on about the Prime Minister sending rockets into Wales because some Teddy bear on television had upset her. So what's it all about then?"

Waiting for a moment she left the rostrum and sat down among the open-mouthed Councillors; the room went quiet. The long silence was broken by the odd snigger from the officers struggling to maintain some dignity and behave like the professionals they purported to be. Almost out for the count, Tomo again lost control of Council procedure and staggered from the room.

"It's his prostate or a very large scotch and water," Ned explained.

"Whatever it is he's done for," Bill said to Janet.

The Chief Executive was incandescent with rage at Crispin's latest 'foot in it'.

"Wanker, wanker and thrice wanker" he whispered to Ruth who, completely misunderstanding his comment slipped her hand into the pocket of his well-pressed Daks.

"Oh my God," he gasped. "That idiot of a Member of Parliament has done it again, Ruth."

Aware of the consequences Bill asked. "So what do we do now, Anderson-Shelta? The lady from the press is snapping at our heels and we need a firm hand at the tiller."

"Yes, come on, boyo," Ned Tonkin added. "You're paid chief officer scale to think for us all. So do us all a favour and do what you're paid to do and get your head round this bloody mess of a meeting."

The situation was reaching boiling point and Anthony's florid features told their own story; the situation had to be dampened down, immediate action needed or the game was up. Clearing his confused head he conjured up his stock answer.

"I had better consult standing orders and check with the legal team."

Bill Jones had a better idea. "Never mind all that standing order nonsense, I'm Central Co-ordinator and will tell you what's to be done."

Pointing at Dee he went on. "As you seem to be well in the know young woman, we can appoint you our official press representative and expect you to keep the others off our back. The Housing Officer will liaise with you and keep you informed at every level." Gordon Kemp looked highly pleased with this arrangement and smiled broadly at his colleagues.

"And what do I get out of all this, Bill?" Dee asked.

"Press releases exclusive to you in the first instance and an agreed fee plus expenses if engaged on Council business."

Janet whispered to Dee.

"Plus sleeping-in allowance! If that creep Kemp has his way."

"I can handle him, no sweat," Dee replied and waved across the room to him.

Unaware that Dee was even better at dog fighting than the Red Baron himself, he smiled smugly at his colleagues and touched his nose.

The meeting relaxed as the ever-efficient Ruth Tremlett eventually committed the final details of the 'secret plan' to paper. In the absence of the runaway Chairman, the Vice-Chairman announced.

"Well, ladies and gentlemen, I must say despite the odd hiccup, this has been a good day's work. If someone would kindly nudge Councillor Hughes and tell him it's all over for the day, we can retire to the Chairman's parlour for drinks."

"That's if there's anything left to drink, Bill, anyway he's having his usual tantrum when things get out of hand." Janet commented as she stretched her legs and stood up.

"Yes, and if Ned has his way, he'd best make the most of it," Bill replied.

Janet asked the Acting-Chairman. "May I say something before you declare the meeting closed?"

"Of course, Mrs Bodkin," he helpfully replied.

"It's Bodmin, and do try to stick to that if you plan taking over future meetings. All I wanted to say is that there's only one obvious conclusion to be drawn from all that has gone on today."

"And what little pearl of feminine wisdom might that be, dear lady," he said with an amused look on his ruddy Welsh face.

She half-heartedly corrected him. "Feminist not feminine! All I wanted to say is that at least no one here can deny that it was a Tory Member of Parliament that leaked it to the press."

Janet pulled Dee to her feet, pushed her towards the swing doors and together held them open for the amused Councillors until the Chamber was clear.

Alone with his paramour at last, Anthony sighed and exclaimed quietly, "It's been a long session, Ruth, I think I'll give the golf club a miss this afternoon. If anybody wants me, your good-self excluded of course, I shall be at home, otherwise I will see you on the morrow."

"Your wife will be surprised, Anthony, shall I telephone her with news of your early arrival, or shall we leave things as they are?"

"Leave things as they are my dear, just in case I have a change of heart. After all, I am told that there are more ways to kill a cat than stuffing it with cream."

Having ascertained that no one was about, he kissed his secretary lightly on her waiting lips, picked up his crocodile skin document case (a gift from the Member of Parliament) and jauntily left the room.

Ruth glanced around the deserted chamber and sighed to herself. Looking into her make-up mirror she admiringly said, "Foreplay or no foreplay, I'll have you one day, Mr Chief Executive, and that day ... or night ... is not far off."

Gathering up her written notes, pens and pencils, she slid them into a large Price-Jones plastic carrier bag and arranged them on top of the fresh pair of knickers she always carried, just in case. Well hidden among her personal bits and bobs was the small, neat plastic case that held her well powdered Family Planning Association Dutch cap.

Chapter Six

"That's some sort of memory, Jan," Dee said. "You're bringing it all back, and so vividly, too. It was a crazy time; I don't know why you haven't written up all that detail. Was it really that long ago?"

Janet laughed. "Yes and an even crazier things went on. I have toyed with the idea of a book, written a lot down, too. The drama group, the Barratt boys, Greenham Common with Aunt Daphne and Luggworth's acting Rector – what was his name?"

"Clive Makepeace," Angela said. "Who can forget him? Such a nice guy, too?"

Dee giggled, "As camp as 'old harry' and terrific fun with it. It would make a great story, perhaps a movie, who knows?

Janet gave it some thought.

"Oh, I don't know if I can put something like that together. You know what I'm like, start off full of it, doodle away for hours and then get bored when I run out of ideas. Believe it or not I've been trying it out, on and off for 10 years. It's all in there and in some sort of order too but I need to find a way of locking it all in." Tapping her head she added. "It takes time but it's all up there in my head and I'm into so many things at the moment."

"Find the time, Jan," Angela said as she slowed down to make a right turn. "You more or less went through a good couple of chapters just talking about Anthony's barmy army."

"And the defence exercise, the widow Tremlett, and the rank and file of Lugworth, and that's not the half of it is it?" Dee encouraged. "We haven't even touched on Aunt Daphne yet."

Angela stopped the car and pointed to a Castilla on the hillside.

"We're about to, it's not so far now, and you can just see the estate across the vineyards."

Way up on the side of a hill was a substantial fortress-like building part hidden by olive groves. In the distance Montserrat could be just about seen above the loitering mist and cloud hovering between the mountain range.

"Better press on," Angela said as she started the engine. It was just over 40 minutes since they left Café Ramble for Villafranca, about 18 kilometres on the main route to Tarragona. The couple of hours spent catching up in the café bar had been well worthwhile. Angela had opened up a few of her Aunt's secrets and explained about the De Banca family, which helped set the scene for her friends. She had decided on the long way round using the smaller roads and it was well worth the diversion. The extended drive through the vineyards was spectacular.

"Can't see any grapes yet," Dee grumbled as they gathered speed along the avenues of olive trees. "Where are they all, Ange?" she mocked.

"Harvested, bottled and on ice waiting for you two. You are now entering Cava country, home to the finest champagne grapes in Spain. The locals recommend rolling it round the tongue, sip it until your taste buds tingle and sup until you are fully quenched. "

The moment she saw the distant castle, Dee was raring to go.

"My God, Janet, is this it? It's gone to my head already, a glass or two would soon rekindle writer's block," Dee promised.

The size of the estate grew bigger with each kilometre and it was beginning to dawn on Janet and Dee that this was more than they had bargained for.

"Blimey, Angie was the old girl tied in with royalty or something, or am I imagining all this? It's a mighty big ranch sister, mighty big indeed," she mimicked in her Sue Ellen drawl.

Angela tried to hide her excitement, it had been building up since she collected her friends from the airport and was bursting to give them the low down on Daphne's secret lover.

"You're almost right, Dee, she was a Marquise, the daughter of a Spanish aristocrat and the nearest we'll ever get to Princess Grace."

"I think she means it, Dee. I've been waiting to get here ever since Angela told me about it."

"Wait until you see the views. It's like magic, a glass of bubbly and a sunset any reasonable painter would die for," Angela replied.

"So you're back to painting again?"

"Yes, Janet, I am. I trained for it, did bugger all about it after I married Tony and with this wonderful place to hide in I'm going to give it another go."

"Bit like getting back on a bike I suppose, Angie," Dee suggested.

"Well not quite, but I get the point. Look over there girls." Slowing the car to a virtual stop she directed their attention to the Castillo by now well within range of the eagle-eyed occupants.

"Good Lord surely that's not all yours, Angela, it's positively palatial. Can you see it, Jan, it's hard to believe?"

Angela grinned. "Seeing is believing Dee but it's not all mine. I have a converted winery tucked around the side."

"The love nest?" Jan said quietly.

"That's right, Daphne's secret hide away. Supper will be laid out on the terrace and we can eat whenever we choose."

Revving up she slewed the car round a sharp gravelled bend with ease. "Done that wheeler before have we not, darling?" Dee commented sarcastically.

"I've had a lot of practice these past few weeks, it handles well on the loose surfaces around here; you're riding with an expert today, Dee Donnington."

"Good thing, too," she agreed. "I wouldn't fancy these stony roads on a dark night."

"There's a new Seat Amosa 1.6 four wheel drive in the garage if you want to give it a go. It comes with …"

Her words were cut short. "Yes, we know it comes with the inheritance. Anything else we should know about, Angie?" And they laughed together.

Swinging the car into a small courtyard surrounded by a high stone wall she parked under the branches of half a dozen olive trees and a couple of ancient fig trees, the cool air was a welcome relief. Three cats, a Siamese, a variegated ginger and a small, dark grey tabby dropped into the back of the coupé from an overhanging branch.

"Hell's teeth, Angie, where did those come from? Could give a couple of old girls like us heart attacks," Janet suggested.

"Speak for yourself, my heart's as sound as a bell according to Gill and she should know," Dee said.

Janet laughed, "Still following in daddy's footsteps is she?"

"It was the right time to quit the Welsh Office after everything came crashing down on Lugworth and the right decision to chuck in the civil service and study medicine. She qualified and joined Daddy's practice. When he died she became senior partner and loves it. We stay in touch. What more could a girl ask for."

As they walked across the yard to the front door Angela asked Dee.

"So all is still well on the home front then? I'm glad to hear it. It was high time you settled down. How long has it been now twelve years and nothing on the side?"

"Would I ever, Angie? Gave all that up yonks' ago didn't I, Jan?"

"She's teasing you, Ange; we both know you've played fair with Gill. If you hadn't you would have answered to us." Janet confirmed.

"If she can ever get away from the practice bring her with you next time. It's always good to see you two together, wherever or whenever."

Pushing wide the big double doors into the entrance hall, Jan and Dee were stunned at the sight and size of the house. From the outside it appeared to be a plain, cream-coated, two-storey building converted from two adjoining wine caverns, one on slightly higher ground and at a ninety-degree angle to the other. The deceptive layout hid the real interior. The buildings were linked by a cleverly designed marbled colonnade and a small wrought iron staircase alongside a gentle slope. Whitewashed walls offset the rich blue and yellow ceramic floor tiles laid between the two safety glass windows looking over the illuminated wine cellars below. Five carved oak doors led into the main living quarters where a delighted Angela gave them the full walkabout tour.

The first door leading into to the pale yellow and white washed dining room was large, airy and at that moment flooded with evening sunshine. Spacious enough for six to eight diners, at a push it could cope with ten if the row of folding glass doors were opened onto the terrace. Outside, a raised wooden deck straddled a sunken walled garden with a small pond and a solar fountain that bubbled gently as the last of the day's sun generated the buzz of the motor. The views across the vineyards towards San Salvador were quite stunning and the group ambled onto the solid deck that took in a major corner of the house. At the far end the three cats, last seen on the leather seats of Angela's car, were lolling about in the warm sunlight, a crude wooden ladder set at a slight angle allowed escape to the garden below.

"This bit must have been Daphne's idea," Janet suggested. "I bet on a clear day the old salt could catch a glimpse of the sea."

"I thought that, too, when I first came over, but I've spotted it a couple of times on a good day. She once wrote to me said she was on holiday with friends and making a ladder for the cats. I didn't have a clue what she was on about; she called it getting back to her guiding days."

Round the corner on a white wooden table three champagne flutes and a bottle of Cava Natural rested in an iced filled cooler.

Picking up the bottle Dee said. "Nicely timed. Who came up with this then? Not you, Angie, you've been with us all afternoon and this ice is really cold." Turning to Janet she mischievously queried. "Well this is a turn-up, is there another secret love affair that we don't know about?"

"Stuff and nonsense, Dee. Where does she get her ideas from, Janet?"

"Still living in hopes for you I expect, Angie, she'll calm down after a few days. You know what she's like when we get together, she still believes she's thirty and flirty," Janet said with an affectionate grin.

"Dear girl, did you ever grow up, Dee?" Angie asked with a sigh. "You're becoming more of a Peter Pan every time I see you? I thought your very own Wendy would have mellowed you by now! For your information and to keep your blood pressure off the boil, along with the house I inherited Diorita. I call her Doris ... the live in maid – well more of an 'annexe at the back of the house' maid. She had been with the two of them from day one, looked after them well, cooked, cleaned, and did the garden. This marvellous little woman manages to cope with most chores and the language. Long may she stay on board?"

"This gets more like the "Ladies of Llangollen" every day, Dee said. "Those two extraordinary old girls lived together for years and years with a loyal maid to help out after they landed in Wales from Ireland. They were the talk of the town in late 1800s, entertaining royalty and the like and became celebrities in their own right until they died. It was rather sad, after the first one died the other soon followed. A bit like Daphne and... what was her name?"

"Consequala, although they tell me Daphne always called her Connie. Ring any bells now?"

"Let's sit down and think about it, Champagne is good for the brain and one of us might remember."

"Chivas Regal opens up the memory, too, Angie," Dee said. "We'll start on that after supper."

The three friends sat down and Angela poured out the wine, it was ice cold and just about perfect. Lifting her bubbling glass Janet proposed a toast.

"To Aunt Dapher's, may she be joined on her last cruise by her beloved Connie and sail on forever?"

"Aunt Daphers" they responded as one.

"That was a romantic and poetic thing to say, Janet. "Especially up here on the bridge."

Dee walked to the railed edge and lifted a waterproof cover from a stand over-looking the gardens. Tucking her head under the cover she exposed a mounted brass telescope and yelled.

"Oh yes, this was definitely Daphne's idea, it's an old brass telescope – naval issue – mounted on a gunmetal revolving stand. Peering through it she announced.

"You could pin-point a cruise missile coming in at any angle with this thing."

Janet immediately went into recall mode.

"Don't mention those, Dee; you know how she felt about nuclear weapons. She'd be shocked to the core if she knew we are probably zapping them into Iraq at this very moment while we reminisce in rural Spain, cut off from Blair's war cabinet and doing bugger all about it. Eighty five or not, Angela, your old Aunt would be outside Number Ten with her banner unfurled and Tony Benn on her arm."

Janet smiled. "It was her own decision to join us on the coach trip to Greenham Common and she was one of the first peace groups to break through security to sit on a silo before getting arrested. I can't believe it's almost 21 years ago since we all set off from Lugworth. What persuaded you to bring her with you?"

"I couldn't stop her. I only went to provoke Anthony; he was living, eating and sleeping Operation bloody Fallout and I had to shut him up. Glad I went though, especially with you two and the Lugworth lot. Daphne simply got wind of it and before I knew it she was on the bus, Girl Guide tent and transistor radio tuned to test match special before we could say 'howzat'."

Laughing at the thought, Janet walked across to the wooden trellis that cut off the cats from the kitchen area; it was covered in deep blue Morning Glory and as she bent to smell the blooms. Angela called out to her.

"Daphne's favourite flowers, they all but covered the front of her cottage at Cowes. She just loved the colour. It was a super place, converted from a row of empty coastguard cottages which she bought cheaply when she retired from the WRNS."

"Fantastic view of the Solent shipping," Dee recalled. "I remember when we all went for Cowes week; she was a great host, just about every bloody Admiral in the Fleet dropping in for a gin and angostura before the sun dropped below the yard arm."

"What happened to it after she died?"

"She was a bit miffed when the WRNS merged with the Royal Navy. "Can't have gals on board battleships, recipe for trouble, mark my words," Angela mimicked. "These days it's now known as Oxbridge House, a retirement home for elderly ex-wrens managed and run by a couple of former Queen Alexandra naval nurses. Recently refurbished and extended with a pool of money to keep it going, it is an established Charitable Trust. I am Chair of the Trust and use the money she left me – I didn't need it – to restore some of the out buildings and add a long, glassed veranda for watching the shipping in comfort. Managed by the WRNS Benevolent Association ex wrens in need of short and long term care live there. Many staying until the end of their days and like Daphne, can be buried at sea if they wish."

"You never told us about that," Janet said. "I'd like to help out. You, too, I expect, Dee. Perhaps your friend Bos could make a documentary."

Angela seemed more than a little emotional as she continued the story. "She made a few protests about women at sea among all the hot bloodied sailors and she even wrote to the Princess Royal, Commander-in-Chief, WRNS, but it didn't do any good.

"Whenever she watched HRH on television all kitted out for Trooping the Colour she would let rip.

"Whoever came up with the idea of an Admiral of the Fleet on horseback should be strapped to the mast and given thirty lashes."

"Ouch," Dee said. "Bit heavy on the Royal backside, did she give up after that?"

"More like caved in. She told me at the time. 'It's no good Angela, it's been all tied up shipshape and Bristol fashion by the Admiralty lot. If I keep whingeing on about it, I'll be on defaulters, off caps and marching orders into oblivion.'"

It went quiet before Ange spoke again.

"At least she went down in flying colours; white ensign draped over the coffin and the light blue braid on her battered WRNS hat as she slipped over the side of the Admiral's ceremonial barge into the 'oggin at Spithead."

"Oggin, what on earth is that?" Dee asked.

"Nautical term for the sea and don't ask me where it comes from, I only know it is. The memorial service was in the Chapel at Greenwich, HRH and First Sea Lord in attendance, a Royal Marine band to see her off and half the defence staff, medal ribbons and all on parade. It was a never to be forgotten day but I'd still like to know who the man in grey suit was who spoke for 'Queen and Country' at her burial service. He seemed a pretty important chap and well informed of her history; he was on board the barge for the final salute- a cannon fired off Spithead. Pretty moving stuff I can tell you, spoiled only by my ignorant husband coming out with: "And what did she do to get all that pomp and bloody circumstance and her camped out at Greenham Common?" But by then he'd had a tot or two from the Rum Fanny when they ceremonially spliced the main-brace, an unusual honour for a woman and one she would have savoured. Tony could never hold the rum; that's what Mons Officer Cadet School does for the character, Gin and Tonic yes, rum no. Lady Anne gave him a withering look which shut him up for the rest of the day, thank God."

"Do we know if the Marquise was at the ceremony?"

"No, it was a private burial at sea, although I do recall a Spanish chap from the Embassy came to pay last respects on behalf of the family; something like that. Although I was executor of her estate, the Admiralty and the Foreign Office did the organising, I've got the list somewhere at home."

Noticing that Janet was still looking at the flowers and had not been fully into the conversation, Angela took a bottle to top up her glass.

"Everything okay old friend? Here, let me top you up."

Holding back tears as well as a shrub or two she was peering into the trellis. "If that's what I think it is, Ange it's been there a good while."

Carefully unwinding the small branches weathered clear plastic bag she eventually freed and gasped.

"Dee, come and have a look at this."

Sensing Jan was upset Dee quickly joined her pals and for almost a minute they stared at the green, purple and white object in Janet's cupped hands. Janet silently carried the tiny knitted, woollen doll to the table. Dee broke the silence.

"Blow me, Angela; are you two thinking what I'm thinking? Daphne made lots of these to hang on the wire fence around the Greenham air base, thousands of them were brought by women from almost everywhere; they became symbols for the peace campaign. The Ministry of Defence heavies and the police tried to pull them off but we just kept putting them back again. Don't you remember Ange, Daphne wouldn't give up and ended up pushing a black American service woman off the fence and telling her that she of all people should be helping support the women, not fighting us? If we hadn't dragged her away she would have been arrested again."

Angela was almost in tears. "She was marvellous wasn't she? Didn't give a damn about authority, all she cared about was stopping the cruise missiles parked on England's green and pleasant land. No wonder she chose Jerusalem for her memorial service."

Pausing for a moment she added, "Look girls, Aunt Daphne wouldn't want us to be mawkish about this; she would want us to celebrate our Greenham friendship. So let's eat, drink and be merry. Doris has prepared supper for us; it's in the hot cabinet in the kitchen."

Wrapping her arms around her best friends she walked them across the patio, Janet, still grasping the woolly doll, laid it on the dining table.

"Another bottle, Angela," she said, the writer in her at last coming to the front. "Here by hangs another chapter in the day-to-day life of Lugworth, circa 1981ish.

Three hours later Angela called last orders.

"It's getting time for body clock changes to take effect and you two must be very tired after such a long day travelling. Your rooms are ready and I'll leave it to you to choose, all guest rooms have en-suite, air conditioning and blinds guaranteed to let in the scented night air and keep out the mosquitoes."

"Thank God for that." Jan said, "If they are going to attack anyone, it's me.

"Because you're rather tasty," Dee said with a grin. "Anyway whatever, I'm for bed, we've got plenty of time for storytelling tomorrow and I shall need a clear head. Are you retiring too, Angie?

"No, not yet, I'm on Spanish time. I usually read for an hour or so, all Daphne's books are in her little 'snug', as she used to call her quiet room; sometimes I sit in there and usually find something of hers to look through."

She kissed her two companions, "Off you go, Doris will have left your bags outside the rooms at end of the long corridor; they open out onto the veranda.

Leaving Doris to clear up, she took her part-filled wine glass into a small side room leading off the main reception area. It was all around her, naval and cricket memorabilia, framed photographs, some old newspapers, a couple of videos titled 'Greenham Years', and one or two colourful contemporary paintings. Two blown up press photos were pinned to a large green baize board. Angela had looked at them so many times since she inherited the house she could identify almost each woman peering through the criss-crossed wire fence between them and the American guards; a military helicopter hovered above them.

Highlighted with a circle was the determined face of her Aunt surrounded by chanting women and taken just before she broke cover and made a dash for the huge silos housing the cruise missiles. The other featured newspaper headlines showing her being dragged away under arrest both made the front pages of most national newspapers. Amused at the historic scenes, toasted her old Aunt "Good on you, Daphne Oxford, you did it, we baulked at it. Lady Anne – God Bless her – was so angry at the time but as she said in her eulogy, she never forgot what you did at Greenham Common."

Taking "Blue for a Girl" written by Peter Hoyer-Miller, nephew of a former Director of the WRNS from a lower shelf, she dusted it down went to her bedroom and laid it on the bedside table alongside a flask of Earl Grey tea Doris had left for her. It was her dear old Aunt's favourite nightcap.

She stripped naked, showered and admired herself in the full-length mirror. Despite her advancing years, her shapely reflection returned a still attractive woman and she smiled back at herself. Recalling what might have been had she succumbed to the 'offers' from 'kindly men' keen to show her that sex after divorce was still worth a go, her affair with an up and coming tenor might have worked out had not the gossip columnists got wind of it.

He turned out to be engaged to a French dancer who dropped him in favour of selling her story to an up market Sunday supplement. Angela managed to escape the media scramble by retreating to Switzerland while her estranged husband, Anthony, honourably took the flack back home. In his defence the tenor claimed she had broken his heart but on a promise from Daphne Oxford that she would break the rest of him if he dared darken her niece's doorstep again, he left the country to join a Canadian Opera Company. Arranged by the Art's Minister, (under orders from Lady Llewellyn), and aided and abetted by her reliable godmother, whose good friend happened to have set up the company in Toronto, she was soon over the affair and back on terra firma in Hampshire again. Wrapped in a bright pink bathrobe,

Angela wandered back to her bedroom, poured out the Earl Grey and flicked through 'Blue for a Girl' published to celebrate the Silver Jubilee of the WRNS in 1960. Before deciding whether she should forgo her bedtime read, the decision was made for her when a small wad of neatly folded lined paper fell to the floor; she recognised the bold pen and ink strokes of her Aunt's handwriting.

"Angela dear,

I hope one day you may find this, a sort of ship's log of a voyage of discovery unexpectedly embarked upon, perhaps too late in life. No doubt you are wondering how we got here and I think it's a fair bet that your loyal friends are with you at some point, if not they should be. I know by the time you find this letter, Consquela will be gone, but I also know she wanted someone of mine to inherit our hide away, all I have is you Angela, apart from my sister. We were never really hidden in the true sense; we simple wanted our life to be ours.

It all began in Cowes a week or two after our Greenham escapade. After my arrest and short break in Holloway, I came back to my sister Ann's feeling a bit worn out and quite shocked by my self-imposed ordeal at the hands of the MOD police. However, looking back I realised it had affected me more than I thought; you thought so at the time and suggested I needed to rest up after all the our war games, an experience I now consider to be one of the best of my life.

After a week or two of Ann's cosseting and occasional reprimands it was time to up sticks and retreat to Cowes for some bracing sea air and space to think. It was still fair weather sailing and a good few boats were anchored off. You know how it is, where seafarers gather, party time follows and before long I was pink-ginning it at the RYS when I ran into Sybil

Martin, (we served together at Lossiemouth just before she married Commander Air Roger Scott-Johnston.) Later, I was promoted to Chief Officer and sent to the Admiralty. Forgive me for rabbiting on dear.

The Scott-Johnstons had retired to Warsash on the Solent and I hadn't seen them for years, so they offered Sunday lunch and I went over on the ferry. It was there I first met Connie, an oncologist working an exchange arrangement between her hospital in Madrid and the Elizabeth Garrett Anderson where Sybil's son-law Ralph, was consultant neurologist. It was Sybil's 65th [h] birthday and just about every grandchild had turned up for grannie's big day – we never seemed to get round to those did we dear? And Ralph invited a colleague to join the weekend party. It was a typical English occasion and the young woman was finding it a bit of an ordeal. However, her English was reasonable and I spoke a bit of Spanish – I was stationed in Gibraltar for a year or so and somehow we got along and, despite the age gap of some 10 years, we managed to convey our interests until Roger raised the Greenham issue. Some of the older grandchildren took my side. They thought it was quite heroic for an old girl like me to do her time in Holloway simply for her beliefs but it was difficult explaining it to Connie. Nevertheless, she got the drift and made sympathetic noises which I thought came more out of politeness but when it came time to leave she suggested she would like to hear more, so I gave her my Cowes' address and left it at that.

Weeks went by most of which were spent at Ann's during the stupid defence exercise, when it all went wrong; I accompanied Anne to London for the State Opening at the House, and stayed on for two weeks to enjoy some culture between medical appointments in Harley Street. From there I went to Cowes for a few *days to lock up the cottage before autumn sets in. The mail had piled up, mostly junk of course, and that's when I spotted the postcard from Spain, some place called Villafranca, it was signed Consuela, I was taken aback by its suddenness. I still have the card. You' will find it pasted on the back of this book, do read it before we go on.*

Angela cast back to the inside cover, the colourful postcard of a vineyard at harvest and villagers dancing barefoot in large tubs of red grapes meant nothing to her. Carefully lifting the top edge, she eased it off and turned it over.

"To Senora Oxford, The harvest of the grape is the special time in my region and this is how we celebrate; you must come and see it one day. My family have all the vines and it is custom to go home to enjoy the festival then I shall return to the Garrett Anderson Hospital for a short time and then return to Madrid for my work. The time has been long since we met at English lunch and I would like us to meet again, I shall be back into London next year if my arrangements are made. I am able to be contacted at the Marsden for another a few days and if you can find me it will please me to hear of you. Consquela de la Barca.

Angela turned back to the letter and read on. You see dear, I could have missed the boat, the card had been posted six weeks before and I hadn't given a second thought that I might hear from her again; she had by them left London and I have to confess to being disappointed. It took some time to track her down, Sybil and Roger had left for warmer climes in Sydney with their son, a county cricketer who coached a local college team during the closed season in England. Eventually I caught up with Ralph at the Marsden – he had been lecturing in America – and he me found the address of the Madrid hospital. I rattled off a letter of apology and awaited the reply; the response came almost by return and to say I was delighted is an understatement. We briefly met again when she made a stopover in London on her way to a World Health Conference in Brazil and our friendship was somehow cemented at Heathrow. From then, like topsy, it just grew. It seems silly to say it was love at first sight but neither of us could understand or dared cope with our feelings, particularly me, with my disciplined upbringing and at my age too. After a series of get togethers here and in Madrid – you remember I kept popping off to Spain for a touch of the sun – by Spring the following year, the time of my birthday, this amusing, gentle and courteous young Doctor had taken a corner of my life and made it hers, claiming the rest as time went on. Believe me Angela, to be swept of your feet at any time in your early life must be exhilarating but at the approach of late middle age, it is a calming, comforting moment that washes you away into timelessness. I simply could not comprehend what had happened or where it may take us, but wherever or whatever, I couldn't give a damn and neither could she. At Easter that year, she took me home to Villafranca. It felt like my first day at public school and I wanted someone to take my hand and see me to the door. It was a huge culture shock going into a historic Spanish connection going back centuries, you' feel it and see it as you wander the estates and quietly enjoy (I hope) our home. I was introduced to her aged mother – her father was dead.

"Mama, this is Daphne – my lover, companion and friend – your blessings Provo." She looked me over and said nothing, Conni held my grip and whispered 'it is custom', smiled and continued, "I am now ready to *share my home and I take the key and then we meet the family at dinner."*

Her mother beckoned to a suitably turned out, slightly effeminate man in his early middle years, Senor Jose de Cabolet the familia lawyer, I expect you to have met him by now., who handed her a large key and stood back. The old lady lifted it to her lips and silently offered it to her only daughter, Conni responded by kissing first her mother's hand and then both cheeks.

I could only stand and watch until Conni raised my hand and gave it to her mother; she smiled enough to show me that her daughter had inherited the gentleness. She patted my hand warmly and still said nothing. We walked across the cobbled courtyard to a huge wooden gate that took us out of the Castillo into the vineyards, and there it stood, our soon to be hideaway home.

Over time, it had been restored and renovated almost to what you see today, our bags were in the door way accompanied by Dorito, who came with the gift.

It is, I hope, now yours, a place of love and peace for my much-loved niece and God daughter to share with her constant friends. I am only sad that I did not share my secret with you earlier. Enjoy our space, tell our story among yourselves and remember me with laughter.

Dear girl, so much love and blessings to you and your friends.

Aunt Daphne."

The following morning Angela was up with the lark, she had a slight hangover and yearned for her first coffee of the day. There was little sign of her two exhausted friends so she wandered onto the terrace for a breath of fresh early morning air. Doris had laid up for breakfast leaving the anticipated strong pot of coffee and hot milk on the terrace table. She also needed a clear head to cope with the next stage of the Fall Out saga. The unexpected letter discovered in the book had opened up a romantic side to her Aunt's nature and she had read it again and again before finally dropping off to sleep. Deciding against showing it to her friends over breakfast, if at all, nevertheless she was moved by the content and privileged to have shared her Aunt's emotions and feeling sand needed time to take it all in. Her thoughts were broken when Dee dragged herself onto the terrace.

"Coffee, strong and black please before I take a shower. God, what a session. Is Jan up yet?"

"Jan is." came the reply from the garden. What a beautiful morning to smell the coffee,"

Carrying Ginger on her shoulder she half skipped up the steps leading to the patio and brightly asked. "How did we all sleep? I went out like a light, slept like a log and woke up with this lovely feline staring at my toes. What a big boy and so heavy, too. Down you go, Ginger boy, while I have coffee, too."

Dee looked at her friend in amazement.

"How does she do it, Ange? She was up at six for the flight from Bristol, then hanging around for hours at airports and a longish train journey here. I'm almost out of it and she looks as fresh as a daisy."

Angela laughed "Yes she does but she never touched the Chivas Regal, did she? You, dear girl, hit it hard. Now have your shower and Doris will serve up a light breakfast; lots of fresh fruits and boiled eggs- if that suits."

"Anything to clear the palate, and more coffee please. Won't be long" Dee promised.

Angie smiled at Janet. "She'll never change. I had hoped she would have calmed down a bit when she finally grew up and went to live in Brecon with Gill. "

"In many ways she has, but do we really want her too? She did try for religious broadcasting at the Beeb but she never fancied, "Thought for the Day,"

"What!" Angie said. "When was this? God only knows what her thoughts would have been. She would have been drummed out after her first 'on air' thought."

Jan hesitated. "It was after our gay Rector promised to marry her to Gill, should he ever become a Chaplain to the Queen."

"I'm not surprised. When he held court at the Lugworth Arms years ago, Daphne always said he was bonkers. What did happen to him?"

Dee laughed. "I'll tell you what I think happened to him. After the defence exercise he ended up as Chaplain to the new County Council, did a stint as tour guide at Brecon Cathedral, (he was hooked on Michael Cain in "Zulu"), moved in with a producer from TV South West and went to live in Bristol. For a while he was a regular on the God Slot but blotted his copy book by speaking out of turn. Now and again I bump into him in Cardiff and we have lunch. He always brings up the drama club meetings in the Lugworth Arms and the day we went to Greenham in the mini-bus.

As I recall, it was Daphne's favourite tale, too; she could recount it in fine detail enough to drive her sister to the gin bottle on several occasions."

"Lady Anne didn't need much driving, she was up for a large Gin and Tonic any time of day but they were both great company and great fun to be with during the build-up to Fall Out. Anthony believed he was ring-master of the whole show and everyone else, apart from Ruth Tremlett, the performers."

"But what about the day you told him it was your duty to go Greenham Common and demonstrate against the nuclear weapons," Janet reminded.

"Never forgot it, Jan, and nor did Daphne. Anthony blew his top when he caught us pitching the tent on his precious Cumberland turf.

Chapter Seven

May had merged quite beautifully into June giving early notice of a very warm summer. The Mid-Bordershire countryside was bursting with natural activity and couplings of every description were common place around and under the hedgerows of Lugworth. Anthony Anderson Shelta absorbed it all as he drove home from his morning on the golf course and felt quite relaxed in the driving seat of his classic, bottle green and beige, Armstrong Siddeley Sapphire. The feel and smell of the leather seats reminded him of Ruth Tremlett straddled across the centre arm rest of the back seat laughing at his inept attempts to do the business while parked on Stanton Hill. His late father-in-law had bequeathed him the classic car much admired by visiting members at the golf club.

The highly competitive match he had won that morning at Brecon had put him into the semi-finals of the Welsh Masonic Hospitals Cup, due to be played at Wrexham; the final scheduled for the St Pierre course at Chepstow in late autumn. Hence he was feeling mighty pleased with himself and keen to get home and tell Angela of his sporting success.

Originally a vicarage built in 1928; he and Angela bought it when he was appointed Chief Executive fifteen years ago. It was a handsome property in good architectural and decorative order complete with original features including stained glass windows. Surrounded by an acre or two of landscaped gardens it had glorious views to the west at the front but more important, the rear garden overlooked the eighteenth green of the county golf club, a fact that had not gone unnoticed when he had been investigating available properties.

Anthony had been lucky to acquire it. He had been advised of its whereabouts by a former Church Commissioner and member of his Lodge. In return for some assistance with a planning application, his fellow Mason pulled a few strings and with the help of a cash injection from his father-in-law he was well able to purchase it at a very good price. Jointly owned with Angela, they both loved the property and soon realised that neither of them would risk losing it to the other. With this in mind he needed to tread carefully in his dealings with Ruth.

Approaching the outskirts of Lugworth he opted for a quick sandwich and a drink in the Lugworth Arms before going home. It also gave him the opportunity to broadcast his morning's sporting success hopeful it would soon reach the ears of the local reporter. A bit of self-aggrandisement never went amiss in Anthony's book. Meanwhile back at the Old Vicarage his wife was turning out the loft.

A striking woman in her mid-forties she had the style and class befitting an only daughter of a retired Brigadier General. Home Counties to the core. She never lost her Englishness despite marrying a Welshman and living most of her married life in Wales.

Angela was quite young when she married Anthony; she had been swept along in the excitement of the officer's mess social life and quickly found herself dressed in white clinging to arm of her proud father to be handed over like a chattel to an eagerly waiting groom.

The honeymoon in Bruges was a reasonable success, Anthony just about managing to get through the consummation ceremonies on a wing and a prayer but it didn't take long for disillusionment to set in. By the time she was thirty five it was clear they were totally incompatible and that she had married the wrong man. However, the death of both parents within a year and the substantial inheritance that followed, freed Angela from the financial ties of the marriage and she became her own woman leading virtually her own life.

She didn't hear the knock on the front door or the footsteps in the hallway. Supporting herself on the oak newel post at the bottom of the staircase surveying the empty scene her Aunt, Daphne Oxbridge, called out in the commanding voice of a former Chief Officer Wrens.

"Is there anyone at home? Angela are you there? Come along, old thing, Admiral's inspection and all that. Stand by your beds." There was no response so she strode up the stairs and impatiently called out again.

"Angela are you up there? It's me, Aunt Daphers. What's going on and where are you?"

At the top of the stairs, she paused again and noticed that the trap door to the loft was wide open and a purpose built ladder propped up against it.

"Are you in there, Angie. Show yourself girl, I haven't got all day."

Advancing a few unsteady steps up the ladder, she called again and Angela poked her head out of the trap door. Her face was dirty and she was covered in dust.

"What the devil are you doing up there, dear?" Daphne asked her.

"Oh it's you, Aunty. I thought it was the Chief Exec back from his busy morning on the golf course."

"I thought he had a finance committee at HQ today."

"You know Anthony, left it to his deputy as usual. His relations with the public are at a low point these days. He thought it would be good public relations to play in the Masonic Handicap, or something like that. Back off, Auntie, I'm coming down."

Angela clambered out of the roof space onto the ladder, it wobbled under their combined effort. Daphne warned

"Steady the buffs, Angie old girl. Hang on until the old legs touch terra firma." Stepping back onto the landing she chuckled out loud.

"This brings back a few memories of the Wrens' quarters, I can tell you."

There was no escaping her Aunt's nautical tales.

"Oh come on then, Daphers, share the joke and make it quick."

""Yonks ago when I was a young Wren can you remember me talking about Biggy Beaumont? We played cricket together for the Combined Women's Services."

Daphne paused wistfully. "Yes I remember Biggy she could turn a ball and make it do all sorts of things. She once had the Women's Royal Air Force all out for fifty seven on a drying wicket at Portsmouth."

Angela was becoming irritated as she waited for Daphne to get to the point of her story.

"Oh do get on with it, Auntie, you always go the long way round a story. Anyway, what's cricket got to do with being up a ladder?"

"What? Oh yes, sorry. Well, we had been to the NAAFI club in Portsmouth for a few drinks with the Field Gun Crew team from HMS Excellent and we missed the liberty boat back to Gosport. We were late back to quarters and knew that the duty officer would never believe our excuse, so we decided to go over the fence. The lads borrowed a ladder, Biggy went over first and I followed her; straddling the top of the fence I shouted at Biggy.

"I feel like a commando!" and I started laughing. Biggy, quick as ever said 'Come on Daphne, we can't go back now."

After a moment to think Angela began to giggle and before long they were almost hysterical, not so much at the story, more to do with the thought of Daphne stranded on a barbed wire fence at dead of night. It took a moment or two before Angela broke the moment. She loved her godmother and all her glorious stories but she really did have to get on before Anthony came home and asked what she was up to.

"Honestly, Aunt Daphne, you really do tell a good tale but I must get this kit out of here."

Stretching back into the loft she dragged out a large rucksack and a waterproof bundle.

"What on earth is that?" asked Daphne.

"My old girl guide tent and camping kit. You remember, you bought it for me. I might need it for the weekend."

Staggering down the ladder, dust flying everywhere, she suggested.

"Better get this out into the garden, it's pretty dirty. Could you manage an end as we go downstairs? It's quite heavy, Auntie, but if we can manoeuvre it round the top of the staircase we can let it go on its own."

At the bottom the two women dragged the large bundles through the kitchen and onto the back lawn. Washing their hands under the garden hose pipe Daphne asked.

"Are you and Tony away at the weekend? You're always off somewhere but not usually together. You two are more like ships that pass in the night."

Angie muttered. "We're not even that these days. When we do meet up, all he can talk about is directives from Central Government, golf handicaps and national conferences at every bloody seaside resort on our shore line, all at the ratepayer's expense of course. He's off on another next week at the Floral Hall, Southport. Mind you, after a few malt whiskies, it's a different tack, he can't control his admiration for the 'Iron Lady' and how he would like to get a pair of wire cutters and have a go at her tin knickers. Let's go inside and have some tea?"

"Love some. It's a pity you never had children, it might have eased things between you." Daphne ventured.

"What! That would have needed a meeting of the Health Committee, approval of the General Purposes Sub-Committee and ratified by full Council. Plus, of course, attendance and sleeping-in allowance. However, for the moment, I think we are reasonably comfortable with each other as we are. Now sit down, dear, and I'll bring the tea over."

Seated at the large kitchen table, Angela poured the tea into attractive art deco tea cups and saucers. They sipped it in silence until Daphne asked, "Where are you off to this weekend?"

"Greenham Common. I'm a little short on hearing these days. Did you say the Greenhams? Are they town or county, dear? I don't seem to recognise the name."

"Bit of both, I suppose."

"Are there many going?"

"Hundreds," Daphne looked at Angela in amazement.

"Hundreds! I say, that's some house party."

"It isn't a party, it's a women's peace camp at a United States Air Force base in Berkshire. You must have read about it."

Daphne looked mischievously at her god daughter.

"Good heavens, Angie, I thought you had passed through your American soldier phase back in the late fifties. Does Tony know about this?"

"Partly, but he will need reminding. I did mention that I might be going, but he didn't take much notice. Anyway, it's got nothing to do with American soldiers, or airmen for that matter. It's an all women gathering."

"Daphne thought for a while before replying.

"Oh, Angie, my dear, you haven't got those sort of feelings have you? I know Tony isn't the best of husbands in that quarter but all girls together, that's a different kettle of fish."

A little flustered she had difficulty in continuing. "I mean. It's not healthy you know. I came across it quite a bit in the services. Had to put up the barrier myself once or twice, but a bit of bromide in the tea got it under control. Pour me another cup will you dear this takes a bit of thinking about."

Pouring out more tea Angela tried to hide her amusement. Daphne insisted on pursuing the conversation.

"You of all people, Angela. You had a good upbringing, Sunday school, Cheltenham Ladies College, finishing in Paris and now you're dabbling in a bit of sexual deviance. It must be your age, dear. What else can one say?"

Angela laughed as her god mother tried to hide her embarrassment.

"Stop it, Daphers, please. I'm thinking of going on a peace march, Women against the Bomb, that's all."

"But you have never marched in your life Angela."

"I have."

"When?"

"With the Guides on Remembrance Sunday."

"Oh yes so did I," said Daphne proudly. "I used to carry the British Legion Banner." Picking up a tea towel hanging over a chair she marched up and down the kitchen, shouting, eyes left eyes front each time she passed Angela's chair …

"Sit down for goodness sake, Auntie, you'll have a wobbly if you're not careful and end up in hospital again."

"You'll have a bigger one my girl, if you march the two hundred miles to Berkshire."

"We haven't quite decided yet and I am not actually marching. A group of peace women set off from Cardigan Bay for Greenham Common some weeks ago and set up camp outside the main gate at the base. They have invited other likeminded woman to join up with them at the camp for a special the weekend. Janet and Dee have booked a mini-bus to take them and other peace campaigners from the district and I'm thinking of joining them."

"You must be mad. What will Anthony think?"

"Maybe I am but I damned if I care. So now you know why I need the tent. Now, I must try and pitch it on the lawn to make sure it's still waterproof. You can help if you like."

Unfolding the tent across the lawn wasn't easy.

"This reminds me of Women's Cricket Week at Colwell in Malvern. We had to pitch a few tents for staying overnight, it was great fun. Now let me help you spread the canvas. Where are the tent pegs, dear?" Daphne asked.

"Help yes; memories definitely no. We've had enough of those for one day."

"Come now, Angela. That's no way to treat your god mother. Come on, let's get this thing up."

Grappling with the guy ropes and tent pegs, it didn't take too long to realise just how big the tent was.

"Steady, Aunty, it's bigger than I thought. It looks like I ended up with the mess tent so do be careful."

Un-aware that Anthony had arrived home, he was halfway up the staircase before she heard him shout.

"Angela, where are you? What are you doing in the roof, hiding a secret lover or something?"

Laughing at his little joke, but failing to get a response he decided to investigate for himself. Tentatively climbing the ladder he peered into the deserted roof space and called out again.

"Where the devil are you, Angela? Come along, dear, this is no time for silly games. Come out or at least say something."

The empty attic unnerved Anthony, so to be on the safe side' he started backing down the ladder whistling 'Land of Hope and Glory', which he always did in difficult situations. Just as his lower body cleared the hatch, the cat leapt onto his shoulder and dug its claws well and truly into his shoulder.

Crying out in pain he yelled. "Bloody hell, Scargill get off me, that hurts."

The cat jumped off his back on to the banister and sat there staring at him. Pausing to catch his breath Anthony muttered.

"Now, Scargill, where's your mother? That's if you ever had one you old bastard. What's she been up to in the attic "

He loved having a go at the cat. It was good therapy, especially as he had chosen the name for just that reason. Walking down the stairs, he wandered into the kitchen, the cat following in his footsteps.

"She's here somewhere, Scargill, there's tea on the go and Daphne's bicycle is chained to the side gate."

Pouring himself a mug of tea he picked up the cat and walked to the large picture window overlooking the back garden; the unexpected sight of his wife and her dotty Aunt trying to pitch a tent alarmed him. Dropping Scargill to the floor, he threw open the kitchen window and yelled out.

"Angela ... Daphne ... what the hell are you doing?"

Daphne clambered unsteadily to her feet.

"What does it look like, Tony? Angela is practising her camping skills ready for the weekend."

"Not on my practice putting lawn she isn't! There's enough camping going on in Lugworth with that trendy new Rector prancing about in his striped blazer and white flannels. That's apart from all that lot in the theatricals, or whatever they call themselves."

"Really, Tony, that's his cricketing togs, he turns out for the village eleven. Anyway, they don't look as outrageous as your plus fours and tartan stockings."

"Hear, Hear!" Angela said from inside the pile of canvas.

"Never mind about that, what are you doing with that tent?"

"I'm sleeping under canvas this weekend."

"Under canvas? That will be the day. Where are you going on this great expedition? Up Everest?"

"No, not Everest, Anthony," she replied calmly. "I told you weeks ago, I'm thinking of going to Greenham Common."

Shocked by his wife's answer he responded.

"What? If you're thinking of joining that ... that rat bag collection of women's libbers. You can think again."

Slamming his mug onto the window ledge, he rushed at the door, and stumbled over the cat calmly seated on the door step. Picking himself up, he yelled.

"Bugger off, Scargill and stay out of my bloody way. Come to think about it you're in everyone's way these days."

In a flash the cat shot out of the door, across the lawn and into the back of the part erected tent. Tripping over a guy rope, Anthony followed on his knees just as his wife poked out her head though the doorway.

"Ah! Tony, be a good chap and hang onto the centre pole for a second while I ease the roof up."

Crawling inside he grabbed hold of the pole and pleaded with his pre-occupied spouse.

"Angela, please be reasonable. You can't go gallivanting off to Greenham Common, not when I'm fully engaged with the defence exercise ..." Before he could finish the sentence, he let go of the centre tent pole and the canvas collapsed on top of them both.

"Bad luck, Tony!" Daphne called out from the sidelines.

"Never mind luck you stupid woman, tell Angela to get me out of here, her blasted cat is clinging onto my plus fours and digging his claws into my privates. They'll be ruined."

Angela scrambled her way out of the tent dragging her furious husband with her.

"Do you mean the plus fours or your private parts, Tony? You really are a wimp dear. How you ever survived Mons I shall never know."

"Were you at Mons, Tony? I'd have thought you were far too young for the trenches."

Angela answered for him.

"Of course he wasn't, Daphne. Mons was the Officer Training School in Aldershot where we first met. Anyway, Tony, what are doing home at this time of day, I thought you had a meeting after your golf match?"

"Never mind about that, Angela, you are not going on that peace women's picnic and that is final."

"It's not a picnic. I told you I was thinking about going and I am. That also is final."

"Yes I know but that was before I had this defence exercise to cope with."

"No it wasn't. This cruise missile threat has been rumbling on for months and I am doing my bit to support you by spending the weekend at Greenham with my friends. Now can I get on with the tent? Realising another domestic was on the horizon Daphne interrupted the conversation.

"Look here you two, you can sort it out between you, I'm off home."

"Shut up, Daphne, Angela knows her place; she can't go trotting off on a peace march while I'm up to my ears in nuclear warfare. It's just not on. What about my standing in this community and anyway, 'she' might be putting in an appearance on the day."

"Who is 'she' Tony?" Daphne asked.

"I'm afraid I can't say. Official secrets and all that but as you probably still have clearance from your naval days, Daphne, I think it may be safe to tell you."

Dropping his voice to a stage whisper he told her. "Suffice it to say that "M" might be coming."

"Who the devil is 'M', Tony. Surely not James Bond's boss?

"I suppose in a way yes it could be."

Almost at wits end, Angela replied.

"Need you ask, Daphne? Surely you know that 'M' stands for Margaret or for mistress, both great loves of his life. Margaret his beloved Prime Minister, his mistress, the greatest official secret of all time, his private and oh so personal assistant, Mrs Ruth Tremlett."

Shaken at his wife's announcement Tony tried to bluff his way out.

"Angela, stop this at once. Don't take any notice of her, Daphne. It's rumour, hearsay and wicked gossip put about by those bloody little left wing layabouts camped on Lugworth Common."

Amused at the way things were going Daphne turned to her niece.

"Are you saying your pillar of the society husband is carrying on with the Commander's wife while he is on active service with MI5 in some foreign field, decidedly not forever England?"

With everything about to come out, Angela began to enjoy herself.

"When Bill Tremlett finds out what Lugworth field his beloved Ruth has been serving my husband in he will head for home on the first gun boat Tony, and definitely gunning for you."

For a moment, Anthony felt he was up for a heart attack. It seemed the only way out, but he knew that he had to at least have a stab at going on the defensive. After all, his entire career was at stake and the press would have a bumper of a week and not just the local media. Struggling to get a belated grip on himself, he let his political training take over.

"What do you know about Bill Tremlett? He's got nothing to do with MI5. He's on some trade mission, at least that's what he told me at the club just before he went away. Anyway, how come you know so much about it?"

"Do you mean about you and Ruth?" Angela suggested.

Daphne interrupted her. "Come on, Tony, you know very well that there are no secrets in Lugworth. It seems there is a little bit more to Ruth Tremlett than meets the eye and you'd have never have guessed it at the WI meetings."

"Guessed what, Daphne?"

"That you and your secretary are at it, Tony, and that's not a guess. The WI is the local gossip in Lugworth."

"Are you saying the WI know about the nuclear defence exercise?"

"Yes and they also know about your extra marital affair," Angela said. "But fair play, they are not too sure if it has reached full monte status yet."

Daphne looked at her watch.

"Caught out on both counts, Anthony. Gosh is that the time? It's well past 'up spirits' and I promised the Major a large gin and tonic while we ponder over the England team for the next test match. He will have dropped Botham because he has grown some sort of facial hair and if I don't get there soon, he'll have given all and sundry his opinion on the Australians padded up like the SAS, scared to death of facing our opening bowlers. That's if Kim Hughes has stopped crying by now." Looking up at the tree she suggested. "That cat will never get down from there; you'll have to get a ladder, Tony. Enjoy Greenham, Angela in some ways, I wish I was going with you."

Taken aback by her offhand remark Tony mumbled.

"That's not the right attitude for a retired Chief Officer WRNS, Daphne."

"Take no notice of him, Auntie. Come on, come with us."

"Don't encourage her, Angela."

"It wouldn't take a lot, Tony, I can tell you, but with my MBE and the JP bit, well, you know the problems. More to the point though, the first test starts tomorrow at Edgbaston and I have a ticket. Be sure your tent is waterproof, Angela. Have I permission to leave the ship, Tony?"

That said she about turned, went through the side gate, unchained her ageing bicycle and wobbled across the golf course.

"Carry on, Admiral," he called back. "She gets dottier every day, Angela."

"After thirty years in the Wrens, who wouldn't. Still, her sister keeps her out of trouble."

"And who is going to keep you out of trouble? You simply cannot go gadding off to Greenham Common on a whim. We'll discuss it when I get back tonight. You know this exercise is taking up all my time."

"Makes a change from Ruth, although I suspect she's involved somewhere along the line. After all, she is the Chief Executive's etcetera … etcetera."

"Enough, Angela. There is nothing going on between Ruth Tremlett and myself that isn't covered by standing orders."

"Or the official sex act, sorry, I mean secrets act. Come on, Tony, I wasn't born yesterday; now about my meeting tonight?"

"What meeting?"

"The peace group, I said they could meet here for a last minute get together."

"You mean that scruffy lot are coming into in my house?"

"Our house, Tony, but we could meet in the tent on the lawn? It will be good practice."

"You want require practice, my dear. It's all academic as far as you're concerned, because you're not going."

"And just who is going to stop me, Anthony, the Lugworth Volunteer brigade? I am going and we are meeting here tonight to finalise travelling arrangements."

Rising to the bait Anthony put his foot down.

"Let's get one thing straight, Angela, you're not taking the car. I'm not having the Armstrong daubed with paint and stickers."

"Don't panic, we're going by mini-bus. Clive has arranged it."

"Do you mean Makepeace, the trendy Rector?"

"I didn't mean Clive of India. Now I've got things to do, so if you don't mind, Anthony, I'll just start on the dishes and you had better have a go at getting Scargill out of the tree."

"Never mind the damn cat. What do we employ a domestic help for if you have to do the dishes?"

"I've given her the day off to get ready for the trip. She's coming with us."

"What? You're taking Mrs Miller with you? Good God what next? And just who is going to look after her brood?"

"Her husband, he's on nights at the cheese factory and he's due four days off."

"And who else is going on this little outing? No, don't tell me, I can guess. Lady Llewellyn and all her socialist cronies, Councillor – Ms with the long S – Janet Bodmin and the great unwashed parked on the common. That Bodmin woman is going too far these days, her behaviour in Council leaves a lot to be desired and a very a bad influence on you, dear. Before long she will have you voting Labour."

Angela smiled broadly. She knew how to wind her husband up and once she had him on a tight spring, she wasn't going to let go.

"What makes you think I haven't, Tony?"

"Haven't what?" he replied wearily.

"Haven't voted Labour already; the Boadicea of Downing Street is enough to persuade me to vote for Screaming Lord Whatsit."

Astonished by the verbal attack on his party leader, Tony was rattled but he knew if he protested too much he would end up in an even bigger hole. However, dignity of office was always a good defence at times like this.

"That will do Angela. I am the Chief Executive Officer of this district and have some standing in the community, I must remain unbiased, although I privately admit to favouring the Tory Party at times."

"Favouring, that's a laugh, you'd rinse your hair blue if you thought it would do any good. So would all those so called Independents on your Council. Come off it Tony, everyone knows you're in Davenport-Jones's pocket. Why else would a case of House of Commons malt whisky arrive every three months or so?"

Anthony was feeling the pressure. The last thing he wanted was any sort of scandal and it was time to nip the situation in the bud.

"Let's be serious for a moment, Angela, I'm warning you that what you may or may not suggesting could be seen as a crisis situation in our marriage."

"Our marriage is an on-going crisis. It always has been, but we get by."

Staring out of the window and after a few moments silence Angela attempted to change the mood.

"Look, Scargill is still up the tree, do try and coax him down."

"Best place for him, up there."

"Her," said Angela.

"No. Scargill is a he."

"I'm sorry to disappoint you, Anthony, but our cat is a she. Try lifting her tail up sometime!"

"Don't be difficult, Angela. Does it really matter? The vet operated, so she's a bit of both."

Changing the subject again, his wife suggested.

"Hadn't you better get ready for tonight?"

"Why?"

"Because I understand, you are dining early."

"Who said so?"

"Ruth Tremlett. She rang to say that the table was booked for seven-thirty at Beales. Expenses again, Anthony?"

"What? Err yes. I'm dining with the County Organiser of the Meals on Wheels service. We are discussing contingency plans for Operation Fallout."

"And Ruth happens to be, as if I didn't know, the local meals on wheels organiser?"

Tony was sinking fast and he struggled to overcome the combination of shock and embarrassment.

"Yes, well it is official. She is a very capable woman and well suited to the position."

"I'm sure she is, Anthony, you'll have made sure of that. Bit of a come down for her, though, or should I say step up. Meals on Wheels and meals at Beales, not bad for the personal secretary of the Chief Executive."

It was then Anthony put his foot right in it.

"Ruth is quite used to dining at Beales."

"Is she indeed and what does the Commander have to say about that?"

"Well, he's away at the moment. Anyway, it's all in the line of duty, Angela, one has to front up at times like this. We all need to pull together if this exercise is to get off to a good start, so Ruth kindly offered her services."

"I bet she did."

"It's only for a short time. We needed a reliable woman, someone to depend upon to join the team. The budget is there for extra personnel and she does do a lot of unpaid overtime, thus a little perquisite from time to time comes by way of a reward for services rendered."

"The way you're going on, it will be Help the Aged next. Now go and organise yourself for your … err … meeting!"

"Right, I will. We'll talk about this Greenham business later."

He walked across the kitchen and into the hallway. Angela shouted after him. "Nothing more to say, dear. I'm going on my trip, you're going on your weekend with the Tory Twit of the Year. Shut the loft ladder away while you're up there please."

Anthony froze. He didn't know how to counter this latest exposure, and the effort of constantly being on the defensive was beginning to wear him down. His normally clear head was awash with confusion as he tried to assimilate his wife's amazing knowledge of his social calendar.

He decided to play it low key and hoped that the nervous twitching under his right eye would go unnoticed. "Did you say Crispin had telephoned while I was out? I told him to ring the office."

"He called earlier and said to tell you that all's well for the weekend in Westminster, whatever that means!"

"Well actually, the Constituency Chairman and I have to attend a weekend conference at the House. Sorry it's such short notice."

"Are you going with Sir Charles?"

"Not exactly, Angie dear. The old boy has a touch of gout and can't make it, so he's sending the Vice."

"Speaking of vice, that isn't who I think it is, is it?"

"Well as a matter of fact, Ruth is the Vice Chairman and she is required to stand in for him."

"Really? She truly is a Jill of all trades … and, it seems, mistress of none. Mind you Anthony, you never did consider yourself trade."

"What the hell does that mean?"

"Think about it. She's not doing too badly so far. Meals on Wheels to meals at Beales and now meals for deals at party appeals."

"For God's sake stop all this nonsense, Angela. It's all in the line of duty. These meetings are an important part of this defence exercise. We must ensure our country is in safe hands."

"My sentiments exactly, Tony, that's why I'm going to Greenham. Now off you go like a good boy or trembling Tremlett will trip over herself to discipline you for being late."

"This is ridiculous, Angela, I'm going to take a shower, perhaps you'll be in a better frame of mind to talk later."

That said, Anthony dashed up the staircase and walked into the loft ladder. The clatter of leg against steel forcing his wife to sigh, leave her chores and climb halfway up the stairs to see what had happened. Legs entangled in the ladder, Tony, cursed out loud as he tried to free himself.

"Bloody hell, Angela, why don't you put things away when you've finished with them."

"Be careful, Tony, I might put you away one of these days."

"What is it with you?" he asked. "Is the change of life making you act this way, a sort of midlife crisis?"

"Have a heart, Anthony, I'm not there yet; the only change of life I need, is a change from you. You're so bloody pedestrian, so boringly local Government."

Stung by her comments Tony tried desperately to hit back at his wife. "These peace women are not doing you any good at all. I don't think you've washed your hair since you have been involved with them."

"Actually, I haven't, my hairdresser does it for me. As for my midlife crisis, take a look at your own. You were born into it and will be carried out of it feet first. Now please go and get ready or do something, I've got to get my tent up."

"Not on my Cumberland turfed lawn, it's only just been re-laid and good turfs are hard to come by in this area."

"Yes and you only got those because they were somehow left over from the landscaping of the fallout shelter. Cumberland turfs on a fallout shelter! Whatever will they think of next?"

"It has to look nice, Angela, it makes the ratepayers feel it's money well spent."

"But do they really know what lurks beneath the eighteenth green on the municipal golf course?"

"No, and they must not know, Angie. Official secrets and all that."

"Not that old chestnut again. Who do that ageing group of well-heeled farmers on the Council think they are, modern day Francis bloody Drakes? I can just see them; putting to the left, chipping to the right as the advancing missiles hit the early warning system. Then they will be under starter's orders for the sixty yard dash to the eighteenth green to scuttle underground like a bunch of rabbits on heat, while the poor old ratepayer doesn't have a hope in hell of avoiding the fallout. Believe me, Tony, your happy band of nineteenth holers, haven't got the collective intelligence to realise that we are in a nuclear bunker and need more than a sand iron to get out of it."

"That's it, that's bloody it, Angela. No more insulting remarks about my Council. Now get that Girl Guide Wendy house off my lawn before I get back … or else!"

"Or else what, Tony? Don't you threaten me. I'm not one of your minions at the town hall. If you don't watch it I shall get all the peace women to camp out on your wonderful Cumberland turfed fallout shelter tonight, and if you attempt to throw us out, I'll tip off Dee Donnington. I can just see it in the local rag.

'Chief Executive attacks local peace women.' What a sizzler of a story! It's a dead cert to make the nationals."

"You wouldn't dare."

"Try me."

"But what about my reputation, Angela?"

"Which one? Lover or lout? I'd do it, Tony dear, I really would, and if *Private Eye* ever got hold of it. Well, I mean … it's goodbye to all that."

"All what?"

"Meals at Beales, parties at the Palace of Westminster."

"My career, Angela, you wouldn't try and destroy that, would you?"

"I wouldn't, dear boy, but I can't speak for Dee. If she ever gets wind of our MP on the 'pop' in the Chairman's Parlour, Mrs Tremlett's perks and the left over turfs on our back lawn, it will take more than a fallout shelter to save you from the flak."

Anthony was gutted. His face grey with shock he slumped onto the staircase and slowly came to terms with his situation.

"Shit, shit, shit," he cried out.

His highly amused wife took two more steps up the staircase, leaned over her stricken husband and said,

"Chin up, old boy, or should I say chins. I really must get on. See you later legislature."

Kissing him lightly on the forehead, she skipped down the stairs and went outside to erect the tent. "Good one, Angela" she said to herself. "Let's see him get out of this."

Chapter Eight

The Sunday lunch time crowd in the Lugworth Arms was missing a few of the regulars and the landlord was decidedly quiet for a change. It was coming up to peak time for lunches and he was in and out of the dining room like clockwork distributing the wine orders from behind the bar. As usual the cricket team arrived for a light lunch and a few beers before departing for the annual needle match with Arrowtown, just over the border.

Since the days of W.G. Grace this was the match that made the Battle of Pilith seem like a Sunday school outing; it was leeks versus roses every time the warring factions met to rip the leather and smash the willow in an effort to maintain national pride.

Tim Taplow, the team captain of Lugworth First Eleven was anxiously trying to hype up his fast bowler Rick Richards, the stockman from Dyke Farm; he was still under the weather after a heavy session at the Village Hall dance last night

"I'm sorry, boss," he moaned. "Me arm's as stiff as a bull's what's it in a field of heifers, I can't even get me leg over the wife let alone me right arm over the bloody wicket."

His captain was decidedly miffed. His public school background and years as a club cricketer with the Law Society Casuals had instilled in him a sense of discipline his team couldn't grasp let alone adhere to. It also irked him that on this day of all cricketing days he had lost not only his fastest bowler but the team umpire as well.

Janet Bodmin had preferred a weekend on a demo rather than officiate at the big match; she could read a bumper from the moment it left the hand of the bowler, and call a 'no ball' soon enough for a batsman to give it some welly. However, Tim disapproved of women on the cricket field, the pavilion was their natural habitat on match days, but he grudgingly accepted that she could be a useful ally especially when the Lugworth tail-enders were facing the opposing heavy mob.

In a manner more suited to the Old Bailey, he questioned his indolent bowler.

"Tell me again, Rick, what happened last night and what caused this injury?" His team answered as one. "The bloody Barratt Boys, that's what happened last night and it's all down to that bloody police woman from Arrow Minster," Rick explained.

"She arrested Sid Barratt yesterday morning for occasional bodily harm, or some' at like that and they've got 'im in custody awaitin' the beak on Monday morning."

"I think you mean occasioning bodily harm, Rick," he pompously announced. "What the hell did he do to warrant that charge?

"He wrapped a banner pole round Mo Morgan's head, leavin' him bleedin'. When the Inspector woman marched him out of the hall he grabbed her truncheon, tried to measure it against his plonker, yelled 'Mine packs a bigger punch,' and passed out."

"What's that got to do with his bowling arm? Tim asked.

This time the wicket keeper answered.

"The rest of the Barratt's turned up at the dance looking for trouble and started messing about with Rick's missus. Rick went after 'im, took a swing and missed."

"So how come you bruised your hand and arm?" Tim queried.

Rick explained. "Ted Barratt ducked, I smashed me fist into the coffee urn, and it keeled over and made a real mess of Sid's Wranglers and ruined his leather boots."

"So what happened next?"

"He yelled for his brothers and we all did a runner via the fire exit, hid in the skittle alley at the back at the Bulls Head and got ratted. At least one or two of us did, the rest of the team decided on an early night skip, ready for the big match." The Vice-Captain added.

Looking at Rick's black and blue swellings, Tim was decidedly unsympathetic. "Yes well that was very commendable but I don't give much for our chances with his hand in that state," he murmured sulkily.

Announcing the arrival of the team bus, the ever-optimistic bar tender called out. "Drink up lads, the bus is here, now stuff it up those English bastards, young Tim. See you when you get back."

"I think you're drifting into the realms of fantasy, Ted, old boy, what with our umpire indisposed, Rick knackered, and the Barratt Boys turning out for Arrowtown we'll be lucky to get away with a draw. Tell George we'll be in after the match as usual."

They motley gathering of white flannelled warriors of the wicket shuffled out of the bar without a decent box among them and a cat in hell's chance of taking a wicket.

Seated in a quiet corner of the snug bar Josh Aiken, Ben Neal and Dick Doby, the planning officer, were deep in political manoeuvrings.

"Of course it will, Josh," said Dick. He's got a vested interest plus the fact that it must be ready for a dummy run during the defence exercise."

"How do you mean vested interest, Dick? Surely he's not been on the fiddle?" Ben said. The planning officer wished he had kept his thoughts to himself. If this got back to his boss, then his promotion prospects were down the pan and flushed away with the turds of the town into the communal cesspit.

Back peddling like mad and with the eloquence of a bard at some local Eisteddfod, he explained, "When I say vested interest, Josh, I mean that he somehow managed to persuade the golf club to allow the fall out bunker to be built under the eighteenth green."

"What?" Josh and Ben exclaimed in unison. Dick nodded.

"It appears that the developers, in appreciation of the goodwill and sportsmanship of the members, kitted out a small ante room in the club house to be used as a private dining room for the committee. Anderson-Shelta also promised places of safety in the shelter for the club president and secretary, plus of course the lady captain for a last bang or two before the big one comes."

His companions were agog. "Has this been ratified?" Ben asked.

"I shall be outlining details of the interior and the facilities next week at the defence committee planning meeting, assuming they all get back safely from Greenham. Oh yes! The developer has also provided the finest Cumberland turf for the practice putting green plus a few square yards left over for Anderson-Shelta's rear lawn to be re-tufted, free, gratis."

Josh could hardly contain his shock. "Bugger me, Ben! If that's not being on the fiddle Dick I'll climb up Snowden with the wife on my back."

"Course not," Dick said Josh defensively; his life in public service is littered with back handers. It goes without sayin'. He believes a man in his position is entitled to a bit of dropsy now and again, that's how they oil the wheels of trade, commerce, and local Government all the way to Westminster."

He caught Ben's disapproving eye. "Don't you look like that, Ben Neal. You've had yer share of selling spuds at the farm gate and I bet you don't pay any tax on yer King Edwards"

Ben coughed as the scotch and water caught the back of his throat. "I'd best be off home, the wife will be fretting."

"Me, too." Dick said. "Best forget what I said earlier. See you at Council on Thursday if not tonight."

"You won't get me in 'ere this evening," Josh announced. "What with the cricket team cryin' in their beer and those daft wimmin back from bannin' the bomb, I think I'd rather watch *Songs of Praise* with the missus." He put his glass down, nodded to Ted and bumped into Anthony as he came into the bar with Hugh Tremlett.

"Talk of the devil," Ben said.

"I'm out of here," replied Dick, his future promotions dimming rapidly. "Bye both."

With a swift movement, he sidestepped his approaching boss and nipped in the gents.

Ben Neal, who had been propping up the bar alongside Josh and Dick, sighed.

"What's up with you then? Got something on yer' mind have yer', Ben?" Josh asked.

139

"You could say that," Ben muttered. "I'm a bit bothered about this ruddy defence exercise; it's going to be a bit of balls up if you ask me."

"Don't worry about it; just think of the out of pocket expenses you'll be picking up,"

Unusually for Ben he wasn't concerned about expenses.

"It's alright for you, Josh, you're only the Town Mayor, I'm on the district bloody Council and if anyone is going to get any flack, it will be me, not you. It's not the expenses I'm bothered about, next year's elections that are giving me sleepless nights. If this goes wrong, Lugworth will vote me out and bang go all the perks."

Josh was puzzled so Ben ordered another round.

"Same again, Ted. I've got a funny feeling about this exercise thing, Josh. I'm not sure Anderson-Shelta is up to it, let alone that halfwit Member of Parliament he worships."

Back from the gent's Dick Dobie hearing mention of his Chief hung around for a little longer despite family lunch in half an hour; if he didn't make a move soon, Glenys would be on the phone. It was worth the risk; her pain in the arse mother was coming to lunch and an afternoon of wild gossip, innuendo and family squabbles was on the cards. She also suffered from bouts of wind. He also needed another pint to get him through the traditional roast Glenys always served on the Sabbath day and another round or two might encourage a bit more juicy gossip about his boss.

"I'll get these, Ted. Fancy a short before you go, Josh, the roast will keep for another half hour".

"Well, why not?" Josh replied. "A scotch with a drop of water please, Ted."

"Ben?" Dick asked. "What about you?"

"Go on then, I'll have the same and then I really will have to get home."

Ted responded with his usual droll comment, "We can't keep the good ladies slaving over the hot stove for too long," and then produced the drinks.

"So there's not a lot of confidence in this defence thing then?" Dick suggested. It seems everyone's falling out over it, at least in Council."

"Not only in Council," said Josh. "Half the town's up in arms over the cost, the ban the bomb brigade are ready for a fight, the 'happy clappy' lot are doin' over time at prayers and the WI is already going on about refreshments and emergency tea tents. Where's it going to end?"

"God only knows," Ben replied, hands above his head. I'm up to here with it all. No one tells us what's going on and it's my bloody town that's got to take the brunt. I'm not happy, Josh, not happy at all. Apart from that we've got the town twinning' weekend at the same time, all those Germans in leather pants and braces knee-slapping through town, high as a kite on cider; it's going to be a ruddy riot come October."

As tongues loosened up, Dick probed a bit deeper "What about the cost of the fallout shelter alone will be a small fortune, and it's still got to be ratified by the Council on Thursday."

"And passed on the nod again," Ben suggested. "What a waste of bloody money. Where is it going to end?"

"Like the wife's Sunday roast up in nuclear smoke if I don't get home before carving."

That said the three conspirators by now more than slightly well-oiled went for a final bladder release and disappeared without paying the tab.

Chapter Nine

For many years the Lugworth Arms Hotel rested on its historical laurels at the top end of High Street just on the edge of the town. A solid black and white inn built around 1690, it was a good example of timber frame construction with a wattle and daub infill that showed off the well preserved oak beams. According to the local guidebook, it was originally a manor house given, along with a knighthood, to a successful sea captain whose heroics on the high seas had warranted a gift from the monarch. Inside it was very well appointed with excellent facilities for the English visitors. High or low season they would flock across the border for their weekend bargain breaks, simply to enjoy the comfort, cuisine and country pursuits offered at manageable prices to the lower middle classes. The main bar was grudgingly shared between the locals and the tourists; pictures and certificates hung on whitewashed walls proving that for many years the inn was the headquarters for a number of local sporting and theatrical activities.

Appropriately it was also the regular meeting place for the Lugworth branch of the 'Odd Fellows'. The landlord fell into the latter group in more ways than one; although of smart appearance and accomplished in his chosen vocation, at times his behaviour, especially in the presence of well-proportioned women, did not endear him to many of the regular drinkers. An orderly house with a good reputation for local ale and cider it was the main reason his customers stayed the course although the occasional practical joke he liked to play on visiting honeymoon couples caused periodic merriment that lingered for days.

It was about nine o'clock and the place was unusually quiet and, for a change, peaceful. The holiday guests were still in the dining room partway through the Thursday gala dinner and dance when a small group of people wandered into the bar. Led by Clive Makepeace, the recently appointed Rector (elect) of Lugworth, he was accompanied by Janet Bodmin and Dee Donnington and a few stragglers bringing up the rear. The small party sought out the largest table in the room and sat around it.

Janet broke the silence. "Pleased with the meeting, Rector?"

"I suppose so. Public meetings in this town don't exactly go with a bang do they? No one seems to care about the realities of life, it's almost as though Lugworth and the world lead separate lives."

"You've got it in one, Clive," said Dee. "If the meeting hadn't been so well intentioned, it would have been hysterical."

"It was Dee! When Clive announced that this was to be the inaugural meeting of the Lugworth Peace Group, forty people gasped at once. It sounded more like a meeting for asthmatics, not CND."

Clive shook his head in disbelief. "I was staggered. What on earth did they think I was on about?"

"Josh summed it up nicely for them, didn't he Jan?" Dee said. "It was mind blowing, at least it blew mine and I've heard a good few oddities in my business."

"So have I," Janet replied. "But when he got up and said 'you'll never get peace in this town, Rector, no matter how hard you try; they've been at each other's throats for hundreds of years', I thought I would burst out laughing at the look on your face, Clive."

"I know but it was such a shock when two thirds of the gathering left the meeting."

"And the rest only stayed for the tea and sticky buns," Dee added. "I tell you, Rector, you've got your work cut out in this town."

"I know," he replied, "but what could I say? I didn't have a choice. The Bishop pushed me into it and I needed a settled, quiet 'living' but I hadn't bargained for this one."

Clive had heard the rumours and gossip about the past Rectors of Lugworth but even when he was appointed to the post no one, not even the Rural Dean gave him a clear insight into the place.

"It was one of the main reasons I would not accept the full Rectorship. I needed to be absolutely sure that I wasn't leaping over the wall before looking as I almost did at Ferndown."

Clive had nearly come a cropper at Ferndown, a breakaway theology college set up in the late seventies where, as a naive young priest fresh out of university, he accepted the post of Chaplain-cum-Warden.

Backed by a small but financially secure low profile splinter group of Anglo Catholics worried about a future that might become dominated by women priests, Ferndown encouraged well-heeled, bright young men and boys with little or no faith to study the misogynistic ways of misguided bishops. Students were sent on to suitable academic establishments to gain their degrees in divinity and then swiftly pushed through the system to become the cannon fodder of the nineties. Once clerically collared they could be dispersed to weakening dioceses armed with anti-women propaganda with the sole intention of rocking the Archbishop of Canterbury's boat.

Once established in post, Clive had had some difficulty coming to terms with the set up and was still trying to cope with the one major hiccup which had blighted his career and had almost cost him his chaplaincy. Foolishly, he had taken the word of the organist and choirmaster that it was acceptable to join the sixth form boys for the ritual midnight feast in the dormitory. On one such occasion, the senior prefect called for a fag who quite properly Clive had taken to be a junior pupil bringing in the goodies, that was until he got the whiff of what he thought was herbal tobacco. Before he could leave, Matron had burst into the room, her face masked in mud and her hair in rollers. Sniffing in large amounts of cannabis-polluted air and gripping her candlewick dressing gown to her non-existent breasts, she made it plain that Dummer junior had reported the smell of burning coming from upstairs and was concerned that the house might be on fire. Reassured by a convincing Chaplain (Clive) that all was well and that he was simply explaining the use of incense in the High Anglican mass, she left the room ever grateful to God that he had sent them such a kind and considerate young parson who would soon bring those with little or no faith into the fold. The fact that the organist had almost lost his left testicle in the hand winding pump of the chapel's ageing Victorian organ at the Founders' Day service, was more down to Macclesfield senior's ingenuity rather than the wrath of Clive's God.

Nevertheless, Clive stayed on for two years before agreeing to come to Lugworth but even now he was very unsure of his position and role in the church community.

Turning to Janet he appealed to her for more information on the lives of past Rectors.

"You've been here a long time, Janet, how on earth did my predecessors cope?"

"They didn't. One early retired to a Benedictine Monastery!"

"Mind you, they did say he liked a drink," Dee joked.

"And the other poor chap left for a tandem tour of the lower Himalayas," Janet added.

Open mouthed, Clive looked up to his heaven hopeful that the Good Lord would offer some great theological explanation for this strange mission. None came so he elected for a more earthly solution. "I could do with a drink. How about you two?" he sighed.

"Better wait until Bill and the others get here, he's parking the car."

Confused and unsure of the truth in the tales being told by his two friends he opened up a new line of enquiry.

"A tandem, Janet? All the way to India without anyone with him? Good God! Why? I can understand the monastery bit, but the Himalayas on a tandem seems a bit over the top."

"The gossip was that his cycle clips, which were usually found hanging on the hat pegs in the vestry, were found once too often on the end of a pair of clerically trousered legs in a prone position at the top end of buttercup meadow."

Dee, by now well into the local hot gossip, encouraged the wild tales of religious hanky-panky by mimicking the Churchwarden's wife, who, slightly squiffy after three glasses of communion wine at the Whitsuntide family service, gave the game away.

"If he wasn't ploughing the fields and scattering' then what was flighty young Gwyneth's dirndl skirt doing hanging on the hawthorn hedge?"

The laughter echoing around the bar drew attention to the skittish group in the far corner. Ignoring it and even more puzzled, Clive queried, "But how did she know it was hers?"

"She had sold it to her at the church jumble sale on the Saturday before."

By now Clive was clearly out of his depth. "But what has that got to do with a tandem ride round Nepal or wherever it was?"

Dee did the honours and explained the finer points of the story as simply as she could and without too much laughter.

"You see, Clive, your predecessor, for reasons known only to himself, took to riding a tandem to and from his pastoral duties. Sometimes, he took the girls home from choir practice on the back of it, they used to take it in turns."

"Doing what?" Clive exclaimed in mock amazement.

"Riding on the back of his tandem. Anyway, the gossip continued and he was warned by the Bishop to take a cold shower, examine his behaviour in the light of the Prime Minister's request to return to Victorian values and piss off out of the parish post haste."

"She's right," Janet confirmed. "He packed his pannier bags ..."

But before she could continue, Bill Jones came across with a tray of drinks. Familiar with the saga, he carried on the tale with a flow of Welsh rhetoric that needed no amplification to distribute it to the entire room plus those not engaged in the military two step at the gala dinner.

147

"So the poor chap clamped his cycle clips to his new fur lined wranglers, cocked his leg over the saddle, lifted two fingers to the Bishop and peddled out of the diocese singing, come ye thankful people come. I say we should raise our glasses to the gallant fellow. Your half of bitter, Dee, lager for you, Janet, and a Cinzano and lemonade for the Rector or under the circumstances, would you prefer a large scotch?"

"Heavens no!" cried the worried young cleric and attempted to hide his glass behind his hands.

"If they see this concoction, the church warden will have me drying out in Talgarth by the weekend."

Bill laughed and sat down between Janet and Dee. "Thought you should know Lady Llewellyn is on her way with Mrs Anderson-Shelta."

"Oh good," said Janet. "I wanted to see Angela and try to persuade her to join the Greenham trip."

"What!" exclaimed Dee. "The Chief Exec's wife on a peace march? You'll be lucky Janet, her stuffed shirt old man won't sanction that one, not when he's up to his eyes with nuclear defence."

Clive's relief at the change of conversation showed in his eagerness to prolong the new issues a little too loudly.

"Nuclear defence! What is he up to now?"

"Keep your voice down, Clive, bars have ears."

Dee was about to go into detail but Bill put his forefinger to her lips and in a stage whisper reminded her.

"Top secret, young woman. Remember our agreement."

Shrugging her shoulders she looked at Clive and in hushed tones replied. "Sorry Clive no can say. You know what it's like, pressure on the press and all that."

Her sarcasm was not lost on the Rector and he responded in similar vein.

"Don't tell me it's 'D-notice time for the Lugworth Daily Press. Wow! They will be bugging our one and only telephone kiosk next."

Appealing for common sense, Janet cut the conversation short.

"Do keep your voice down, Dee. Lady Anne is here and if she gets wind of the situation it will be raised in the House of Lords on Monday and the shit will hit the fan on Tuesday. Sorry, Rector, but modesty goes out the window at times like this. Good to see you again, Angela, you, too, Lady Ann," she said with genuine pleasure.

Bill pulled up two chairs and the two women sat down. Angela responded warmly, she was very fond of Janet and was always keen to see her, particularly if it involved stories of her husband's latest war games.

"How nice to see you again Janet and so soon," and kissed her on both cheeks with genuine affection. "You, too, Dee," she said with more than a hint of humour. "Now what scoop have you got for us this week? "Naked choir boys prancing about on Rectory lawn!"

Clive almost choked on his Cinzano. He had become used to Angela's teasing; she was Chair of the Parochial Church Council and well known for her witty remarks when meetings reached boredom point. However, it was quite clear that tonight she was more light hearted than usual and Clive was not ready for it. His assumed sexuality was sticky ground in some parts of the parish and at times needed to defend himself.

"Careful, Angela. I shall be a complete wreck well before I am confirmed into the Rectorship, although after what these three have been telling me, it's doubtful that I'll ever survive the course, never mind make the grade."

"I'm so sorry, dear boy, have they been telling you about the last of the brave Rectors of St Dick's. Better not wear your 'Gay is God's word, too' at evensong anymore."

Smiling at his concern and with more than an average twinkle in her eye, she laughed when he said:

"That isn't funny, Angela."

"Of course it isn't, Clive. It's living the life of Mrs Anderson-Shelta, he brings out the worst in me sometimes."

"He brings out the worst in all of us" replied Janet trying to ease the situation. "Talking of the Chief, Angela, how are things at base camp?"

"Base camp? Sorry, Janet, I'm not with you."

"You know," said Dee, "down at mission control."

Angela got the point. "Oh, you mean Fall Out headquarters. Well I'm afraid it's a case of Anthony the Unready ... for anything. I left him playing Monopoly with his management team. If you pass go, collect your ticket to the fallout shelter, chief executives and personal assistants first of course."

Lady Llewellyn, despite a small impairment in her hearing, had taken much of the conversation on board and contributed little, irritated, more than likely because no one had yet offered her a drink. Tugging sharply at Angela's cashmere covered arm.

"Angela, dear," she said quietly, "don't go over the top, he does try." Then, turning swiftly to Bill Jones, she uttered in a tone more suited to the Upper House. "Is anybody bothering to get this Peeress of the Realm a large brandy or do I have to get it myself out of my meager attendance allowance?"

Bill was on his feet in a flash, he was a big fan of the socialist Baroness; she was a good party worker and he admired the way she took on party leaders of all persuasion's if they didn't come up to scratch.

Bill beckoned towards the bar and called out: "Large brandy for her ladyship and a gin and tonic for Mrs Anderson-Shelta. That's your usual tipple isn't it, Angela?"

"I'd rather a malt whisky please, Bill. The Chief has 'acquired' a case or two and I'm glad to say I've become rather hooked on it, although Tony hasn't cottoned on yet."

"Make that a large malt with the brandy and cancel the gin and tonic, unless you want it, Dee?"

"Not for me, Bill, I'm only part through this bitter."

The landlord who had slipped away from the gala dinner, heard the order and always keen to chat up her ladyship, he whisked the tray from the barman's hand and took it to the table.

Whatever the occasion, George always dressed well and it showed in his Saville Row suits and handmade shoes. Tonight though, in his role of 'mine host' at the gala dinner dance he cut quite a dash in his evening togs and patent leather dancing pumps. There was the look of an ageing Lionel Blair about him; his fashionable maroon velvet jacket edged in silk binding of a lighter shade was new and he sported it with the style and relish of the winning competitor in the final of *Come Dancing*. Choosing his moment and with a particular eye for Lady Llewellyn-Llewellyn he glided towards the group and placing the tray on the table he took her hand and kissed it. To the amusement of all around her she responded with her usual curt display of reticence.

"For God's sake, George, do stop these ridiculous displays of so-called admiration, you're like an over-sexed peacock. All I want is a bloody drink not a long-term courtship."

Never a man to be put off his stroke, he announced to all and sundry. "But, Lady Anne, you promised me a tango one day, and as I can hear the Peggy Comfrey Light Orchestra tuning up for 'Temptation' what better moment for the two of us to cling together and chaises across the room as one?"

He caught her eyes knowing that hope would never spring eternal and that his unrequited desire to hold her wholesome Welsh body close to his would never be fulfilled.

"Chaises off back to your ballroom, George, and find yourself a buxom bargain breaker to troll around the dance floor with you. Now be kind enough to leave me to enjoy the company of my friends and send one of your minions across with another round of the same."

Turning to address her companions, who, like the rest of those in the lounge bar, were tear struck with laughter. It was always worth an extra penny or two on a pint, just to hear George and her Ladyship's banter.

"I trust another round is suitable to all."

"Anything you say, dear Lady," George replied. "The same again I presume."

"Well, I suppose I can manage another," said Janet, "although I do need an early night for a change."

"Don't we all, darling," Dee replied. "The Gladstone's under the eyes are beginning to show these days. How about you, Angela, are you keen to get home?"

"Never been less keen in my life, especially after a finance committee meeting. Anthony will be hell bent on giving me every minute detail of next year's budget proposals from blue-collar wage demands to the cost of plastic forks for the school meal service. That should cover the hours until the dawn chorus, by which time he will be so high on cash flow that he will get some sort of an erection and suggest that we might try a little conjugal wrestling. But by the time he is up on his elbows, it's all over for him and was never on for me."

Lady Anne was aghast at this outburst, she had not heard Angela speak like this before and was quite taken aback. For the first time in years she felt defensive towards Anthony and attempted to reprimand her niece.

"Angela, dear, that was uncalled for; he does his best at being a husband despite his peculiar ways. Whatever you say, dear, he does try."

Angela had been feeling edgy all day. Her marriage was well and truly off the rails and perhaps it was time to re-think her life and start seeking a new challenge; something that would excluded Anthony. There was no other man in her life, her upbringing had instilled in her that loyalty to one's spouse was paramount whatever the differences but she was at the end of her tether with the situation and Lady Anne's sudden defence of Anthony was just not on. Public place or not it was time to put the record straight. Sensing the atmosphere, Bill excused himself and took George to the bar, the others adjusted their positions and waited.

"Try! It's me that should have tried ... tried him out before we were married, but he was so damn moral about pre-nuptial sex, his mother evidently disapproved."

Lady Anne was taken aback and tried to halt the embarrassing flow before it got too far, the others – eyes wide open – waited.

"Steady, Angela, time and place and all that."

"Please let me have my say. What on earth would your sister, my God mother say if she knew what he was up to. Believe me, Lady Anne, the only thing he ever tries is my patience, life is so boring with him. I really will have to do something to shake him up."

Keen interest flooded Dee's face provoking Janet to nudge her in an effort to warn her off, but Dee, always on the lookout for snippets of social gossip for the nationals, prolonged the conversation enough to tempt Angela into revealing all.

"Do I note a hint of domestic crisis amid the hierarchy of Welsh local Government? I shall have to leak it to Dempster and make a fast buck or two," she joked.

Angela was undeterred. "Crisis! Life is one permanent bloody crisis with Anthony. Would you believe that yesterday he came back from the golf club in utter panic, he had somehow got the knitted bobble cover of his number one wood caught in the zip of his plus fours. He stood in the door clutching his crutch and acting like an inexperienced flasher caught in the act of indecent exposure outside a school for blind girls. He makes such a fool of himself, so much so, I just can't laugh at him anymore. Yet he's convinced he's down for a CBE in the next honours list, surely the PM isn't that stupid?"

"No one is that stupid" Janet said. "Come and sit over here next to me and be careful what you say in front of the news hound or you will be headlines before too long."

"As if I would do that, Jan," Dee said with a hurtful look. "You know I'm an old softie at heart."

"Yes, well that's what some say I suppose, including the doctor's daughter I hope."

Bill strolled back to the table.

"Domestic over and done with, ladies? I'm off now so take my chair, Angela. I can't stay, I'm taking Gladys into Cardiff tomorrow she's being measured for her nuclear fallout knickers, see you all at harvest festival. I understand you will be launching forth, Clive."

"Is that right, Clive," asked Janet. "You're using the harvest festival as a political platform?"

"Well, actually yes," he said glaring at Bill Jones.

"Tell them what you're up to Rector. Goodnight all."

With a brief wave he left the small group with just enough information to keep the parish pump flowing for a couple of hours.

"Bye, Bill," Dee waved. "Now, Lady Anne, what's going on? You must be in the picture with your connections on the church Council. Tell all please."

Lady Llewellyn was cornered and reluctantly offered an explanation; they hung onto her every word, Clive kept his head down.

"I understand that the Reverend Hayden Williams, one time hell fire and damnation brigade and former Rector of Lugworth is coming out ..."

Before she could finish the sentence Dee clapped her hands gleefully.

"Coming out! I knew it. He always spent a mite too long in the choir vestry after evensong. Things are looking up in this funny old backwater."

Lady Anne was appalled. "Miss Donnington, kindly get your mind out of the gutter and let me finish. The past Rector is coming out of retirement simply to oppose young Clive's political views. You know how he feels about young, trendy vicars, don't you, Janet. Well he's up in arms about Clive using the pulpit as a platform for his CND activities."

"I really don't understand the man," said Clive. "Surely any self-respecting cleric would be up for peace and goodwill across the world and that there is no place in God's plan for the wholesale slaughter of our enemies."

She responded sympathetically. "Of course we understand how you feel, Rector, it goes without saying but the old boy is set in his ways. Look what he had to say about York Minster burning down, he spent an entire sermon blaming it all on the Bishop of Durham and his comments about the Virgin Birth and the erection."

"Don't you mean the resurrection?" Janet politely prompted.

Her Ladyship flushed as she tried to correct the statement. "Yes! Yes! Well you know what I mean. Don't look so concerned, Clive. Tell them what his harvest message is going to be."

"I believe his sermon is going to be 'All is safely gathered in' or words to that effect."

The alcohol was slowly seeping into Angela's system. She had had two or three glasses of wine at dinner and it was beginning to show as she cut into the seriousness of the conversation with a bit of a giggle.

"Yes, well I wish he had said that to Anthony when his zip stuck. It might have reassured him."

Her elbow slipped on the shiny surface of the table and an empty glass hit the floor, the crash silenced the banter of the locals at the bar who began to realise that there could be a bit of fun on the cards.

"Can't someone be serious for a moment?" a concerned Clive asked. "I'm not absolutely convinced of his ability to preach anymore; I mean, he doesn't get frocked up much these days let alone climb into the pulpit. He must be up to something."

"Frocked up! This gets better and better" said a delighted Dee.

Lady Llewellyn was not amused. "Miss Donnington, please, Janet, do try and exercise some control over this exasperating young woman; she's bad enough sober but with a few drinks inside her, she starts thinking more like the editor of the News of the World instead of the nice public school girl she used to be."

Janet gave her friend a long hard look. "Shut up, Dee, you're over doing the reporter bit. As for the old Rector, his hell fire might have gone but he's still pretty strong on damnation but using his beloved St Richards as a platform for a CND campaign goes against the grain for an old die hard like Hayden. Anyhow, Clive, both sides have to nail their colours to the cross … if you'll pardon the expression."

Despite her dressing down, Dee was as enthusiastic as ever. "It seems to me that all this nuclear warfare stuff is breaking up what peace we have in this town, not encouraging it. I can just see the headlines in the Courier if Jonno gets onto it, 'Unrest at Evensong; All God's gifts (tins only) to be delivered to the local fallout shelter care of the Chief Executive."

"Doesn't she ever give up" said Lady Anne with just a hint of amusement. "Fleet Street come and get her, she's driving us all batty."

Pushing herself up from the settle she announced to Clive.

"Come along, Rector, you and I must be on our way, we've got to sort out the travel arrangements for Greenham."

"Is there still that to do?" responded a weary Clive. "I thought we were up to date on everything."

"Not quite, dear boy."

Turning to Angela she kissed her on the cheek. "I'll walk home, my dear, you stay and chat about your domestic crisis or whatever you call it. I'll see you all on the bus on Saturday, sleeping bags, primus stoves, sandwiches et al.

As for you, Miss Donnington, let's have a bit of decorum if you're travelling with us. Come along, Clive, your arm if you please."

Ignoring the ribald comments of the landlord and his cronies who, well and truly under the influence of Welsh bitter, had been filling the heads of the visitors with expansive tales of yore, she moved across the room.

"Goodnight, Gentlemen ... goodnight, George and take your hands out of your pockets when I'm in the room, you'll spoil the lining of your new Daks."

It took a moment for the penny to drop. The flushing landlord accepted the laughter of his pals before replying "Message received and understood, your Ladyship, see you Sunday lunchtime as usual."

"Not this weekend you won't. We are all off camping."

"Taking the new Rector with you, your ladyship?" came the unknown voice from among the lads by the dart board in the corner.

"Yes she is," Clive replied a little too nervously. "It's a peace campaign that's all, there's a coach party going from Lugworth and it's a very worthwhile trip."

"Come along, Rector, take no notice, they're just winding you up. You should know by now that they love a bit of tittle tattle in this town and if it wasn't you it would be some other poor soul. Just see it as your Christian duty to take the flack. Anyway it's none of their business what you get up to under the blankets. Now open this door and let's get out into the fresh air."

"Who's for another then?" asked Dee as she waved goodbye to the odd couple.

"It's my turn," said Janet. "Get them in please, Dee, I want to have a quiet word with Angela."

Dee wandered over to the bar while Janet put a friendly arm about Angela's shoulder; the alcohol was having its usual effect of casting care to the wind.

"Look, Angela, don't think I'm interfering in your domestic life but have you thought about coming with us on Saturday. It will do you good; show you what women for peace are all about."

"What, me march to Greenham? You're insane. Firstly, I cannot march anywhere without him in tow and don't forget he's up to his eyes in this defence exercise."

"Bugger the defence exercise. You couldn't choose a better time to fly, Angie, you said you needed a new challenge so show him you really mean business when it comes to nuclear warfare."

"That will be nothing compared to the warfare with him when he finds out how I feel about the subject."

"He knows already, he waffles on about it in the Mayor's parlour."

"I know, I know, but he's a bit more touchy these days now that he's C in C of the Lugworth Bunker Brigade. Seriously, Jan, he is worried about this defence project."

"I should think he is! Your husband hasn't got a bloody clue about it. No one has. The real panic is not nuclear fallout, it's community fall out. Who's in charge of this, who's not in charge of that. I tell you, Angie, it's not just Lugworth; all over the damn country they play these silly war games. It's farcical, it really is, and if it should happen … well it doesn't bear thinking about."

She went quiet for a moment until Angela nudged her.

"Come on, Janet, don't be so pensive, we are supposed to be having a laugh at the Chief Exec and the atomic cock-up of all time. Will we ever see Lugworth defending itself against Russian rockets! How ridiculous has life has become. Where has Dee got to with the drinks?"

She was coming towards them muttering out loud.

"Sorry about this. I wish George would get some extra staff on gala nights. Thank God for Dai Davis, he got me one in while I was waiting."

"So you're one up on us already are you, Dee?"

"Don't worry, Angie, I've got us doubles. By the way, Janet, I've switched us all to malts, if we are going to make a night of it, let's do a proper job."

Angie giggled, "This looks ominous. In for a penny in for a pound I say. How about you, Jan?"

"I suspect I'm out numbered. Now what's the delay this time, Dee? George run out of bitter again?"

"Nothing quite so simple. Our devious landlord seems to have got wind of the secret we are supposed to have kept under wraps and is taking bookings for spaces in the cellars just in case the bomb falls upon this green and pleasant acre or two."

"You mean they've heard a rumour and think it's for real?"

"Spot on, Janet. That's why I wanted to do a piece in the Express and Journal, just to avoid this sort of local hysteria, but your power crazy husband, Angela, shoved his official secret act down my throat and D-noticed me. Stupid bastard. I told you, it's gone to his head," Dee said and sat down.

Pointing to the gaggle of farmers and their boys propping up the bar she added.

"Anyway, that lot over there are negotiating like hell for places in the cellar and Ted isn't helping by shouting, "If we're going to go out with a bang, best may as well go well and truly pickled."

"So Lugworth's top secret is out of control. What on earth will my husband do now? Hold a bloody inquiry I suppose and then sentence the offender to ten years before the mast."

Angie dropped her head onto the table. After a moment or two she announced. "I think we need another top up. Same again girls."

"I'll go and at the same time have a word with George. He must have picked it up from someone in the bar. Ted will bring the drinks over"

Looking worried she came back to the table and sat down.

"It was Elwyn Price told him," Janet said quietly.

"What! Elwyn Price from the Methodist Chapel, never in a month of Sundays. How, what where and when and what has it got to do with her?" Dee gasped.

"Shush! Keep your voice down," Jan whispered. "George said she found a copy of 'The County Plan for Defence (Nuclear). Fall Out Shelters for the use of."

"Shit, Janet! Where the hell did she find that?"

"In the magazine rack at the Family Planning Clinic."

The laughter was more of a strangled cry as the three women choked back their delight. Dee, utterly amazed, spoke first.

"I don't believe it. I just do not bloody believe it!"

"I can," Angela said. "I believe anything can happen where Tony is involved."

Aware that the room had suddenly gone quiet Angie suggested.

"Voices well down I think girls. We appear to be lowering the tone of the bar. How did it happen, Janet?"

"It seems that our thoroughly organised Council has planned for everything. Fall out, families and free contraception for those wanting a bunk up in the bunker. Somehow a copy was left behind and put in the magazine rack and Elwyn (mother of five) Price spotted it while waiting to catch her wayward daughter with a handful of Durex."

Angela, by now soaked on whiskey, was agog.

"It's so ridiculously funny, Janet, it's almost frightening. I'm definitely coming on your Greenham adventure, if only to reassure myself that there are people who take this matter seriously."

"Good on you, Angie," Dee gleefully stated. This will stir up the locals and give me some great copy." Angela looked concerned. "Will the papers be covering Greenham then?"

"At this rate masses; nationals, TV, radio and me covering the Lugworth story, my goodness, Mrs Anderson-Shelta, you've seen nothing yet. They will all be there, breaking the news and agonising over what peace women do in their makeshift tents at night."

Janet added, "From what I have been told already that any hope of sleep is destroyed by helicopters deliberately clattering overhead until dawn eventually blowing the bloody tents away. The photographers will, of course, avoid the shots of police truncheons striking any unsuspecting young women daring to ask the way to the bog."

Janet's sarcastic overtones had not gone unnoticed by Angela. "You've become serious again, Jan. Okay girls, I'll join the club but he isn't going to like it."

"What can he do about it anyway; you're free to do your own thing aren't you?"

"I suppose I am really, he's so bloody right wing that he can't make allowances for anything. You know what he's like, Janet."

"Indeed I do. So what's got up your nose this time? Something has. Come on, out with it."

"I really shouldn't let him get to me … but last week I happened to pass the courthouse when he was on the bench and I dropped in to wait for him. "

"He is the Chairman," Dee said.

"I know but it was so embarrassing. Old Mrs Thornton, you know her Janet, she lives in the lovely old cottage on the edge of the common. She's got all those cats."

"Yes, Ange, I know who you mean."

Dee cut into the conversation. "I know what you're going to say, I covered the case, Jan."

"Well, I didn't. Go on, Angela, tell her what happened?"

"The old lady stood in the dock, looking quite frail, charged with stealing a tin of cat meat from a pet shop. When the evidence, provided I might add, by the owner himself the old girl broke down."

Janet was shocked and muttered to herself, "bastards." and said, "Carry on, Angie, this is awful."

"You haven't heard the half of it. Tony gave her a dressing down, a conditional discharge and told her not to do it again. I was beginning to feel quite proud of him until he addressed the court and said. 'This is the sort of case that a spell in the British Army would have cured'."

"He said that to a seventy-five year old woman?"

"In a nutshell," Janet, "in a bloody nutshell. He makes himself utterly ridiculous."

"Ridiculous, Angie! He's a first class idiot. How do you live with someone like that?"

"I really don't know. When I asked him about it later all he would say was that he had had a belly full of yobbo's all morning and it was about time they brought back conscription." I said that she was a seventy-five year old woman trying to live on a meagre pension, not a bloody vandal. It was water off a duck's back and he spent the rest of the evening muttering, "Riff-raff, nothing but elderly riff-raff."

"Where on earth did you find him, Angela. You're so incompatible? Dee said, "Let's have another drink and you can enthral us with tales of your courtship."

"Do you think I should? I've said too much already. Oh sod it, why not? He won't be home for hours yet, some Masonic do at the lodge. I need the loo so I'll get another round in on the way back."

Angela was more than slightly tipsy and she swayed slightly as she crossed the room, nevertheless it did not deter the looks of appraisal from casual admirers at the bar. Her middle years had brought about a sensuality which unknowingly caused eyes to glaze in lustful appreciation of a body that offered many things to many people, including Dee. It was as if seeing her for the very first time as she sighed to herself in silent worship. The moment had not gone unnoticed by Janet.

"You alright, Dee? You've gone quiet."

"I was watching Angela, she is just lovely. I look at her sometimes and think what I would give for a long weekend in Tuscany with her by my side. It brings me out in a cold sweat."

"One thing you wouldn't give is your right hand, that would render you useless. So clear your head of such insatiable appetites and get your feet on solid ground. The lady's not for turning."

Angela reappeared at the bar and Janet quickly broke up the conversation.

"She's on her way back, Dee, so please try to remember that what she tells us tonight is between friends, not you and your readership; and don't look so hurt."

Angela grinned as she placed the tray of drinks onto the table. "I took the liberty of getting large ones again. It's almost last orders and the gala dinner dancers will be thirsty, so a little stock piling is called for. Ted will bring another round over before closing time."

Chapter Ten

"Crikey, Angie, at this rate we will be stupefied by closing time" Janet said.

"That's a reasonable state of mind for discussing marriage. Now where were we?"

"You were going to tell us why you married the Chief Exec?" Dee said.

Angela took a mouthful of double whisky before launching into the biggest mistake of her life.

"I met him when he was doing his stint in the army; he was a Lieutenant in the Education corps. Daddy was commanding the 'A' division of the Parachute Brigade in Aldershot and we lived in nearby Farnborough Park. Desperate to lose his Welsh accent, Daddy suggested he went to my elocution teacher who made quite a good job of it actually. Anyway, Tony took a liking to me and we drifted into some sort of relationship, fawning all over me in the officers' mess he even signed on for a six year short service commission just to impress Daddy."

"You must have had other admirers, Angie?" queried Dee.

"Lots! But being an army family we never stayed in one place long enough to sustain a regular courtship. There was this chap at university; he ended up a researcher in ancient Egyptian history at the British Museum. He was obsessed with the Pharaoh's and far too boring; anyway Daddy wasn't all that keen on boffins so it just petered out. Looking back, though, compared to local Government, Egyptology would have been a laugh a minute.

"Before long I found myself carried away with the social life of the mess and became heady with the romance of it all. In those days Tony was handsome, attentive, considerate and really quite nice. Although not strictly my type he was good company, too, but before I could put the brakes on I had a diamond ring, prospective Welsh in-laws and parents who were 'jolly pleased I was going to settle down to an army life; after all it had done well for them'. Little did they, or I, know that Anthony had no plans for a military career, he had political leanings, but by then it was too late. The engagement was announced in *The Times* and *Tatler*, gold edge invitations sent out and the regimental silver polished."

"And the wedding Angie. What was that like?" Jan asked.

"I was marched up the aisle of the Garrison Church of St George, Aldershot to the strains of the 'Trumpet Voluntary' on the arm of a proud father in full regalia and medals and handed over to a waiting Tony, starched up to the eyeballs in mess undress and with no idea how to control his ceremonial sword. The Chaplain General, Daddy's old drinking chum, stumbled though the service stinking of brandy and peppermint unable to take his eyes off my cleavage highlighted by the low cut of my Chanel dress."

"Well I can see his point," Dee said. It must have been a sight for sore eyes?"

"Shut it, Dee," Janet responded. "Let Angie get on with this fascinating story. It's better than Barbara Cartland."

"Formalities over with, I was promenaded back down the aisle again by a rather smug husband, accompanied by a camp organist from the Royal College of Music who heavy pedalled the wedding march as if he was in the Tower Ballroom at Blackpool. Outside in the sunshine I was manoeuvred through the archway of raised sabres for the confetti and rose petal moment to be faced by a waiting crowd already emotionally moved by Elgar's 'Pomp and Circumstance No 1' played by combined band of the Blues and Royals, as a personal favour to Mummy (in return for what I shall never know). Photographs by David Bailey and then a first class reception in the senior officers' mess, provided of course by the very best chefs from the Army Catering Corps.

Oh yes, the Welsh contingent, we mustn't forget them. Tony's family and friends, and I use that term loosely, arrived in a coach from Cardigan much to the dismay of Mummy's family and the military police. All that was needed to make a perfect day was a bloody male voice choir."

Pausing to finish her whisky she waved at Ted to bring over the last order leaving her two friends stunned, they had never heard Angela in such full flow.

"I think we've all had a bit too much. Perhaps we had better call it a day," Janet said with some reticence.

"Not likely," Dee replied. "I want to hear the end of this story. Anyway, we've got another drink to go before closing. Thanks, Ted."

Ted made room for the drinks and then cleared away the latest empties, while Janet, thoughtful for a moment or two and stared into her fresh drink before sipping it.

"But there must have been some highlights, a few good moments to remember?"

"Of course there were some good moments, Janet, certainly in the early days, but it's getting late and George wants last orders."

"Bugger George, Angie, you're on a roll and we want to know the works about you and the Chief Exec. It's never too late for the confessional, best tell all and get it over with, otherwise Dee won't sleep tonight." Jan said. "Come on, Angie, it's not all that late, and as long as the bargain breakers are still in the bar we locals can stay, anyway the lads are still around."

Dee called for another round. "Same again, Ted. Now Ange, how did your husband get to where he is now, after he left the army. You must have gone along with it."

This time, George brought tray across and ignoring his usual sexist quip, they waited until he it placed on the table. Angela was already a whiskey in hand; she loved the light and easy friendship she had with Dee and Janet and decided it was time to open up on the real Anthony Anderson-Shelta.

"Okay, seconds out for round two," Sitting back into the big armchair she felt more relaxed than ever and grinned at her companions. "While we were in the service, I was still wearing my rose tints and he was still hanging his heart on his sleeve but once he resigned his commission everything changed; he wanted success and I wanted it for him as well, but the pressure was on to start a family and I was keen on that, too. Fair play, he had worked hard to get all his qualifications letters after a name impressed him, he even turned down a business partnership preferring to smooth his way up the ladder of local Government. Once he spoke of going for Parliament which terrified me. I couldn't have coped with selection procedures and his disappointment at not being chosen."

"So how did he get on the local Government gravy train?" Jan asked.

"He saw an advertisement for a Town Clerk in Hampshire and against all the odds got it; from then on our future and his promotions were set and I could do nothing about it. His rise to power came earlier than expected, in fact it was almost forced on us following major changes in local Government administration in the early 1970s. It was also about this time that my parents died."

"What both of them?" Dee asked. "How come."

"Daddy dropped dead on a brigade reunion in Cyprus and mummy, after enjoying a brief period of widowhood drove her new Lancia off the road in Monte Carlo a year later. The inquest never really identified the male passenger except to say he appeared to come from some defunct European Royal family. It was a great shock, my entire family were wiped out within a year and all I had left was Anthony."

"But what happened to your own plans for a family?" Janet asked quietly.

"Down the drain I'm afraid, we soon discovered that we couldn't have children, something to do with his sperm count although he wouldn't admit to it; all I had left were my joint godmothers, Daphne and her sister Lady Anne. They were my mother's oldest friends and went to school together; Daphne never married and in a way she was all the family I had I suppose. After what seemed an endless pause, she drew out a long sigh, before carrying on.

"Anthony was very supportive throughout it all and we rubbed along well for a year or two until he found a new love, golf. Later he was appointed Chief Executive at the Mid Border District Council and that dear friends, was when we parted company, so to speak. I didn't want to live in Wales with nothing but rugby, golf, chapel, hymns and bloody arias, but he gave me his lecture on wifely duties and all that crap and stressed that after all he was a Welshman. From then on it was downhill all the way.

Dee was shocked. "Bloody hell, Ange, pulling you out of your Home Counties roots, just like that, for desolate Mid Wales, takes some beating, it really does."

"I suppose it didn't mean all that much at the time, Daddy was posted here, there and everywhere and I was used to moving on, but somehow I wasn't ready. We rowed until I grudgingly conceded defeat on condition that I used some of my substantial inheritance to purchase an apartment in Hampstead and debenture seats at Covent Garden."

"And his conditions for you?" Dee asked.

"Fronting up on all public occasions, like conferences and civic do's, which seemed reasonable at the time – until he got really hooked on bloody golf and joined the Masonic Lodge. I couldn't cope with that. He spent more and more time teeing off with a celebrity in some charity tournament or examining male nipples at the Lodge. However, we eventually worked out a way of life that suited me more than him but even that is beginning to pall."

"Have you still got your London retreat?" Dee asked.

"Yes. I couldn't exist without a bolt hole." she replied. "The opera, theatre, all that culture, it's the breath of life to me and I miss having it on tap. You must come for a weekend sometime, both of you."

Dee was the first to reply, her eagerness took Angela by surprise. "That would be great. When shall we go, Janet?"

"Not yet, Dee, there's lots going on at the moment. Anyway I can't think clearly, we're all a bit sozzled. I suppose we ought to start winding up the evening while we can still walk home."

Angela laughed out loud. "I must tell you one funny story before we go. It was when Tony took me to his first NALGO conference at the Flora Hall in Southport. He had been invited to speak in a debate on 'The New Way Forward for Local Government' and he was ready to give the unions some stick.

"What happened?" Dee asked.

"You mean what didn't happen. He said it was going to be a second honeymoon, our entry into the top level of local Government society; the road to Number 10."

"What!" said Janet. "He was thinking that high?"

"Yes and he even cocked that up. He was just about to deliver his first paper 'Down the Drain' to conference, something to do with sewage reclamation in rural areas, when some chap in the front row sighed and said, 'Oh shit. Beaming husband was so impressed someone had already tuned into his thinking, he dropped his papers, bent to collect them and caught his foot in the microphone cable. For one joyous moment he held his balance and then, almost in slow motion, he fell off the front of the platform."

Jan and Dee roared together, "I'd like to have witnessed that one, Jan. How about you?" Dee asked, but Angela had not finished.

"Wait for it, girls, that's not all. He went arse over head into a trough of floral arrangements at the foot of the stage, fused the lights and ripped his new pinstriped trousers on a rather spiky conifer, and that wasn't all he ripped. He left the hall escorted by a kindly St John Ambulance Brigade lady and the gentleman who shouted shit moved next business. Poor Tony couldn't sit down for a week let alone cope with a second honeymoon."

Still laughing, the noisy group looked up just as George approached them. No one could speak at first, they were laughing so much, but Janet managed to wipe her eyes and ask, "Was there something, George?"

"Haven't you three got homes to go to? It's after hours you know."

"What's it to you, landlord?" Janet had drunk far too much. "Are you going to kick us out then?"

"He'd better bloody not," Dee said as she tried to stand up and sat down again. "You've still got a few left in here drinking and they're not bargain breakers, not with the local copper propping up the bar with them." She shouted across to him, "Alright, Dai?"

"Very well, my dear," replied the amorous policeman. What about sharing your joke with us, ladies?"

"You wouldn't even begin to understand it, Dai" Janet replied. Anyway we're going soon."

"That's if George doesn't chuck you out first."

"He wouldn't dare. Would you George?"

"Ten more minutes, dear ladies, and then I'm locking up the bar except to residents."

"Fair enough, landlord," Jan said. "Well Dee, I don't know what you think, but Council meetings will never be the same again. Now, Angie. What about Greenham Common are you coming or not?"

"She's got to now, Jan, just to keep us laughing on the bus. Come on Angela," Dee pleaded. "What have you got to lose?"

"Only Anthony," Janet said.

"In that case count me in. It's about time this worm turned."

The whisky was having its usual effect on Angela; the domestic balloon was going up as she began to confide in her drunken soul mates.

Drawing her companions closer she announced to all and sundry. "I'm up to here with his boring local Government ways and his boring local Government floosy, Mrs Ruth Bloody Tremlett. The woman who thinks 'knocking off at four' no longer means going home early."

"Is that still going on?" Dee asked.

"Only when the commander is away," Janet confirmed.

"Of course, and he still thinks I don't know about it."

"Surely it's nothing but a quick fumble under the Council table?" Dee suggested.

"It's bit more than that," said Angela. "He takes her off to conferences now. They call it official business these days."

"Don't worry about that it's only her knockers he's after; he's just a knocker man that's all. These days he only has to meet a woman with big tits and his Y fronts do the splits. It's common enough. I know a retired vicar in religious broadcasting who behaves the same way; if the production assistant has big knockers he delivers the best daily service for weeks."

"I'd like to know what his "Thought for the Day" was," said Janet before putting her head on the table.

"Time to go home, ladies" George called out again.

"Right oh," Dee replied. "Come on you two, on your feet it's home time."

The three women stoically supported each other as they giggled their way across to the exit. As they passed the bar Angela called out to a grinning Dai. "We're only slightly drunk, Constable Davis."

"So it seems, madam. Mind the steps as you go outside."

"You're not going to arrest us then?"

"Why? What have you done?"

174

"Got pissed with my friends."

"No law against that, madam, unless you do something you might regret in the morning."

Leading her friends to the main door, Janet suggested. "Come on, Angie, we need coffee.

"What for?"

"Coffee. Your place or mine, Dee?"

"Yours, Jan. It's nearer on foot."

"Is Angela going?"

"We are all going," Angela said. "Even Constable Davis. I want him to tell me some stories about ghosts and fairies."

"Not tonight, madam. Some other time but let me walk you all to Ms Bodmin cottage."

That was when Angela decided to sit down on the stone steps leading to the street. They tried to get her up, but she wouldn't budge unless Dai agreed to go for coffee.

"Come on, Dai, for God's sake. She'll sit here all night. I've got a bottle of Glen Fiddich if that will help you change your mind."

""Bollocks to him," Angela replied. "Are you going to tell me about the fairies or not? Otherwise I'm going to sleep here."

"Oh no you're not," Janet said. "If you're staying here then I'm staying here with you."

"And I'm staying here with you, too," Dee insisted.

"Nobody's staying in my porch. Just get 'em home Dai, please," George pleaded.

"On your feet, girls, let's get some coffee," Dai encouraged. "Come on, up you all get and let's move on."

"Alright, Constable, alright. I'm coming. You won't forget the stories about the fairies?"

"No he won't forget about the fairies will you, Dai?"

"As long as you don't forget to keep filling my glass, ladies."

"Will do Dai," Janet promised.

"Right then off we go. Now what particular fairy stories do you want. The ones about the boys who live in Bottom Lane or the fairies at the bottom of my garden?"

Chapter Eleven

The following morning Janet woke up with a corker of a headache. Each throb told her in no uncertain terms that it had been an idiotic decision to go back to the house last night. The session in the Lugworth Arms was bad enough, but Angela had insisted that Constable Davies came in for a drink, as she put it, after 'kindly seeing us safely home'. Angela had never been included in a Dai Davis gathering before and was unaware of his obsessive interest in the supernatural, thus her naivety showed the moment she asked him, "Do you believe in fairies, Constable, or is only a naughty rumour?" Thanks to the last drop of Glenfiddich she never understood the answer and the first of the dog watch's slipped by un-noticed.

The sunlight flooding through the bedroom window reminded Janet that she had not bothered to close the curtains before she had finally crawled into bed. For a brief moment her eyelids lost the fight for survival and she was just about ready to drop off again when the simultaneous sound of the telephone ringing and the cat wailing for its breakfast forced her to face the day. She managed to grasp the phone long enough to cope with Ruth Tremlett's husky voice reminding her about the four o'clock meeting of the Lugworth Defence Committee and that the venue had been changed from the town hall to the assembly rooms. Coping with the hungry cat balanced on her shoulder and she had no choice but to get up. It was ten fifteen when she eventually hit the tin opener, cured the cat of its hunger pangs and then put the kettle on. While it boiled she collected up *The Guardian* and the post from the mat in the hall, walked back into the kitchen and made a pot of coffee which she carried into her small dining room. Taking her special blue and white Italian cup and saucer from the pine dresser she poured out the coffee strong and black and sat down at the table. The mail wasn't worth opening so she glanced at the paper and sipped her coffee. She had already missed the deadline for two phone calls she should have made and she still hadn't finished the history paper she had been commissioned to set for Cambridge University Examination Board. The thought of completing that, followed by three hours of Anderson-Shelta and his management team finalising defence day, was daunting enough and she still had to pack her kit for the weekend at Greenham.

Janet Bodmin had lived in Lugworth for almost ten years. Her roots were Home Counties, although a good deal of her early working life had been spent in London. Having missed out on a formal education, she became a mature student at London University's Birkbeck College, where at the age of thirty-two, she obtained an honours degree in Social and Political History which took her to a teaching position at a girls' public school in Hampshire. Encouraged by her head mistress, she studied for and obtained a Master's degree and after twelve years at the school she was offered the position of deputy head mistress. She turned this down in favour of a part time senior lectureship at The University of Wales, this allowed her the time to gain her Ph.D. And to supplement her income, she marked GCE history examinations papers and joined the lecture circuit. Her election as a district Councillor had been unexpected and brought her representative appointments to the board of The Welsh National Opera and the Llangollen International Festival committee but turned down the offer of Justice of the Peace. The black and white cottage she had purchased in Lugworth was her haven and the pleasure it brought made up for her lack of family ties, although her elderly mother spent many pleasant periods with her during the summer and at Christmas time. Her family and friends made regular visits, staying for fun filled weekends in the country, some bringing their children, but in the main she enjoyed her own company and the space it gave her. Whether or not she would one day return to the Home Counties was a question she often toyed with, but today she had other things on her mind.

The doorbell announced the arrival of her close friend bright as a button with no hint of a hangover.

"Morning, Jan, how's your head? I see you've got the coffee on the go?"

"Awful. I've just brewed up. If you want some grab a blue cup from the shelf."

Reaching up she took a cup and placed it on the table. "You do look rough, Jan. I suspect that you're not feeling up to the defence committee today?"

"I'm not up for anything at the moment. I'll kill Dai when I see him. Angela was scared half to death by his weird stories. God knows how she's feeling today?"

"I haven't seen her yet. Mind you, I've just bumped into Lady Llewellyn and she doesn't look too pleased with us."

"Us, Dee, not us. It was you who invited Angie back in and she was well and truly plastered by then. What did Lady Anne say?"

"She shouted across the road to me when I was parking the car. Something about leading people into

179

temptation. Seems my reputation is catching up with me again, Jan."

"Yes well, we had better gloss over your so called reputation. Are you covering the meeting today?"

"Of course, you know I have carte blanche on the press statements. By the way, have you seen today's Guardian?"

"Briefly, why?"

"There's a small write up announcing that the Prime Minister will be visiting Mid-Wales sometime in late autumn."

"Does that mean Lugworth?"

"Could be. I think it's time I contacted the doctor's daughter and find out what's new on the Welsh Office front."

Jan grinned, "Haven't you seen her lately! Not losing your touch are we, Dee?"

"Not my touch, dear heart, change of venue that's all. Anyway, I only dropped by to tell you the news. Oh! – one other thing, Crispin's in town, he's parked up at the Lugworth."

"Please, God, don't say he's coming to the meeting." Jan pleaded.

"If he does, that will cure your hangover Jan! Shall we go into Brecon tonight; they say the wine bar is worth a visit?"

"Let's see how the meeting pans out. Anyway, after last night I'm off the booze for a while."

"Fine, until the next round, I'll catch up with you later. Lots of black coffee, Jan, that will do the trick, or a hair of the dog in the 'Cricketer's' at one-ish, if you feel like it."

"That's the last thing I feel like, Dee. I'll see you out, and then I'll take a shower and prepare to face the day."

"Want any help with the shower," Dee said, with more than a hint of humour in her voice.

"No thanks. Keep that for the doctor's daughter, you might need to prime the stove before you put the kettle on especially if you want the low down on the PM's visit. Sorry to disappoint you, 'bye for now."

"Heartbroken, darling," she flirtatiously called back. "See you later."

Closing the door, Jan topped up her coffee cup, took it upstairs and ran the shower, above the sound of running water she heard the distinctive growl of Dee's MG roaring off to her next assignation. Smiling to herself she stepped into the cascading hot water and reminded herself that she really did enjoy her friendship with Dee; it was solid, reliable, good humoured and affectionate even though at times it could be exasperating but on the whole the rapport they had with each other was special. Lingering under the hot water for as long as she could, it took the edge of her tiredness and she dared herself to let go of the cold control, gripping it tight, she pushed herself to the edge and twisted the tap. The shock to the system almost blew her away, her strangled cry forcing the cat out of the airing cupboard like a bat out of hell.

"Jesus Pankers, why the hell did I do that? It could have killed me." Shivering, she grabbed a large towel, already warmed in the airing cupboard, wrapped it tightly round her expanding waistline and flopped into her mother's old wicker chair with the big soft cushions. Quickly drying off, she creamed her body in Crabtree and Evelyn Patchouli skin cream, its heady perfume clearing her mind enough to think about the afternoon's meeting and Davenport-Jones's arrival in town.

The cat, looking distinctly put out, poked his head round the part open bathroom door, wide eyed and hopeful he produced his usually silent word-speak and leaped onto her warm lap.

"It must be something big if the Sloane Rangers turned up midweek," she muttered. "Something very big indeed. Roll on this afternoon and let's see what secrets and lies are on the agenda this time."

Lugworth Defence committee was meeting at the Assembly Rooms in the town square for the first time, it had just reached the yawning stage when the noise began; Ben Neal heard it first. Jumping up from his seat he dashed towards the window tripping over the outstretched legs of Crispin Davenport-Jones who was desperately fighting the effects of a long liquid lunch.

"Will somebody help him up and let's get the sensitive matter of expenses out of the way and get onto the D-day, otherwise it will mean yet another meeting, Anthony announced. The thought of another day of expenses brought smiles to the faces of his officers. Janet and Dee were sitting nearest to the two floored men and helped them back into their seats but the incident had jolted Crispin into what life he had left in him. Thinking that he had missed something important, he asked quietly.

"Are we lunching her in the Council Chamber or at the Lugworth Arms? Perhaps the Council Chamber would be better under the circumstances, it will be easier to keep the socialist gate crashers out."

"Lunching who, Crispin?" The Chief Executive asked, "What lunch are you talking about, the civic, or the next Rotary Club meeting? We can't sort those out today you know."

Crispin realised that he had said too much and tried to back track. "What! Gosh I think I've let the cat out of the bag. Forget what I have just said, Tony, didn't mean to cause a flap. Please don't record that, Mrs Tremlett."

Ruth was unusually flustered, "What do you wish me to do Mr Chairman?"

"Hold on for a moment, dear lady," the Chairman replied. "Let's hear what our Member of Parliament is trying to keep from us. Are you aware of any special luncheon arrangements, Chief Executive, or you Mr Treasurer?"

Arthur Yorkshire consulted his paper work and flicked carefully through it before replying.

"Nothing recorded, Mr Chairman, although I do have, at the Chief Executive's request, a rather high contingency refreshment allowance for the day of the exercise," he smirked, "I have tried to extract a fuller explanation for the figure, but to no avail."

"Pompous bastard!" Anthony muttered to himself as he tried to counter the treasurer's unwanted comment and turned to his personal assistant for support.

"Mrs Tremlett, perhaps you could look this up after the meeting. Now I think we had better get on."

"I think it would be best if we cleared this little matter up now," Bill said. "Why has this money been set aside and who will be taking lunch with whom?"

Ben Neal, who, by this time was more confused than ever, decided he would stick his oar in, especially if it concerned freebee lunches."

"Let's have an answer then, Mr Davenport-Jones, it's the ratepayers' money we are talking about here, not yours I assume?"

It didn't take long for Dee Donnington to figure out what was going on. "It's the Prime Minister isn't it Crispin? She's coming."

"What?" said Bill. "The Iron Lady coming to Lugworth? What the hell does she want to do that for?"

"Spot on Ms. Donnington," Crispin acknowledged. "Now tell me how did you know it's on the cards when it's supposed to be top secret."

"Nothing is ever top secret in this town," Janet said. "They hinted at it in *The Guardian* today."

"And just how long have you known about it?" Bill Jones asked the Chief Executive. "From day bloody one I suppose. So, what's the real plan for D-Day? We all rush around like blue arsed flies playing bloody war games, while you lot entertain the PM and her retinue to a slap up lunch. Let me tell you this, if Tomo gets to hear about this, he'll find the biggest bloody padlock and weld it on the booze cupboard in his parlour, otherwise Dennis will hit the Gin and Tonic like it's going out of fashion."

"Hold on a moment, Bill, no worries on that count, Councillor Thomas and his good lady will be at the do," said Anthony. "After all, he is Chairman of the Council and he and Marjorie will be hosting the luncheon."

"As long as she isn't cooking it," Josh Aiken said. "Otherwise you can count me out."

"So there is going to be a lunch do Chairman?" Janet enquired.

"Seems like it, Janet," Bill confirmed, "and not even approved by the committee."

Looking towards the windows he queried. "Has any one any idea what is going on outside?"

"Music of some sort," Dee said, "and it's getting louder, I'll take a look."

Moving to the nearest window she calmly declared.

"Crikey, it's the town band, or at least two thirds of it, for some reason they're trying out the German national anthem, oomph style. For the life of me, why is the town band playing German tunes. It's been going on for weeks in the square which I can only describe as

'Woodstock revisited' coupled with a few escapees well past their sell by date, from some vintage CND campaign."

"Will someone please tell us what the hell is going on out there?" Bill Jones asked.

Hanging over the window ledge Dee continued her commentary. "It looks like someone has got wind of your war games Bill and intends stopping them," she replied.

Anthony was up on his high horse again. "I'm going to call the Chief Constable and insist he nips it the bud now. We don't want any riff raff upsetting the Prime Minister, do we, Crispin?" Shouting at his secretary as if she was on the moon he yelled. "Tell them to clear off Mrs Tremlett, I won't hesitate to call the police if they don't move on."

Upon hearing her master's voice Ruth was on her feet; skilfully avoiding the pit falls of Crispin's outstretched legs, she leaned out of the open window. Whether it was her over hanging bosoms that caused the final notes of anthem to fade into silence will never be known, but whatever it was, it did the trick.

"Thank you, Ruth," Bill said," Now can we get this PM mess sorted out and get on with the agenda?"

Extracting herself from the window she said in a voice that indicated that there was trouble brewing, "There's a lot of people with banners."

"Banners! What do they say?" her agitated boss demanded.

"Something about Krauts go home," she replied. Her breasts heaving from a serious rush of adrenalin, she calmly sat down and fanned her flushed face with her lemon hanky.

Encouraged by the chaos below Dee confirmed. "My God she's right, Jan. There's quite a crowd in the square carrying all sorts of banners; one says that you're something very rude, Crispin."

At that moment, the chanting started. "Nuclear fallout, no thanks! Don't bomb the border land, just ban the bomb! Bomb the Council, too ... not us!"

It was too much for Anthony and he rushed to the window, cautiously opened it and leaning out, he confronted the agitated gathering below. His appearance brought a brief silence which he took to be recognition of his position of power and he pompously went in with both feet. Raising his arms, preacher style, he smiled and asked.

"Please, ladies and gentlemen, lower your banners and cease your songs, there is no need for all this commotion. Nothing untoward is happening up here, I can assure you. Quite simply, we, your Council, have been chosen by Central Government, via the Welsh office of course, to host an event of such national importance that I am not allowed to expand upon it just yet."

"Why?" asked an unknown voice in the crowd. "We've got a right to know what you are up to in our name."

"Nonsense, these are matters of state we are discussing and I suggest you all clear off or I shall send for the police."

The big frame of Police Constable Davies, stationed close by to oversee possible trouble, made his way to the front.

"The police are here already, sir, what would you like me to do then?'

"Clear this lot away, officer; we're trying to hold an important meeting up here."

"Important to whom, Anderson-Shelta?" Came the mystery voice from the crowd, "You can't fool us, we know what's going on up there, you're planning to spend our rates on your bloody war games."

"Yeah! Power to the people, man," said another of the demonstrators.

Anderson-Shelta felt very uneasy. "Do your duty Constable Davies and clear the square, this could get nasty."

"And when it does, sir, then I will act, but so far this is a peaceful demonstration and we are not obliged to act."

By now a worried man, it was time to pass the buck again. Backing away from the window he stood over his MP.

"Sorry old chap but it's time to stand up and be counted, you're on next, Crispin."

The tension in the committee room was building as the chanting outside grew louder. Dee and Janet left their seats and moved to an adjoining window to commentate on the happenings below for the rest of the committee. Pushing a reticent Crispin towards the open window, Anthony quietly encouraged.

"On your feet and address your constituents, Crispin, there's a good chap, after all you are the Government representative, but try not to wind them up any further. When you're ready I'll announce you and you can take it from there."

Crispin was extremely nervous and dithered for a while before approaching the open window. Turning to Dee he whispered. "I'd be better off jumping out of the window, Ms Donnington, than face that lot."

His pathetic laugh did little to reassure the meeting that the situation was under some sort of control. Warmly slapping him across the shoulders, Anthony edged him towards the open window. "When you feel ready, Crispin, can we get on with it?"

"Perhaps I need the hand held megaphone to get the message across?" Crispin suggested.

"No you don't, this is not the Tory Party Conference. Now be a man and get on with before that lot down there get out of hand and storm the battlements."

In fear and trepidation, the man of the moment approached the window and looked down. He hadn't a clue who they were and what they were up to, the Party PR machine had not prepared him for this. Straightening his Guards tie and brushing his hair back with the flat of his hand, he peered over the window ledge.

"Oh God!" he cried. "I can't do it, Tony," his chum was right behind him.

"You can and you will, Crispin, now, are you ready for me to announce you?" Anthony addressed the gathering for a brief moment.

"As I said before Ladies and Gentlemen, this is a particularly important meeting and we must be free to get on with it; afterwards we will prepare a bulletin to keep you informed."

The mystery leader of the pack replied, "But why can't we know now? If it's going to affect Lugworth why aren't you telling us?"

"Because, my dear fellow, it is still an official secret. However, we are fortunate that in this very room, working alongside us is our own Member of Parliament, the Honourable Crispin Davenport-Jones. Over to you, sir."

Overcome with anxiety, Crispin thrust himself out of the window just a little too far and dropped the entire contents of his top pocket into the crowd below. The laughter built up as the items were examined and then announced to the rest of the gathering by the self-styled spokesperson.

"What have we here then?" he asked.

"One silk handkerchief nose for the blowing of."

"Yes!" Yelled the crowd.

"A gold Parker pen, letters for the writing of."

"Yes, yes!" they repeated.

"A very nice nail file complete with cuticle buffer."

"Ooooh, what a lovely boy!" called out the anonymous joker.

"And … wait for it, everyone, a smart green and gold packet of three, sold only at Harrods and the House of Commons' souvenir shop for doing the upper class business with … whatever that might be."

The crowd, encouraged by the laughter, steadily increased and cheered noisily at every comical statement, embarrassed by the comments Crispin was forced to back off.

Inside the meeting room, Janet and Dee were pitched into laughter as they watched the activity below.

"Who's the funny guy causing all the fun, Jan?" Dee asked.

"Haven't a clue, but he's got a great sense of humour. Mind you, I'm glad it isn't my personal effects that he's going through."

Visibly shaken by the jesting below Crispin pulled himself together enough to stick his head out of the open window and give it another go.

"Hallo again," he said, his handsome good looks creasing into a grin. "Sorry about that, dropping all my little knick-knacks over you all. May I have them back later? Right, now as Mr Anderson-Shelta has already explained, things are hotting up in Mid-Border country and you good people are standing on the threshold of history."

"And you'll be history very soon if you don't spit it out, mate," replied a big fellow at the back the crowd.

"Look, everybody, these things happen all the time. Nuclear defence exercises have been happening the world over, and it's time they happened in Wales; it is in your own interests to try and understand. However, it will be such a grand occasion and the Prime Minister, bless her, has kindly consented to join us for lunch on the big day. Isn't that rather splendid?"

"Get him inside for God's sake," Bill Jones demanded. "He'll spill the beans all over the county if we don't shut him up."

Anderson-Shelta quickly obliged and grabbing Crispin around the shoulders he yanked him back into the room watched by the gob-smacked committee.

The momentum carried them both across the room and straight into the waiting lap of Ruth Tremlett who, unable to resist the unexpected physical contact with her lover, used the moment to lightly squeeze his balls. For the first time in many years, Anthony experienced a strong erection which pressed, unintentionally, into Crispin's rear end, causing him to sit up sharply and giggle.

"Whoops darling!" Dee shouted. "Lucky old Anthony, he doesn't know which way to turn."

Red as a beetroot, he tried to extricate himself from Ruth Tremlett and yelled at Crispin. "Wipe that silly bloody smile off your face and get off my lap. Are you alright, Mrs Tremlett?"

"Wonderful, dear, thank you; I quite enjoyed myself, I do like new experiences."

Bill Jones was also experiencing something, but it wasn't new. Despite Anderson-Shelta's assurances, he had started to have grave doubts about the whole project and had the distinct feeling that things were on the slippery slope to total disaster. Something was going wrong, yet he couldn't quite pinpoint it. However, it was becoming clear that whenever Davenport-Jones lingered around the fringe of Council business, he felt a strong need to do a runner. Not just out of town, but out of the entire Principality, yet he knew that his was the only steady hand on the tiller. Quietly observing the mood of the meeting, the look on the Anthony's face said it all.

He was fighting for his political survival yet again and he knew, as did his officers, that if he didn't get a grip on Davenport-Jones, the whole exercise was down the pan and his career prospects with it. Over the past few years, he had just about come to terms with Crispin's brain patterns but today he had quite obviously miscalculated. The man was a walking disaster with enough bluff to get him in and out of any situation and leave everyone else dangling over the precipice, thus Anthony had no choice but to stay on the end of the rope. He needed the friendship of the Member of Parliament; it opened many doors placing him on a social plane that could not be reached without influence. What he had to do now, though, was to salvage what he could of the plan and try to make a silk purse out of the pig's ear. All around him, Councillors and officers were awaiting his leadership and, encouraged by the warm smile of his secretary, he gathered his thoughts and made his decision.

"Right, ladies and gentlemen, in view of the unexpected interruptions from below, we cannot continue with this meeting. However, I suggest that as we have tackled the main problems and broken the back of the basic planning for Operation Fallout, we adjourn this meeting 'pro tem' and reconvene on Thursday next. By this time, one would hope that the Voluntary Services Liaison Officer would have finalised her plans and submitted them for discussion. All this, of course, subject to your approval, Chairman."

Janet Bodmin repaired to her seat. She was intelligent enough to understand what was going on, but being a virtual newcomer to Council, she was shell shocked by the brick wall attitude of local politics. Watching the clownish behaviour of two, so called, leading local dignitaries wasn't helping Bill at all and she waited for her highly experienced Chairman to bring the situation to a head. He did and with some force. Striking his fist upon the table brought immediate silence to the room and he spoke with more authority than expected, surprising even the hardened officers. Turning on the Chief Executive he argued.

"It appears, sir, that people outside of this Committee are more well-informed on the Operation Fallout exercise, than those serving on it."

"Well yes, I do take your point, Chairman," Anthony explained. "However, you surely agree it is somewhat difficult, security-wise, that certain matters have to be kept a close secret until nearer the event."

"Who the hell proposed this visit anyway?" Ben Neal queried. "It's a bit shabby, dropping it on us like this. After all Lugworth is my town and if the PM is coming then we have got to spruce up the town and that will take cash, something Lugworth Town Council is short of at the moment."

Arthur Yorkshire cut in quickly. "I have to say, Chairman, that along with hospitality grants, nothing has been set aside in the budget for titivating Lugworth."

"Contingency allowances, Mr Treasurer, it can come out of those," said Crispin, sticking yet another unwanted oar into a very delicate situation.

"And what has it got to do with you, Crispin?" Janet asked quietly, "You are the ex-officio member of this committee. It is not one of your House of Commons financial get-togethers, expenditure is our problem not yours. So don't give us advice on what to do with our budgets. Anyhow, who are you to invite the Prime Minister to lunch in our town, at our expense and without any consultation?"

"Well said, Ms. Bodkin," Ben replied. "It's time we local Councillors took a stand on this decision." The chorus of "Hear, hear" caused momentary panic for Anthony but before he could come between question and answer, Crispin dropped him in it again.

"Actually, it was the Chief Executive's idea. He was hoping that it would get him an invite to the Queen's Garden Party this summer, which it did and he took you with him didn't he, Ruth? He thought it would help towards his Knighthood if he was seen in the right places."

Josh Aitkin was not best pleased, "So you take your personal assistant to Royal Garden Parties then?"

"What about the lovely Mrs Anderson-Shelta, why didn't she go with you?

Anthony was sinking fast. How he was going to get out of this one was any one's guess? If only that upper class twit would stop shooting himself in the foot and mine, too, he might have salvaged his already diminishing reputation. Thinking on his feet, he turned to Ruth for support.

"Was not my wife a little off colour at the time, Mrs Tremlett?" She smiled and nodded her agreement.

"That's right, my wife hadn't been too well and I thought it would be a nice gesture to take my secretary along. She has been with me a long time and it seemed a suitable reward for her long service to our council."

Smiling weakly he looked around the table for general support but none came.

"Nice touch, Anthony," Bill said. "For services rendered you say? Well it's up to you, of course, who you choose to whisk off to the wicked city but if this gets out, well … it wouldn't look too good if you booked her in as the missus."

"Indeed he did no such thing." Ruth replied indignantly, "I must ask that your statement be removed from the minutes."

"You're taking them, dear lady." Bill said. "We shall leave it to your discretion. Now I think we had better bring things to a close as the natives in the square seem to be getting more than a little restless and I am not prepared to run the hippy gauntlet for you, Crispin. You can go first."

Dee nudged Janet and pointed at Crispin, "Look, Jan, he's gone as white as a sheet, it's all those tales that Dai Davies has been feeding him during Saturday morning clinics in the Memorial Hall."

"Which ones?" Janet said.

"You know; his favourite. The one about the Welsh massacre of the English in the Lugworth valley leaving the river running red with blood."

"Oh not that old chestnut?"

"Old or not, he scared the pink jockey shorts off poor old Crispin. He thinks that's what going to happen if we go outside?"

"What do you think? Just look at him, he's shaking in his shoes."

Everyone was packing up their papers and preparing to leave, except Crispin so Dee walked across to him and tried to help him off his seat,

"It will be okay on the day. Bill will make sure of that and you can show your leader that we are all systems-go in Mid-Wales."

"Rather, she won't be best pleased if the crowds are anti during her visit. The Chief of Police should arrest the blighters now, that's what I say."

"You would, you right wing twit," Janet muttered as the over eager reporter propelled him towards the door. "On your way, Crispin, English to the front Welsh to the rear. Are you man enough to go first or shall I put on my butch pose and lead the assault"

"I say, steady on, Dee, it could be a bit dicey out there and this is my new jacket, handmade at Gieves and Hawkes. I don't want it ruined by that pack of left wing loonies. " He nervously peered out of the window. "There's a good few more there now, Dee."

Dee laughed, "That's because they know about your supply of Harrods condoms to give away in exchange for their vote at the next election. Now let's get out of here everybody, it's getting close to opening time and I need something strong after all this. No not you, Crispers old love, I mean really strong, like a large gin and tonic. If it helps your ego, you can buy the first round, you too, Mrs Tremlett, I'm sure you could manage a large brandy after what you have been exposed to this afternoon."

"And likely to be exposed to tonight," Janet whispered, "Anthony hasn't yet recovered from the stimulation of the afternoon. Look at him, he's still sitting with his hands in his pockets and he isn't playing with his pennies."

Their laughter echoed round the upper room of the assembly hall as the committee members picked up their motley collection of briefcases and bags and meandered down the wide stone staircase chattering about everything except the defence of the realm. Outside in the square a loud cheer went up as the first of the few appeared on the steps and banners were lifted to the opening bars of 'We shall not be moved'. Acting as decoys, Janet, Dee and Bill made their way to the Lugworth Arms leaving Anthony, complete with golf clubs, to escort his smiling secretary and his Member of

Parliament off the premises via the rear entrance and into his waiting classic car. Crossing the square, Dee tucked her friend's arm under her own. "All set for the weekend then, Jan?"

"As I ever will be?" she replied.

"Then let's have an early one for the road. Preferably in the Cricket, if you don't mind, Jan. I can't cope with another five minutes with that bunch."

"Just the one, Dee, I thought, we were going into Brecon for supper. After that near farce, I could do with a breather. Remind me how I managed to get involved in this political pantomime? I must have been mad when I agreed to stand for election. It's going to be one enormous cock up, I can feel it in my bones, but what can we do?"

"Plod on, dear heart," replied Dee wearily, even her usually high spirits were beginning to flag but for the sake of her friend she kept up her good-humoured banter.

"Let the clowns get on with it while we watch them bring the big top down on their conceited heads, at least we'll have a laugh about it one day. Our outing to Greenham on Saturday could turn out to be a laugh a minute too."

"Yes I suppose so, but I really believe in what's going on in Berkshire, I mean, all this Operation Fallout fiasco is a bit of a mockery when you realise that hundreds of women are camped beside cruise missiles while these idiots are playing war games like little boys. It's frightning, Dee."

"I know, but we have to go with the flow and do our bit for the Greenham women and if that means camping out for a weekend or highlighting the stupidity of our Councillors, present company excluded of course, then let's do it. If Lady Anne can rally our collective consciences enough to get Anderton-Shelta's wife on board then it's surely a worthwhile challenge? Now buck up and let's get a quick one in before we set out for Brecon."

Chapter Twelve

On the following Friday the official business at the Annual General Meeting of the Lugworth Amateur Pantomime Society (LAPS) was almost over, apart from the Director's report and any other business.

The upper room of the Lugworth Arms contained well over fifty disciples of the Janet Bodmin style of writing and directing, including the landlord, himself a keen performer on the boards. His theatrical enthusiasm was anchored firmly to a Gordon's Gin bottle from which he swigged large mouthfuls before uttering a line or making a move in front of a packed Memorial Hall audience.

The boring matters of officers, elections and financial reports had been hurriedly nodded through but what the well-oiled members were waiting to hear was news of this year's Christmas offering, nevertheless, they still had to undergo the annual 'knuckle' rapping from their good humoured director. In the eyes of her contemporaries in the Home Counties, Janet Bodmin must have been overcome by some sort of inexplicable rural madness when she agreed to resurrect the local drama group after a heavy night on the pop at the British Legion. Soon after she had settled into the town culture, her theatrical credentials were discovered and she underwent a complete rundown of Lugworth's chequered history on the entertainment front.

Over the centuries, a variety of dramatic and musical extravaganzas had taken place in the town's ancient Assembly Rooms; it was also rumoured the great actress Miss Sarah Siddons and her company of travelling players 'stopped over' on the way to Brecon and gave a stirring performance of Elizabethan drama that had yet to be surpassed, that is, until the Lugworth Pantomime Society was established in nineteen seventy six.

For decades, the local entertainment went in peaks and troughs; egos were alternately swollen and then deflated but throughout it all, the inherent talent of the indigenous Lugworthian remained below the surface until roused by a creative incomer with the stamina to resuscitate a dying breed. It is still quoted in some quarters that if a Lugworthian wasn't copulating in some field, he or she was always keen to perform on stage. Thus, over the years, the cultural and physical desires of the township were easily quenched by the rise and fall of a red velvet curtain or a patchwork bedspread.

In her first season as a newcomer, Janet had unwillingly been coerced by Dee into donating her "very creative attributes to a artistically starved community." After a good few Southern Comforts – she took up the well-worn mantle of the town's theatrical past, dusted it down and persuaded the recalcitrant pack of rural thespians that lounged around the main bar of the Lugworth Arms, to get back on the boards again. An act of worthiness Janet has regretted ever since. Tonight, she addressed her disciples with a calmness that betrayed her inner feelings, but with Dai Davies closely observing her over a pint pot of Welsh bitter, she knew there was no way she could chuck it in. Her anxious apostles waited with baited breath for her announcement.

"After much deliberation I have decided to …" Dai Davis coughed three times, "give it another year, but with one proviso," she said. The applause was well over the top.

"The ground rules will have to be tightened up." She was the teacher again, but it had to be said: "Rehearsals, punctuality and line-learning are vital and to avoid the chaos of last year's production of Cinderella, if you can't commit, don't audition. May I also remind everyone that alcoholic infusions may help calm the nerves but the clatter of glasses falling from scenery ledges did little to enhance the mood of the trio in the orchestra pit. The back stage stank like a brewery, and it was fortunate for us and the set designers, that only the front row could actually see that Cinderella's kitchen had been decorated with pink varnished copies of Gay News."

She allowed the predictable laughter to die down before sternly issuing a final warning.

"However, if we are to continue with our much improved theatrical output then we must also earn the respect of our audience by behaving ourselves outside our theatrical circle while having fun inside it. I make this point if only to emphasise the repercussions that followed the concert we held on the eve of the nuptials of The Prince of Wales and Lady Diana Spencer."

She waited for the laughter to die down again and was hardly able to contain her own.

"Without doubt, it was most artistic of our backroom boys and girls to change one letter in the flower bed display outside the Assembly Rooms, but 'Good Fuck Charles and Diana' did not go down well with the old Rector, the Council and the Street Party Committee. We lost a lot of goodwill over that and if our celebration concert party had not raised enough cash to cover the street party and the evening barbecue disco, things might have gone very sour on us."

She sat down and waited for the expected response from the casting committee chairman.

"Be that as it may, Jan, are we in production for this Christmas?"

The rising murmur of the gathered members demanded a positive reply.

"Time and Council business permitting, the answer is yes. It's a tossup between an "Old Time Music Hall" and a localised version of Dick Whittington, depending how many thespians we can muster. Auditions will be held early in October when hopefully, certain Council activities will be over and done with; so let's raise some much needed cash for repairs to the memorial hall stage."

The club secretary was up in an instant, "All those in favour say aye." The membership was undivided. "Right then, that's carried," he said, "Any other business? No, then let's get down to the serious stuff in the main bar. First round is – as usual – on mine host and then it's every thespian for him or herself."

"And get your tongue round that when you've had a few," said Dee.

Clive called out from the back of the room, "I hope we're not going on too long, some of us have got early starts at the weekend."

"Nothing will stop the Greenham bus leaving on time." Dee replied. "Drama tonight and comedy tomorrow for us lot it seems, so a few G and T's won't harm our motley crew. Come on, Janet, last to the bar sits next to Lady Anne on the mini bus."

It was just nine o'clock when Janet walked Dee to her car, it was a clear night and the weather forecast was good for the weekend.

"Fancy a coffee before you go home, Dee?"

"Better not. I've still got to pack a bag and sort myself out for Greenham. Is Angela still coming?"

"As far as I know, but mind you, you never can tell with Angie. What she says to us in her cups and what she says when sober are two different scenarios."

"Not this time, Jan, she seems very determined. Still, I expect we'll find out in the morning. Good night at Brecon the other evening, smart wine bar. We must do it again."

"If we can find the time. What with this crazy defence exercise stretching through to September and then Panto rehearsals, spare time will be at a premium."

Dee grinned, "Oh come now, dear heart, I expect you'll find a little moment for an old and faithful friend along the way."

"I expect so," Jan said affectionately. Come on, this time tomorrow we'll be eating around the camp fire and do remember the baked beans."

"Don't worry, if we don't Lady Ann will. Oh by the way, where did you get your sub-title for the panto."

"What! Fifty Miles to Lugworth Puss and Not a Dick insight. From you, Dee, don't you remember? I picked it up when you were doing your impressions of a Principle Boy in front of your latest principle girl?"

"Blow me yes! That weekend you invited your arty friends down from the home counties."

"And some of yours, from Cardiff, it was a good night, though." Talking of good nights, I had best be on my way, its mini-bus at dawn for us Jan."

Dee leaned across her car door and lightly kissed her friend. Sighing out loud she said. "We're good together girl and let's not forget it. See you soon."

Janet strolled back to her cottage acknowledging a few familiar "goodnights" from the shadows along the way, the cat was waiting for her on the doorstep and she scooped him up and carried him inside. As she closed the door on her strange little town she felt more comfortable with herself than ever before. Switching on the radio, she made a cup of tea and sat down; the weather forecasters had kept faith and she was looking forward to the weekend adventure, totally unaware of what might lie ahead.

The sun was up early and so was Janet. It was almost five thirty and because she had made her preparation for the trip before she went to bed she dozed for a bit before giving Dee the promised wake up call. Reaching for the bedside phone she dialled and announced in her deliberately husky stage voice, "Your early morning call, Ms Donnington." There was a long pause before she replied, "that will do, Dee," and put the phone down.

Showering in record time she fed Pankers and left instructions for the neighbours who will be looking after her while she was away. Knowing it might be the last 'proper meal' she might get, Jan made a good breakfast and quickly scanned *The Guardian* that had dropped through the letterbox. Planning to read it on the journey, folded neatly and tucked it into her backpack. After washing up the breakfast things she double checked her baggage and she went upstairs for a last pee. Relaxing for a few minutes in her cosy bathroom, she reminded herself that her next bodily function was likely to be in some impersonal earth based latrine part hidden by a rough piece of pegged canvas, she hoped and prayed that if Daphne Oxford turned she would likely bring her Harrods' Portaloo. Finally ready for the off, she picked up the loose change from the hall table, slipped the catch on the front door and hoisted her pack onto her back. With a final goodbye to the cat she closed the door and ambled towards the Shire Hall.

Pete the Postie passed her halfway up the street.

"Got a few letters for you, Miss. Want them now, might give you a bit of reading stuff for the bus ride?"

"Won't have time, Jack, what with all the fighting, shouting and naughty tricks us women will be getting up to. Just stick them through the door please and I'll read them when I get back."

"That's if you ever do, Miss. You 'ave a good time now and don't forget the bum roll. I know what it's like in them there trenches."

He chuckled and called back. "There's a big crowd outside the Shire Hall waiting to see you all off. The Barratt boys have got banners up and half the town band have roused themselves enough to toot a bar or two of Land of 'Hope and Glory'.

"Oh shit," Janet muttered. "That's all we need. The town oiks and half the bloody silver band lined up. What we women do in the name of peace!"

Broad Street from the top end was a sight for sore eyes at any time of the day, but early morning and the sun on its way up it was something more than special. The dew still lingered on the bits of weed and algae which had somehow escaped the annual spraying on the cobbled stone pavements, but it was the distant Shropshire hills, framed between the black and white cottages by the ancient pack horse bridge truly captured the landscape.

Mr Morgan's green and white mini bus was already parked in the lay-by alongside the churchyard railings it had been thoroughly cleaned for the Greenham trip. Usually caked in mud, it must have passed through Josh Hadley's car wash a dozen times and then polished like glass by the stoical Mrs Morgan and her four daughters. It looked as good as new and so did Mr Morgan who appeared to have also been scrubbed up for the trip to England. Used regularly by Lugworth United Football

Club, for away matches and for the last three years it had taken some stick. Lately, the team had not won one game away from home and the disgruntled supporters took it out on Mr Morgan and his popular vehicle. Nevertheless the interior was tidy and the engine was sound, thanks to Mr Morgan's ability to 'tinker' any engine to Rolls Royce perfection. His mechanical skills were the envy of local mechanics both sides of the border and the only man in Wales allowed to touch Anthony Anderson-Shelta's prized classic car was his claim to fame. Indeed he was the only man Anthony had any honest regard for, other than his Member of Parliament.

By the time Janet had reached the top of Broad Street, she could hear the half-hearted efforts of the band and the aggressive chanting from the Barrett boys and was glad to see Angela turning into the nearby car park. She waited for her to catch up.

"Glad you could make it Angie, I see you've got the Girl Guide kit sorted out."

Angela staggered slightly under the load. "Don't know why I parked the car and walked this lot, I should have dumped it on the pavement by the steps, unloaded and then parked up. I must be mad, Jan."

Catching sight of the unruly scene at the Assembly Rooms, she gasped. "Good God. What on earth is going on? Are all the riff-raff joining us and what's happened to Mr Morgan's bus, I've never seen it so clean?"

"No, it's the lads having a laugh at our expense."

Angela cringed. "Not those awful Barratt boys again. I've often said to Anthony it's time he stuck a custodial sentence on that lot when they next come before the bench." Spotting Clive with his clipboard she shouted, "You're looking rather dashing in Levi's and matching dog collar, Rector."

He tried to hide his blushes by helping Mr Morgan stow the back-packs on the heavy-duty roof rack. "We're not the last are we, Rector?"

"Not at all, Angela," Clive replied but before he could finish the hecklers started on him.

"Got yer' airwick for the journey Rector, you'll need it with all those 'ippies in there, they could all do with a bloody good wash!"

Moving across the road to remonstrate with them Janet intervened. "Ignore them Clive, come on, we can wait for the others in the Coffee Shop. We can watch for them from the window and I could do with a brew. How about you, Angela?"

"I never say no to a caffeine top up and we can get some peace and quiet before we set off."

Once inside, they were cut off from the obscene chants from the Barratt boys' efforts to compete with the silver band's tuneless rendering of the Dam Busters' March and waited for Liz to bring the coffee.

"That's the stuff to give the troops, as Aunt Daphne would say. Is she coming Clive?"

"I haven't a clue Angela, but somehow I doubt it."

Quietly sipping their coffee they waited a while before until Janet looked at her watch and then out of the window.

"Are we all here then?" she asked.

"Almost. Bill has gone to the gents and Lady Ann hasn't turned up yet, but she's always late. How did Anthony like you joining us this weekend?"

"He didn't Jan, it went down like a pair of lead knickers. He almost cancelled his trip to Westminster and then I would have felt guilty but tear-filled Trembling Tremlett telephoned and saved the day with her purple prose and he capitulated, thank God. Anyway, wild horses won't stop me now, so come on, Clive, let's get this show on the road."

"Where is Dee?" Janet asked. "I gave her a call to make sure she was up."

"Gone to find Anita her press photographer chum." Clive told her. "She's coming on the trip to take pictures for the Welsh papers and wants a group photo before we set off."

Angela went pale and dropped her head onto the table. "Oh no! This will kill Tony. His good lady leaving town with a bunch of feminist hippies planning to infiltrate a United States Air Force base."

She was stopped by Janet. "No time for second thoughts, Ange. "Look! Here comes Dee, let's get outside and be on our way before your idiot husband turns up and makes a scene."

Janet paid the bill and followed the others into the street while Clive began sorting out the photo call.

His powers of persuasion worked wonders on those inside the bus, most of whom preferred dozing to posing but they reluctantly agreed to front up for the press. The yawning women and their sleepy children peered through the windows blinking like lost moles on a sunny day and eventually they staggered onto the pavement.

Barratt senior yelled. "They looks half asleep. I bet they've been on the weed already. They ought to ban them, not the bloody bomb, and they're taking their kids with em' too. It's shameful."

"Shame on 'em all," said a motherly figure standing close by. "It shouldn't be allowed, taking little uns' on a trip like this and venturing into England, too."

Turning on Clive she taunted. "You should be stopping all this, Rector and be putting yer foot down in the name of God."

Sid Barratt intervened. "Shut it up, Jessie Albright. What do you know about kids? Most of yours are in care, best keep your trap shut if I were you."

Sticking two fingers at him she responded. "Bog off home, Sid Barratt, and tell your ma to teach you some manners instead of shouting about things you know nothing about."

By now the small group of people had become a crowd and attention was drawn to Angela by a scathing President of Lugworth WI, Barbara, 'just a small double gin and tonic' Jameson. Woken up by the noise she appeared at the upper window of her adjacent Georgian town house.

"My goodness me, I do believe it's you, Mrs. Anderson-Shelta. Whatever are you doing with this rabble on a Saturday morning when you should be pleasuring your dear husband and cooking him a big breakfast. It's your wifely duty, don't you know?"

Egged on by his brothers Sid Barratt kept up the banter. "You don't want to be cooking breakfast for that pompous old fart when you can be domestically pleasuring me and I'll vote Tory for the privilege."

Angela was aghast, "For heaven's sake Barbara, don't play into their hands, I thought the WI were behind the Greenham Brigade; shame on you for not supporting us."

The upper window closed sharply but not before her husband's familiar tones escaped from the bedroom. "Domestic pleasuring, don't preach about things you know nothing about, woman."

The vulgar sniggering faded and Dee Donnington took control. "Let's get this picture underway and can someone organise the line-up, please? Where the hell is Bill? Must have you and Bill in the picture, Rector, even if you're the drivers and can't go on the actual march."

208

The wheat from the chaff was soon sorted but the bickering between the locals and the travellers continued.

"So much for the 'good life brigade' Jan, I thought we were the peacemakers."

"Yea! Peace to have a bit of a lie in," Sid Barratt shouted. "We'll soon wake 'em up for yer, won't we lads? Up with yer banners boys and let's get on with it."

Within two minutes there was uproar. From behind the caretaker's gate at the side of the Assembly Rooms a dozen or so local youths and a few young girls hoisted rough banners made from white tablecloths clearly nicked from the Shire Hall laundry basket.

The wording was vulgar, sexist and in some cases very basic, but the message was crystal clear and to the point: "Peace women are OK. Give 'em one from us, Rector."

Blushing bright red, Clive rushed at them and tried to wrestle the banner to the ground.

"Bugger off Padre, this is ours!" Sid shouted.

Janet tried to lead him away. "Don't take any notice, Clive. It's just the local yobs having a bit of a laugh at our expense."

Ignoring her pleas, the rabble formed a circle around the bus and started thumping it hard, a cut glass voice sliced through the chorus.

"I say, what on earth is going on? Cut it out, chaps do, we'll have enough banging and crashing from the local constabulary when we get to Greenham Common."

"Bog off!" the youngest Barratt shouted. "They're nothing but upper class tarts off to service them Yank's. Ain't we good enough for yer then?"

Seeing his beloved bus under attack and before anyone could stop him, Mr Morgan lunged into the circle trooping around his prized vehicle, grabbed the first person he could lay his hands on and kicked him hard up the rear end.

"You leave my bus alone you bunch of bloody hooligans or I'll get the lot of yer I will."

Dee screamed at her photographer. "Get some shots in, Anita, this is front page stuff."

Nimble footed Anita dashed about, clicking like mad, until Dee told her to stop but not before Mr Morgan went down like a ninepin, struck on the back of the head by a banner pole. He hit the pavement in silence and the jostling group gathered round, including Mrs Morgan and her daughters who hearing raised voices watched from her kitchen window overlooking Sisters of Mercy Lane. She arrived on the scene just in time to see her man go down, head bleeding; about to make a grab at her husband's assailant, (her arm lock was well recorded) Janet forced them apart.

"It's not worth the court's time Wynn Morgan. Let's get Mr Morgan onto his feet and then we'll take care of the yobbo who struck him down. Rest assured that whoever it was has been recorded on camera so the police won't have any trouble finding him."

The pronounced Black Country accent of Acting Police Woman Inspector Patti Lloyd brought a sudden silence. "Thank you, but I can assure you madam, that this police officer won't have any difficulty identifying him either. Now what's going on here then? I thought this was supposed to be a peace outing. It sounds more like a punch up between Birmingham City and Wolves supporters. Now who's in charge of this fiasco?"

"Bloody 'ell," said Sid Barratt. "It's that woman copper, the new Inspector from over the border, she's been sent in from the Midlands force. I've seen her in action at the big footy games and she can swing a bleeding baton. Anyway, what you up to this side of the border then?"

Stiff as a ramrod she looked him up and down, took three paces towards him, adjusted her baton and tapped her Inspector's pip.

"I will tell you why I'm here, Mr. Barratt. Oh yes! I know very well who you are. I'm here to keep the peace both sides of the border, so what's yow bin up to, and why all this rowdiness early on a Saturday morning. Don't tell me Lugworth United are playing at home today when we both know they are away to Borth Rovers?"

Rounding on Janet and Dee, she eyed them both up. It was rumoured throughout the Mid-Border force that she was bi-sexual, nevertheless she was strictly straight when it came to policing.

"Councillor Bodmin I believe and you are Miss Donnington, news correspondent from Cardiff."

Leaving them open mouthed, Dee muttered. "Strewth Jan, Dai never mentioned this fit bobby, what a surprise.

Turning her attention on Clive. "I assume by your clerical collar that you must be the Reverend Clive Makepeace Priest-in-Charge of the Parish?"

Quietly admitting to his identity, he stuttered "Ah, well actually I'm acting Rector at the moment."

"Well, you don't seem to have lived up to your calling Father, now is any one going to tell me the cause of this untimely breach of the peace and in particular, why this man's head is bleeding?"

Before anyone could answer Clive spotted Bill coming down the street with a two other people.

"Here comes Bill now, Lady Llewellyn is with him, and I think there's someone else."

Angela, who until now had been standing on the sidelines during the commotion, peered up the street. "Good heavens! It can't be," she exclaimed.

"It is," said Dee and Janet in unison.

"Surely Aunt Daphne isn't coming with us. I was only joking with her when I suggested that she could carry the peace banner. What have I done?"

"That's what we are about to find out Angela, and what has she got with her?"

Officious as ever, Inspector Lloyd butted in, "Excuse me could I ask you something, Councillor?"

"By all means, officer, but there is no need to refer to me as Councillor."

"Oh but I must. I have the utmost respect for all those in authority, at least when I am on duty — as I happen to be at this precise moment in time. What I'd like to know is, which of the two ladies coming towards us is actually, a Lady, if you see what I mean?"

"You mean her Ladyship, Lady Ann Llewellyn-Llewellyn. She's the one on the right."

"And the non-titled one on the left is whom, Councillor?"

"Miss Daphne Oxford of the Cambridgeshire Oxfords, and if you have your notebook ready, Inspector, I suggest you write this down."

She paused while the ever-efficient police officer extracted her regulation black notebook from her regulation black leather shoulder bag.

"If you're ready Inspector, then I shall begin. Miss Oxford was Chief Officer, Women's Royal Naval Service, the past Captain of the Combined Women's Services Cricket team and current Chairwoman of Selectors for the forthcoming England Women's tour to New Zealand."

She waited for the Inspector to catch up. "She is also Aunt-cum-Godmother to Mrs. Angela Anderson-Shelta, standing over there, who also has the misfortune to be the wife of the Chief Executive of the Mid-Border District Council. Does that complete the picture for you?"

Unconcerned by the forthright response the fast track police Inspector was obliged. "Yes it does and I'm very grateful to you Councillor." she replied.

As she approached the two women, Angela looked at her Godmother in amazement; so did everyone else, including the now silent Barratt boys.

Daphne Oxford stood before them in an overly large naval duffle coat, baggy ex Wren slacks, an ancient Girl Guide hat, and seamen's socks and boots. She was carrying a very smart wicker picnic basket in one hand, a sleeping bag under her left arm and a powerful pair of naval binoculars hung from her neck. A top-quality transistor radio dangled from a strap about her wrist and a small purple, green and white knitted doll was part-stuffed in a pocket. Unaware of the effect her appearance was having on the gathering her jocular mood outshone them all. Her unforeseen arrival was completely out of the blue but was enough to encourage the sleepy women out of the bus and onto the pavement.

"Oh my God what have we done?" whispered Angela as Daphne launched her tack onto the roof of the mini-bus.

"Stow that away there's a good chap." Mr Morgan did so without a hint of concern for his head wound. He was happy in the knowledge that just a glimpse of Miss Oxford would have rebuffed the entire Zulu nation at Rork's Drift with or without the assistance of the Third Foot the Welsh Borderer's, let alone the Barratt Boys seated in hysterical turmoil on the steps of the Assembly

Room. Even the normally self- assured acting Inspector Lloyd stood in awe as the distinguished ex-Wren addressed her.

"Morning officer, nice day for it?"

"For what, madam?" she enquired.

"For the cricket, young woman, the cricket."

"And what cricket might that be, madam?" Inspector Lloyd, her police officer's witty answer already forming. "Surely not Jiminy?" she chortled', her copper style joke irritating Daphne Oxford.

"Do buck up, Inspector, the Ashes match, fourth test, and it's close one."

She caught Clive's eye, "We can whip 'em, can't we Rector and send 'em back to the Antipodes with their tails between their legs?"

"Looks like it, Miss Oxford, I see you've brought your radio to keep us informed of the score."

"Absolutely, Rector. Now, what is my sister looking so concerned about? Come on, Anne, what's on your mind?"

"You are, Daphne. I had no idea that you were actually coming with us. I thought you were ambling down here to see us off. Do you think you are up to it, dear?"

"Of course I'm up to it, Anne. If you are then I am. Angela said I could come on aboard, didn't you dear?"

"Yes I did. It will be good for her. She's got so much energy and will be useful at the campsite. Besides, some of the women at the camp are a lot older than Daphne and have been camped out for months."

Lady Anne disagreed. "So it's all your fault is it? I might have known. Do you know Angela, she had me up half the night searching the cellar and the loft, looking for her naval uniform? Thank God we didn't find it."

"Thank God indeed," said the Rector.

"Amen," responded Janet to Dee. "It could have been the start of World War Three had the old girl turned up in that. It's bad enough now."

"Quite right, too!" said Inspector Lloyd. "Your sister could have been charged with wearing a naval uniform without the Sea Lord's permission, your Ladyship."

"Balls, officer!" Daphne cut in. "Don't you go quoting your little law book at me. I know Queen's Regulations and Admiralty Instructions inside out and backwards, so if I were you, *acting* Inspector, I'd keep my thoughts on the matter buttoned up until you've got some time in, dear girl."

"But, madam, I have to uphold the law and ..." Her voice was drowned out by Lady Anne.

"I should quit now officer while you're in front, my sister has contacts in extremely high places and so have I."

"But your Ladyship I feel ..."

"Feel nothing, Inspector, except a healthy respect for your peers, titled or otherwise. Now I suggest you make yourself useful and clear away the riff raff and allow us to be on our way."

"Not without a photograph," said Dee. "Round 'em up Rector and form a group on the steps of the Shire Hall. You too, Inspector, it will be good for your PR image."

Clive persuaded everyone onto the steps and dashed round to join them just as the flash exploded. Anita focused again allowing time for Daphne to push to the front central position.

"A picture it is then. Have I got everything?"

"I should hope so," said Angela. "You're laden down with stuff."

"What's it all for Daphne?" Janet asked. "If it wasn't for Clive and Bill propping you up you'd fall down."

Daphne slowly revealed each item. "A little woolly doll for tying to the barbed wire fencing, a naval sleeping bag, my reliable field glasses to help the old eyes when I'm on watch for helicopters, a tot or two of rum, and some Fisherman's Friends in case it's cold. You see I've swotted up on the subject, Angela."

Angela grinned, "It's not a Wren's reunion, Auntie. Still, you're here now so let's get on with the picture. I'll stand next to you just to show Anthony that we're in this together."

"Oh crikey! I've forgotten about Anthony."

"So have I Auntie. I really don't know what we have let ourselves in for, but it's time to front up."

"I don't either," said Dee. "And neither does Greenham Common. Now hold it everyone."

She slotted into the group just a second or two before the flash of artificial light lit up the mixture of faces frozen into a variety of smiles.

"Nice one, Dee," said Anita. "I'll have them ready for Monday."

A few minutes later, the bus loaded with luggage and various types of camping kit waited for the passengers to settle down for the long drive to Greenham Common. A bandaged Mr Morgan gave last minute instructions on the route to Bill who had earlier volunteered to drive the first stretch of the journey.

"It will be quicker if you take the Wye Valley route and then through Chepstow and over the Severn Bridge; then it's straight down the M4 until the A34 junction to Newbury."

"And with a bit a luck we'll never see the nutters again," yelled Sid Barratt as he struck the rear of the moving bus with his banner. Cheers rang out and the bus drove out of town, but it wasn't to help the gallant crew on their way. The cheers were for Acting Inspector Patti

Lloyd as she frog-marched Barratt the elder to the local nick.

Chapter Thirteen

Crispin Davenport-Jones allowed his new Lancia convertible to glide to a dignified stop on the gravelled car park at the Border and Usk Golf Club. Unaware that he had parked on the Lady Captain's reserved space, he looked at himself in the driving mirror ruffled his fair hair and smiled at the result. Easing himself from the grey leather driving seat he carefully shut the door behind him, casually securing all doors with his latest toy, a remote control locking device. For a brief moment he lovingly gazed upon his new acquisition. The warm July weekend had seduced him into wearing his latest designer casuals, a style that completely erased his normal conservative approach to fashion. Today, his colourful outfit highlighted the effeminate side of his nature which occasionally encouraged a cry of "backs to the wall boys, it's Bertie" whenever he paused in the gentlemen's toilet at the Lugworth Arms.

He had been spending the weekend at his cottage near Rhyder and was on his way to Cheltenham for the first night of Romeo and Juliet at the Everyman Theatre. His partner, actor Duncan Duberry (Dunkie Darling to his fans) was playing Paris and Crispin never missed his first nights or the usual after show party. On the way he had agreed to meet Anderson-Shelta for lunch at his golf club to tie up a few loose ends regarding the possible visit of the Prime Minister during the defence exercise.

He was about to climb the steps to the entrance when he was stopped in his tracks by an indignant female voice.

"I say." Crispin looked around somewhat surprised. "Yes you. You've parked in the wrong place. Kindly move it."

He turned towards the unknown voice "Have I really," he said. "I hadn't noticed," and walked back to his car.

The woman was leaning over the bonnet of the Lancia reading the Westminster parking permit stuck on windscreen. She was a tall athletic woman with very good looks and a Victoria plum accent; her quality sports clothes had the Lilywhites look and her splendid striped blazer and badge confirmed membership of the 'Combined Women's University Golfing Society'.

"You Londoner's can't just park when and where you like on your occasional forays into countryside. This is the Lady Captain's slot. Nice car though!"

"Thank you. You are the Lady Captain I suppose," said Crispin."

"Actually I'm not, my mother is. She's away at the moment and as I'm up here for a week of golf with Daddy I will be using Mother's bay, so please be kind enough to remove your car to the visitors area."

Crispin strolled to his car aimed the remote and casually slipped into the driving seat; reversing out he narrowly missed the MGT of his antagonist. Climbing out he nodded impatiently at her and strutted up to the steps with the elegance of a peacock; the athletic young women effortlessly overtook him.

"I am the Member of Parliament for this area," he said as she passed him.

"And I'm the Lady of Shallot" she replied waving her hand as she turned left towards the ladies' locker room.

Anthony was waiting in the foyer ready to sign him in and had seen the slight confrontation.

"Crispin, my dear fellow. Good of you to come. I see you have met Lindsay Hay-Lewis our Lord Lieutenant's one and only daughter."

"Oh is that who she is? I didn't know Peter had a daughter. I suppose she's between finishing schools?"

"Good God no," Tony replied. "She's through that stage, she qualified a couple of years ago, chemical engineer or something like that with the South Anglian Water Authority."

"Really, I'm impressed."

"And that's not all. She has spent the last year on secondment with Voluntary Service Overseas in South Africa working on irrigation schemes with the natives."

"I thought she had a good tan. Still, not my cup of tea, Tony, stuck half way up the Orinoco without so much as a bottle of Bollinger. What's she doing here then?"

"Home on three months' furlough, although I gather she makes the occasional appearance at company headquarters in Norwich. I actually thought that she might be keen enough to give the troops a bit of a talk on water pollution, what with radiation fallout and all that. It could be useful during the war games."

Crispin was showing signs of boredom. His staying power on matters practical was a common complaint from the members of various select committees, but today it was his anxious digestive system that was causing him greater concern.

"Shall we take lunch straight away, no point in going to the bar, I'm driving to Cheltenham this afternoon; not from the first tee I might add." He chuckled at his little joke, "I've got the new Lancia outside."

"We'll go straight in then," Tony suggested, preferring not to be dragged outside to view the latest top of the range sports car.

The headwaiter escorted them to the Chief Executive's usual table overlooking the 18th green and they settled themselves comfortably into the well-upholstered carver chairs.

"That's my house, just through the trees. It's a former Edwardian Rectory. I acquired it rather cheaply some years ago through a member of my Lodge; he had something to do with the Church Commissioners. Lovely spot, lovely house don't you think, Crispin?"

"Certainly is, old boy?" he said with a sigh. He had heard it all before and all he wanted now was a good lunch and a run down on plans for the PM's visit.

"I say, Anthony, how did you fair in your semi-final this week. I take it you've played it?"

"Played and won it hands down but no final at the San Pierrie for this golfer."

"Why ever not? Crispin asked with a grin." No don't tell me, you've twinged the groin getting your leg over La Tremlett."

"Ah would it be so, old boy," he bluffed. "Nothing quite so delicious as the soft, warm open thighs of dear Ruth, that would somehow have eased the blow. Would you believe the damned defence exercise, is on the same day."

"Bad luck, sir. Still you'll be getting the chance to meet the PM and all that goes with it; honours and all that, perhaps even a K!"

"What honours, Crispin? Have you heard something? Come on out with it."

"Look, Tony, you know how it is. Everything's a bit under wraps, all I can say though is there's been a hint that if the project goes well, there could be something in the New Year list, a gong of some sort. That's all I can tell you."

The elderly headwaiter was hovering around, his ear eager to catch a hint of gossip likely to secure him a large tip at some time in the future. Anthony was well aware of his reputation.

"Say no more, Crispin," he said tapping his nose Shylock fashion. "I fully understand. Now are you ready to order? We'll take the à la carte waiter, not the table d'hôtel today thank you. What about a half bottle of Bollinger, Crispin? I always have one on ice these days."

"Splendid, Tony. It should go well with the fresh Wye salmon."

The lavish meal was ordered and digested without too much chatter. The golf club's cuisine was superior and the Italian chef, coveted by hoteliers throughout Wales and the Heart of England had been secured by the Golf Club catering committee at unexpectedly short notice.

Word had it that the Euro-Member of Parliament for the Mid-Borders and Valleys, a non-playing member of the club, had often dined (expenses paid) on Franco's culinary delights in Rome.

However, following rumours of a possible major scandal concerning young ladies at a superior finishing school nearby, the Chef jumped at the chance to leave Italy for Wales and start a new life with his wife and family. The golf club was for all time indebted to their non-playing member for not only increasing the turnover and profit of the club but also ensuring a recurring Egon Ronay Star rating that confirmed the "Short Shaft" restaurant a must for any discerning diners on local government expenses willing to pay over the odds. Needless to say, the MEP and his guests had free gratis access to the menu whenever he was in the area, which had become more frequent than his past record showed.

It was well after three thirty when Anthony bid a final good bye to his Member of Parliament. He was such a useful and obliging ally but he did take up a lot of Tony's time especially when he could hardly grasp the realities of life, let alone the logic behind plans for local Defence of the Realm.

The odd pair had spent the entire meal moving the condiments around a tablecloth battlefield, the only moment of excitement came when the saltcellar keeled over and Crispin tossed the salt over his shoulder shouting 'good luck'. Unfortunately, the gentleman and his lady seated at the next table miss-heard and suggested that he kept that sort of language for the House of Commons.

Finally waving his MP off, the walk across the course to the Old Rectory cleared Anthony's head; the house was unusually quiet for a Saturday afternoon. Angry that despite his wishes, Angela had gone off on the ridiculous excursion to Greenham Common with a bunch of odd ball women; taking her kooky Godmother with her, was the last straw.

What with Lady Llewellyn, Councillor Bodmin and that 'woofter' of a parson, it was hardly the right company for the wife of a Chief Executive. "Whatever did she think she was doing?" he muttered as he approached the kitchen door.

Inside, he made a strong pot of tea – his military roots char-wise had never deserted him – and took it into the raised conservatory from where he at least he could see the golf.

No sooner had he settled down in his favourite wicker chair. Scargill made a beeline for his lap and he affectionately stroked his head. Despite the occasional show of animosity he liked the old cat but at the end of a bad day who was there to kick but the family moggie. The throaty purr of his fair weather friend lulled him into a quiet doze and his Anthony's head dropped back as.

The distant ringing of the doorbell forced his eyes open, the cat had farted and as the pungent smell invaded his nostrils he threw him off his knee in disgust and staggered to the door.

He was surprised to find Ruth Tremlett anxiously standing in the front porch.

"Anthony!" she exclaimed. "Thank God you're alright, I've been ringing you for ages but there was no reply."

Her seductive voice jolted him into life. "Ruth! It's you, what on earth are you doing here?" and looked at his Rolex watch. "Is that really the time? I must have dropped off. Come in, my dear, come in, I'm in the conservatory, that's why I didn't hear the phone. I've had a long lunch with Crispin and drank rather too much for a lunchtime, you know how it is? I had to get him straight regarding the PM's visit and …"

He couldn't continue because Ruth had placed her forefinger across his mouth.

"Hush, no office chatter this weekend. You promised me your undivided attention would be scattered upon me like rose petals. We were supposed to be going out tonight," she said rather sharply. "Remember, you promised that with Angela away for the weekend we would have ample opportunity to enjoy a few of life's pleasures."

She smiled at him with half parted, lightly pinked lips that brought the kiss of life to his ailing lower regions.

"We shall, beloved, we shall. Now what would you like to do? I could call up the Apple Tree in Hereford and claim our usual table or would you prefer something else?"

"The something else seems decidedly more appealing my lover" she whispered huskily. "What did you have in mind?"

"How about a little white wine on the terrace while we toss a few ideas around. If you would care to step out onto the patio, dear lady, I'll check the wine cooler."

Before he could take three strides across the room Ruth was out of the wicker chair and into the doorway, her breasts heaving with a passion fit to burst. She blocked his way into the kitchen and, as if by accident, grasped his crutch with both hands and said. "Never mind the ideas, Tony, I'd rather toss this handful around for a minute or two and see what develops."

A tremble of trepidation wrapped up in a gasp of sexual release caught him off guard and for a fleeting moment he thought to himself "go for gold, Tony, and never mind the condom," but he knew that a man of his calibre and class could not cast care to the wind so easily.

He quickly rescued himself from her untimely act by pressing the small of her ample back just above her bottom cleavage; a touch she enjoyed and he used to calm their un-consummated love games. This, together with the difficulty he had sustaining an erection, was causing more than minor difficulties in the physical side of the relationship, notwithstanding of course the embarrassing moments in the back of the Armstrong Siddeley in the Elan Valley.

Ruth's giggling responses didn't help much either, they often left him feeling sadly lacking; he had hoped that tonight would lead to a successful coupling, but he feared the consequences.

With Angela away it was a chance he had to take, but somehow in his beloved old Rectory it didn't seem proper and guilt had set in earlier rather than later.

One or two ghosts were still hanging about the place and Angela's presence was never far away. With his hands at the small of her back Ruth responded as expected; she loosened her grip and dropped the ball so to speak before running towards the patio in a state of disarray.

"Don't do that, Anthony. You know I can't cope with being touched just there. Why do you do it at such a critical moment? All these delaying tactics must cease."

"Time and place, Ruth dear. Everything in its right place at the right time," he replied.

"Exactly, Tony. Many's the time you could have been in the perfect place at the perfect time but you've got this irritating habit of stumbling at the first fence."

Anthony was taken aback by his paramour's unexpected insult. He was well aware of his own shortcomings in that field and over the years he and Angela had come to an understanding.

Fumbling with Ruth in the back of the car and the undignified scrambling on his office couch during the lunch hour were one thing but full on with the mistress was another. The problem was that Ruth had passions beyond reasonable satisfaction and he wasn't quite the full Monte when it came to the sexual menu. He was more a snack man not à la carte, and although Ruth tried hard to bed him, he always managed to wriggle out at the last minute which seemed only to challenge rather than deter his salacious secretary.

He began to sweat as he thought up his latest swift excuse but the look in her eye wasn't helping to settle his sexual energy, especially as her nipples, larger than ever, had threatened to burst through the supple softness of her low fronted cashmere top. Without doubt, he was very fond of her; she suited his purpose and was good for his ego; he also enjoyed the nudge-nudge, wink-wink atmosphere and ribald comments that floated about the town hall whenever they were seen together.

However, his colleagues and staff made little effort to disguise their own predilection for 'Raunchy Ruthie' as she was known throughout the Council offices and they were often seen sniffing around her hotel room at NALGO conferences.

It was taken for granted that the 'boss-man' was regularly 'giving her one' and they were green with envy that the Chief Executive with the beautiful wife was having his cake and eating it, too. Little did they know! But today was fronting up day for Anthony, the moment of truth when the months of teasing, foreplay and false promises had to be accounted for, his ladylove was panting for it and would not desist until she got it.

Ruth's plans had been laid weeks ago when she had learned that Mrs Anderson-Shelta was a likely recruit for the Greenham away day. She had persuaded Anthony to plan an unconfirmed trip to Westminster which could be shelved at the last minute and allow the secret half-lovers to enjoy time alone in home-comfort surroundings.

The good Commander Tremlett, RN was still away on foreign office business overseas and as far as Ruth knew, was not due back, until the autumn. However, on the other hand, he could be recalled to home base at short notice. This did not deter his errant wife from striving towards her ultimate goal; her desire to have her Chief, body and body – never came into it. It had been smouldering for years but never really caught fire until a year or two back when she had contrived (against all procedures) to sit next to him at a full Council meeting and there she remained for all future committees, sub-committees and any other meeting on the Council calendar.

This had seriously offended Councillor Mrs Williams, her Methodist upbringing instantly branding Ruth a 'brazen hussy' from that day forth because, she announced at a Wednesday gathering of the Women's Bright Hour, she could clearly see "naughty hands, with naughty plans," exploring knicker lines and down below areas under the Council table."

This devious change in seating arrangements had almost caused the resignation of the Council's Legal Officer who thought it was his place to be seated next to his Chief just in case he dropped a difficult clanger, thus ensuring his seniority in the pecking order. The letter of intent was soon withdrawn after the Chief Executive had clarified that he would be prepared to nominate his legal eagle for a position on the Association of Local Government and County Council Advisory Committee (good perks, expenses and sixteen away days a year). Anthony also promised that he wouldn't let on to the appropriate body that his legal officer was, against local Government rules and regulations, still practicing with a local partnership on the side. Although Anthony did not have to use his final ace; that would come in useful at some later date. Nevertheless it was always good to have a peccadillo or two tucked away and his legal officer's occasional late night trips to Cardiff had not gone un-noticed. On one occasion he was forced to intervene with the Chief Constable at a Masonic Ladies Night when the legal officer's car had been seen 'kerb crawling' in the Tiger Bay area.

But now, with Ruth on a sexual wind up, Tony new he had to grasp the nettle with both hands.

"Ruth dear, let me get the wine and then we can calm ourselves down and talk through our plans for the weekend."

Easing her into a particularly comfortable cane chair, he kissed her flushed cheeks, French style and whispered "Soon my love soon," and hurried through the glass door into the kitchen.

Busying himself with bottle and cork, he waited for a few moments while his buoyant lady-love simmered down and absorbed his unexpected statement.

The silver tray shook slightly causing the glasses and bottle to clink together as he approached the conservatory, the glow in Ruth's eyes and the rosy flush that had spread from her breast upwards gave notice of the unprovoked orgasm his words had caused and he knew that her Janet Raeger silk knickers would be damper than ever just on the strength of the promise in his words.

She gasped slightly as she spoke. "Weekend my love. Are we to spend the weekend together at long last and I haven't brought a thing with me, clothes, night attire, cosmetics ... precautions"!

An unlikely coyness had overtaken her usual brash approach and it began to dawn on her that tonight could be the night and she tried to appear light-hearted.

"Penetration at last, Anthony, and my Dutch Cap in the Council Chamber," she giggled and got up from the wicker chair with some difficulty. "It isn't easy trying to stand with ones legs crossed but I do need to use the bathroom. May I go up, beloved?"

She moved towards him and took a flute of white wine from the tray that now seemed to be frozen in Anthony's hands. "Shall I take this with me and see you up there, darling?" Tony's lips as well as his vocal cords were also frozen and he tried to get some sort of response from his brain; before he could stop her, she was half way to the staircase singing, 'Non Regretta Reinne' with more joy than sadness.

The telephone stopped her in her tracks. Anthony dropped the tray with a clang causing the sleeping cat to take off from his bean bag at a speed greater than sound and shoot up the stairs, almost taking Ruth's sturdy legs from under her ample figure.

A badly shaken Anthony grabbed the phone and then put it down again. "Bloody hell Ruth it could be Angela and I'm supposed to be in London. What shall I do?"

Ruth came into her own on these occasions. "Nothing, my love, I shall take care of it," and returned down the staircase. "If it is important they will ring again and I shall answer per usual."

"No you bloody won't." His panic stricken voice responded.

"We are not at the bloody office, Ruth, we are in my house, my home and I'm supposed to be at Westminster with Crispin, who just happens to be in Cheltenham watching his 'woofter' boyfriend in Romeo and bloody Juliet at the Everyman. If it rings again and it's my wife and you answer it, then I am well and truly undone."

"You're going to be undone whether or not the phone rings again and I'm going to help you, my dear, so for goodness sake do stop panicking and calm yourself before it does. I've never seen such conduct unbecoming a Local Government Chief since the NALGO conference in Brighton ten years ago. As regards the matter of your behaviour, in the interests of inter office stability, it has been glossed over. Anyway, where on God's earth do you think your clever little wife will happen upon a public telephone kiosk on the barren wastelands of Greenham Common, unless of course she has broken into the officer's mess with her pals and sipping

Bourbon on the rocks with some Purple Hearted General in the United States Air Force."

Before begging his usual grovel, the phone rang again. "Leave it Ruth," he snapped. "And just stay still and quiet for one brief moment please."

He nervously picked up the phone again; a sharp answer was already forming in his mind, just in case. "Four seven nine two three, Anderson-Shelta speaking." The sweat caused the receiver to slip in his hands as he awaited the Home Counties accent. The voice at the other end of the line could not have been sweeter.

"Gooda evening sir, pardon the intrusion. This is Georgiou from your favourite trattoria, will you and the beautiful lady be taking your table tonight. We are what you say, over the bookings and if you are not dining with us, then we seat another party."

The colour flooded back into Anthony's face which creased into a relaxed smile conveying 'an all is not lost' look to his anxious lover.

"Georgiou, my dear fellow, good of you to call. I had intended to call you but have left it rather late. Got caught up in the clubhouse, by all means let the table go. Kind of you to call. Goodbye."

He replaced the hand set with a coolness that did not deceive his mistress. Looking down on him from mid-staircase, she leaned over the banister causing her dress to dip low enough to cause a sharp intake of breath as he explored the depths of the lightly perfumed channel between her fulsome breasts. A momentary headiness overcame him and he grasped the newel post at the bottom of the staircase. Seizing her chance she progressed Busby Berkeley style down the staircase, her cotton dress hitched high above the knee as she deliberately swung each leg towards him; his panic-stricken eyes immediately locked on to her suspender-clad thighs. She mistakenly thought his bewildered gaze was the clue to his pleasures.

"Take me here. Now," she cried in undiluted joy. Let this be our stairway to heaven. Touch me my Antonio, touch me at your pleasure and let us writhe together on your plush Harrod's carpet and feel the velvet moment that will unite us forever."

That said she wrapped her thighs about his waist and caught off balance they fell to the floor with a thud. Laying there quite breathless Anthony opened his eyes, looked up and to his enormous relief saw that his mother's grandfather clock was still standing; it could have crushed them both. Good God he thought to himself, "Born in England and for brief moment I might have died in Wales."

It was then, just as the shock waves hit his aging bones that common sense prevailed but not before his un-constrained lover powered her way to a striding position on top of him. He tried to struggle free, but his left arm had become lodge in the bottom banister rail and any sudden movement could cause his discs to slip.

He raised his voice beyond its normal limits. "Hells bloody teeth woman, get off me. You know I have a trapped nerve in my back. My osteopath will disown me if he finds out about this, it could cause untold damage and I've got a Masonic golf match next week as well you know." he paused to catch his breath. "Besides aren't we getting a little old for this sort of caper?"

At first Ruth looked a little disappointed and then broke into hysterical laugher "True big boy, true but I won't get off until you promise to continue with this later."

"You have my word, Ruth, if I'm up to it that is, although after this all in wrestling it's unlikely I'll be up to anything ever again." Still on dangerous ground, Tony knew the situation required a conciliatory word or two, so he looked deep into the dark eyes that were perilously close to his and uttered seductively. "But who knows, perhaps in the comfort of one's bed would be preferable."

"And this you promise with all your heart," Ruth demanded.

"With all of my everything dearest, Ruth," he replied with all available fingers crossed. "Now please, let's be dignified about it and let me up. If ever I needed a very large scotch I need it now, so on our feet, sit down quietly in the lounge and plan what's left of the evening."

Breathing deeply, Ruth struggled to contain her passions, she slowly extracted her perspiring body from her man and eased herself onto the first stair her ample buttocks could reach. Small beads of sweat hung on the fine hairs on her upper lip as she stretched out and helped her lover to a similar position on the staircase. The unlikely lovers sat silently for a while, each reviewing the situation from differing angles.

Anthony got to his feet first, brushed himself down and lifted Ruth to hers; silently they went into the large airy sitting room. Anthony crossed to the sideboard just as Ruth collapsed onto the feather cushions of the jumbo-sized Edwardian settee. "Gin and Tonic please, my lover," she called out. "Heavy on the gin and plenty of ice, I'm going to need this one strong."

"You and me both," he muttered to himself. He had already knocked back a swift malt and was eager for another if he was going to get through this situation unscathed.

Taking the drinks over to the settee he placed the tray on the small colonial occasional table; Ruth took a long draft from the antique crystal glass, rested her head against the soft cushions and closed her eyes.

Anthony settled into the arm chair to the left hand side of the settee; after a quick gulp of his whiskey he carefully jiggled the cubes of ice around the tumbler and prepared himself for the awkward conversation to come. Struggling to find his opening gambit, he tapped the glass against his knee before speaking to his paramour.

"Ruth my dear, whatever we do we must not fall out over this."

"Who's falling out, dear?" she said with a hint of sarcasm. Terms of endearment crept into Anthony's cautious approach. "You know what I mean, dearest lady. In matters of the heart, we must let things take their natural course, bickering can only get in the way of the bigger picture. This is the first time we have been alone on terra firma so to speak so let's not waste a moment of it."

"Words, Tony, it's all words and no real action from you these days. We have been letting matters take 'your' natural course for almost two years and we have hit more dead ends than I would care to remember. What we need is a sexual ordinance survey map to find an open road for you to discovery. As regards terra firma, if you mean we are now on solid ground rather than in the back of your bloody classic car, then the sooner we get down to the business the better. Dutch cap or no bloody Dutch cap, another gin and tonic if you please I've just about had enough of your verbal manoeuvres to last me a lifetime."

"You see," said Anthony as he took her empty glass and walked to the drinks tray. "You're making mountains out of mole hills again."

"I'm doing no such thing. Make that a large one if you please. If Mohammed doesn't come to this mountain and hit me with his rhythm stick, I shall take myself into the Brecon Beacons and offer up my tormented body to the entire officer's mess of the Welsh Guards. At least I shall get some relief from the sexual urges that have been tearing me apart ever since you, my stumbling and stuttering lover, discovered my up market elastic."

In his anxiety, Anthony overfilled Ruth's glass with gin and hastily carried it to her.

"Look, my dear, what I'm saying is that whatever happens tonight we must not fall out with each other. We are here now so let's make the most of it. I'll phone the golf club and ask them to send over a little light supper for one for us to share and then the night is ours."

"Why?" she asked. "Can't I have my own supper or will that draw too much attention to us ... while Angela is away?"

"Not at all, dear lady. I have been advised that making love on a full stomach can cause heartburn I believe?"

"Yes and the rest," Ruth said. "What you don't want is a few suspicious comments from one or two members at the club. All right, but simply tell them that you're hungry and get a bit extra while you're at it. Meanwhile I'll have a wash and brush up before it arrives. Shall I use your bathroom or Angela's?"

"Better use the main guest room, there's plenty of towels and the bed is made up."

Ruth got up from the settee and walked to the door, Tony took the empties to the kitchen.

Poking his shoulder she took her glass. "I'll take mine up with me thanks. So I'm relegated to the guest room am I? Well I shall have to try and be the perfect guest and behave myself."

Lips slightly parted, she kissed Anthony on the mouth, lingered for a brief moment and said, "You had better ask the steward for a packet of three when you order the supper. I understand there's a machine in the junior members' locker room."

She laughed all the way to the top landing before looking back at Anthony's puce features.

The supper from the golf club was superb and although the young waiter had seemed a little too questioning it was nothing a heavy tip would not cure.

Snatching another large scotch before battle commenced, Tony tried to get his head together. In fear and trepidation he climbed the stairs and approached the guest room and calling out to Ruth.

"Just slipping into something more comfortable, dear," he said, a nervous giggle escaping as he dashed into his dressing room to brush his teeth and dab the underarms with Gucci deodorant. Looking at himself in the full-length mirror and despite the foreboding mood, he agreed with his image that he looked pretty good for a man for his age.

"Speed it up, beloved," came the clear request from the guest room. "I am simply panting for my lover, and for his big present."

In the bathroom, Tony was perched on the lavatory seat, bent double as if in prayer. "Please God let me get it up; just this once. That's all I ask."

Slipping into the silk dressing gown, a treat from Angela during a trip to Paris, he tied the belt tightly. "In for a penny in for a pound," he hoarsely whispered and gripped his weakening knees.

Ruth lay in wait for him, her naked Rubenesque body bathed in soft light and smelling of the expensive talcum powder left in the adjoining bathroom for sole use of guests. She could not stop the smile of achievement that played about her full mouth and she threw back the sheet and patted the vacant space beside her. Picking his way through the assorted items of clothing that Ruth had hurriedly cast off on her way to the bed he struggled to dislodge the Janet Reager knickers that were wrapped round his left slipper.

"Why are you wearing your dressing gown and pyjamas, Anthony, while I lie here naked awaiting 'the big one'?"

"Indeed not, it's a matter of manners, dear lady. One should not assume." he quietly added.

"Assume, Tony! As far as I am concerned it's a foregone conclusion. I have been waiting for this moment for a very long time and I am not letting your Liberty nightwear come between us now. In you get my lovely man and I'm not bothered if you enter me or the bed first."

Anthony went pale as he looked down at Ruth and tried to struggle out of his dressing gown and slippers, with the silk knickers still attached to his foot he didn't know whether to laugh or cry. All he knew was that his impatient mistress was becoming very agitated, drumming her fingers on the oak headboard and sighing in frustration. Finally she reached out and grabbed his nearest leg causing him to fall across the bed and pinning herself under him.

"Take me, take me," she cried out in glee as she attempted to claim his limp penis still hidden behind his spotted pyjama trousers. Grappling with the elastic waistband he grabbed her hands to prevent her from discovering that yet again he was unable to get natural lift off. Instead he touched her heaving breasts and was about to suck her nipples when the telephone interrupted the action.

"Don't answer it," she cried. "Please Tony let it ring, it will be picked up on the answer machine."

Happily released from the moment, he whimpered in mock dismay. "I have to, beloved, it's only ten thirty and the lights are on all over the house; they know I'm at home because supper was delivered from club."

Somewhat relieved he jumped out of bed picked up the receiver.

"Anderson-Shelta residence," he said, a hint of breathlessness undermining his pomposity. "Geoff what can I do for you at this ungodly hour on a Saturday night. I'm not playing in the foursomes."

Ruth, having regained her composure was restless and bored by the unwanted intrusion.

"Not the bloody golf club secretary at this time of night," she mouthed at Anthony. "What does he want?"

Before he could answer his face drained to chalk white and he motioned to her to shut up. His left eye began to twitch and his voice petered out as he tried to speak and swallow at the same time.

"Good of you to let me know, old chap," he stuttered." Damn good of you under the circumstances, I'll see you at the club sometime and put you in the picture so to speak. Thanks again, old chap"

He let the news set in and as he quietly replaced the receiver he shook from head to toe; closing his eyes sat down on the bed and beat his right fist into the palm of his left hand.

Realising it was something serious, Ruth grabbed his hand and asked him.

"Good God! What is it, Anthony? It's not Angela is it? Has there been an accident…?" Her concern was genuine. "Say something, love," she pleaded.

Speechless for the first time in his life, he leaned across the bed, picked up his dressing gown, wrapped it round his shoulders like a child's comfort blanket.

"No it's not Angela, or an accident, my dear. I suggest we get dressed and as calmly as possible take this unexpected news one stage at a time, together with a large drink."

"For God's sake tell me what's happened."

Ruth was very calm but Anthony knew it wouldn't be for long. Taking a deep breath he blurted out the news.

"The Commander's back from abroad and having a drink and a snack at the club house because, as Geoff put it, the memsahib is not at home."

Anthony's swift hand movement managed to stifle the anticipated scream just before it exploded into the silence.

"This is all I need," he muttered. "All I bloody need with a Knighthood up for grabs. Ruth, tell me, did you know he was on his way home?"

She took a while to calm down and digest the situation. "I swear I hadn't got a clue but I never do; after all his work is supposed to be so top secret he doesn't know where he is off to never mind when he is likely to return home. All I do know Anthony, is that he'll be pacing about wanting his rights and wondering where his lady wife is this late on a Saturday night."

As the initial shock subsided, Anthony was working out ways of saving the situation. Glad as he was at getting out from under the covers with Ruth, he had to be sure she was quite calm and collected before going home. She, too, was very good at getting them out of awkward moments and no doubt will front up again but what they both needed now was another stiff drink and time to think up a suitable explanation for Ruth's absence from home. As they went down stairs he placed a kindly arm around. "What a bummer Ruth," he sighed"

"Indeed it is, Anthony, so near and yet far. We might have to cool it for a while."

"More like smother it," Anthony mumbled to himself as they walked into the kitchen.

"A large gin and tonic please, Tony. No ice just lemon. He poured it out and gave it to her. "Don't forget you've got the car outside."

Always one jump ahead in awkward situations she replied.

"No I haven't. To be on the safe side I biked round the back lanes and if Dai Davies stops me for being drunk in charge of a pedal cycle, I'll knock his bloody helmet off."

Concerned more for his own situation, he asked. "How will you get home and what will you say to the Commander?"

Much calmer now Ruth suggested, "Same way as I came and if I can get back before he does, I shall tell him I've been sitting with old Mrs Evans while her son went out for a bit of fun with the lads. That will hold water long enough for me to prepare for what he's been missing this past twelve months or so and make a change from trying to get it from other sources … and you qualify as the other source, dear heart."

A weak smile flickered across Tony's face and he tried to make a joke of it. "What's source for the goose is source for the gander, so they say. I'm so sorry it all went wrong for us Ruth but we mustn't fallout over this."

"No you're not, my lover," she said. "You're mighty relieved. We just have to put it on hold until he returns to active service. Now I'd better get on my bike and pedal off in the moonlight."

Putting her glass down, she kissed Anthony on both cheeks and smiled at him.

"Now, my love, see me to the door and off the premises," she said as she picked up her handbag from the table.

Anthony opened the door and tossing her dark hair she blew him a kiss and dropped her bag into the wicker basket fixed to the front handlebars of her bike propped up against the garage wall. Hitching up her skirt she straddled the leather saddle.

"This will be the best ride I'll get tonight, apart from the commander and that will be more of an expedition. See you at the meeting of the Defence Committee next week and make sure you have the right finger on the pulse. It's the last one before the big day."

Another time another place she muttered to herself as she wobbled off down the public bridle path without lights; casting a last look over her shoulder she waved goodbye to her lover as he closed the door on her infectious laughter and wiped the sweat from his brow.

"Yet another close encounter of the wildest kind," he muttered to himself as he picked up his whiskey glass and stared into the mirror at the bottom of the stairs. Taking a large gulp of his finest malt, he toasted the safe and timely return of the man from MI6, his reflection was shared with Scargill sitting wide-eyed on the third stair up staring at him with the contented look of a cat who had just swallowed the cream and crapped on the forgotten Janet Reager knickers on the landing.

Next morning he was up early and ready for the meeting with the planning officer. There had been a problem over the completion on time of the proposed fallout shelter and the golf club and with just a few weeks to go before the defence exercise kicks off, he needed to go through changes to the original plan. In the back of his mind he had a niggling feeling that all was not well with the arrangements.

Chapter Fourteen

Two weeks had slipped by since the three women friends had met up in Villafranca; they had walked the vineyards, sailed the coastline and did the Barcelona cultural scene; Gaudi, Picasso and Montserrat. They also enjoyed a day trip to Collioure, a little coastal town on the French border famous for its connections with Henri Matisse, a colourful artist favoured by Janet and Angela. Dee agreed to join them only after persuading them to see Barcelona, said to be the world's second richest football club, play their greatest rival Real Madrid at Camp Nou. Other than that most evenings were spent dining in the town and generally talking themselves silly. They had also been invited to lunch with the family at the Castillo. Keen to get to know more about Daphne's life they happily agreed and just about every member of Consuala's clan from six to sixty had been asked to attend the special Sunday lunch. Many had travelled long distances for the not to missed family event, not to turn up was considered bad manners. For the three friends it had been a delightful, on your best behaviour occasion which they enjoyed to the full.

On the substantial tiled dining table colourful paella's piled high on traditional olive wood platters were served with fresh seafood, baked aubergines stuffed with tomato and cheese with huge bowls of green salads to accompany the main meal. The wine of course, was plentiful and the dessert, home-made lemon ice cream proved the point; no other puddings were on offer.

"Tough if you don't like it!" Dee whispered to Jan as she sensuously spoon-fed her a second helping from her glass coupe dish. Getting to know everyone made it a joyful day for everyone.

Two days later they were still talking about it as they motored to Barcelona Airport for the flight to Nice. Angie had promised them a relaxing break at the luxurious Negressa Hotel on the Promanade Anglaise.

"It's some family Daphne got herself hitched to," Dee said. "How she could keep it a secret for so long beats me."

"Well it would. You're into gossip and can't keep anything under the hat," Jan replied. "It would have been nice to share it with her; it must have been so exciting."

Angela smiled. "It would, but she never once gave the game away, I knew nothing about this place or her love-life until I read the letter she left for me. She did a lot of travelling when she retired and then spent most of the summers at the Cowes cottage. Now and again she did mention Connie but I thought she was simple an old friend from her naval days. Whatever her reasons for keeping quiet, she has, in her own way, told us now. Who cares as long as she was happy and she obviously was?"

"I wish I could boast an old Aunt like Daphne in my life." Dee recalled, "She was a star turn at Greenham particularly when she got arrested by the MOD police for sliding down a silo and yelling it's better than the Big Dipper at Blackpool,"

"Yes, Dee, we all know what happened. Six of them were arrested and carted off in the police van; Daphne ended up in the cells yelling police brutality and caused a hell of a rumpus in Newbury magistrate's court by insisting on telephoning her lawyer, a London based Judge, before she said a word." Jan added, "In the end they all pleaded guilty and Daphne received a seven day suspended sentence for obstructing a police officer and stealing his helmet.

"And it's still in my loft," Angela added with a smile. That's why we were a day late arriving back in Lugworth and in trouble the moment the bus stopped outside the Lugworth Arms.

"No need to remind us, Dee, but I suspect you are going to."

"Not me. Jan's the narrator here, after all, she was always in the thick of it so it's back to the ranch, as they say and let's get on with it.

Jan sighed. "OK it's down to me to keep the story ticking over and I shall need liquid sustenance to get me through it, you two to just sit and listen. The old memory isn't so clear these days and I'm not quite sure of where to start."

Pausing for a while she began, "I suppose it all kicked off again when I rang George at the Lugworth to warn everyone that we had been delayed for a couple of days due to Daphne's a court appearance, meanwhile Mr Morgan would bring back the rest of the party as planned and we would follow in a day or two."

Angela chucked in, "What Anthony will make of it all, I really don't know. He kicked off when I told him Aunt Dapher's was coming with us but when he hears about her arrest he'll hit the roof. He pleaded with me 'not to take the silly old bat' on such a stupid trip and even suggested that if she took all that camping gear, too, there would no room for her on the bus. What he didn't know was that Lady Anne stood down in favour of her sister claiming she only agreed to make up the numbers."

Eager to be reminded of the fallout when news broke that Daphne was under arrest for sitting atop of a guided missile, Dee hoped another bottle of Carva might loosen Janet's tongue even more. Topping up the empty glasses, she announced. "Okay sisters, curtain up on part two, the homing coming. Cheers."

It was Sunday morning and apart from a few weekend visitors the informal group of Councillors and officers seated in the lounge bar of the Lugworth Arms were keeping a very low profile. Having consumed more than average of pre-lunch pints, there was serious concern over wild rumours that three or four women from Lugworth were under arrest for breaching the peace when Clive Makepeace dropped his clerical pants at two female police officers.

"Surely that won't delay the meeting" Joe said.

"Of course it will Dick replied, "As usual the CEO has a vested interest in all this, we must be ready for a dummy run during the defence exercise or we will miss out on the grant."

"How do mean vested interest, Dick? Surely he's not been on the fiddle," said Ben.

The planning officer wished he had kept his thoughts to himself. If this got back to his boss his promotion prospects were down the pan to be flushed away with the turds of the town into the communal cesspit. Back peddling like mad and with the eloquence of a bard at some local eisteddfod, he explained.

"When I say vested interest, Joe. I mean that he somehow managed to persuade the golf club committee to agree to a nuclear fallout bunker being built under the nineteenth green."

"What?" Joe and Ben exclaimed in unison.

Dick nodded. "It appears that the developers, in appreciation of the goodwill and sportsmanship of the

245

members, kitted out a small ante room in the club house to be used as a private dining room for the committee. In return Anderson-Shelta promised places of safety in the shelter for the club president and secretary, plus of course the lady captain for a last bang or two before the big one comes. I shall be outlining details of the interior and the facilities at next week's Defence Committee meeting, assuming they all get back safely from Greenham bloody Common. Oh yes! The builder has also provided the finest Cumberland turf for the practice putting green plus a few square yards for re-turfing Anderson-Shelta's rear lawn, free gratis."

"And that's not being on the fiddle, Dick?" Ben commented.

"Course not," said Joe defensively; life in public service is littered with back handers. It goes without saying that a man in 'is position is entitled to an occasional 'back pocket' donation now and again. That's how they oil the wheels of trade, commerce, and local Government all the way to Westminster." Catching Ben's disapproving eye he challenged. "Don't you look like that, Ben Neal? You've been selling your spuds at the farm gate for years and I bet you don't pay no tax on yer King Edwards."

As the scotch and water hit the back of his throat, Ben coughed. "I'd best be off home, the wife will be fretting."

"Me too," Dick said. "Best forget what I said earlier. See you at Council Thursday if not tonight."

"You won't get me in 'ere this evenin', "Joe announced. "What with the cricket team cryin' in their beer after losing again this week and those daft wimmin due back from bannin' the bomb, I think I'd rather watch *Songs of Praise* with the missus."

He put his empty glass down, nodded at the bar staff and bumped into Anthony as he came into the bar with Hugh Tremlett.

"Talk of the devil," said Ben.

"I'm out of here," replied Dick, his future promotions dimming rapidly. "Bye all."

With a swift movement, he sidestepped his boss and nipped in the gents. Ben Neal sighed.

"What's up with you then?" Joe Aiken asked. "Something on your mind?"

"You could say that, Joe," Ben muttered. "I've been thinking about this ruddy defence exercise all weekend. If you ask me it's about to go tits up before it even starts."

"Don't worry about it, matey, just think of the out of pocket expenses we will pick up. I might even take the wife away."

Unusually for Ben, this time he was less concerned about perks, he was more worried about the possibility of losing votes come the local elections.

"It's alright for you, Joe, you're only the Town Mayor, I'm on the District bloody Council and if anyone is going to get any flak, it will be me, not you. It's not the expenses I'm bothered about; next year's elections are giving me sleepless nights. If this goes wrong, Lugworth will vote me out and all the perks with it."

That said, he upped and left without another word leaving his surprised companion pondering over a fresh pint of dragon ale.

Lunch at the Border and Usk Golf Club was, apart from a few lady players catching up on the local gossip, unusually quiet. But today, their close-knit conversation was broken by raised voices on the patio outside the gentlemen players changing rooms This was followed by the crash of a pair of expensive golf shoes hitting the tiled floor. Anthony Anderson-Shelta, livid at losing the morning session to the inept efforts of his playing partner Crispin Davenport-Jones, appeared to be yelling offensive advice to his Member of Parliament.

"Call that idiot with you a caddy. He couldn't carry a bag of tea without falling over, never mind a bag of clubs. What did he tag along for any way? Shouldn't he be rehearsing Shakespeare or some other theatricals miles away from here?"

Hurt by the personal attack on his close friend, Crispin snapped back.

"Dunky is resting at the moment and doesn't like to be alone at Borth; he gets sea-sick whenever the waves come splashing over the sea wall and onto the patio outside by the bungalow room. Anyway, Tony, he is my partner and if he is good enough for the House of Commons bar, then he's good enough for my constituency golf club. Now can we get changed and have lunch, I assume you have booked our usual a table?"

Showered and changed into smart casual clothes and shoes, the three diners ate the usual Sunday roast in partial silence, at least until dessert. In spite of this, Dunky, having overdone the wine, boldly flirted and blew kisses over the sweet trolley wheeled by the attractive young waiter from Italy. With little knowledge of conversational English and etiquette, the young man blew a friendly kiss back prompting the headwaiter to slap his wrist and send him to the kitchen with the sweet trolley in tow, leaving Crispin smirking and Anthony embarrassed.

"Good God, man, does he do that sort of thing in the House?"

"Not to give to the game away, old chap, there are a few chaps around here keen to respond. Best I take him home before he gets carried away." Crispin said with a giggle.

Exasperated, Anthony hissed back. "Being an actor and all that stuff does not excuse him. Dressed like that in pink slacks and shirt, he'll soon be wearing the Queen Mother's hats."

"In private, of course, we already do, Chief Executive, and with a string of pearls, too. You should try it on the good Mrs Tremlett, Hugh does it when he's home from abroad; God only knows what he gets up to in Thailand," Dunky suggested and with a deep curtsey swaggered to the gents cloakroom.

Anthony was shocked. "What does he know about Hugh Tremlett's affairs overseas that I don't?"

Crispin laughed. "And you never will, Anthony old boy. It's not called the secret service for nothing, Guy Burgess made sure of that. Now we're off to Borth for an evening dip, subject to high tide of course and it's time you were off to Lugworth to receive the dear wife back from her exploits with the USAF at Greenham Common. Will see you at the defence exercise, hopefully with the PM."

"Is she definitely coming then?" Tony asked excitedly.

"Wait and see, Anthony, we must wait and see. Be prepared is the motto, especially with the rabble on their way back today; the lady wife accepted of course. Do give her my regards."

Tony sat quietly until he was confronted by the waiter with the bill.

"Caught again, sir, I'm afraid, the MP and his chum have already left the club. Sign here please."

"I think I know where to sign by now, Alfred. Despite his Westminster expense account, the tight bastard always manages to slip away when the bill comes. One day, Alfred, one day and I shall have him."

"I believe you will, sir and I hope I am here to see it. Shall I have the car brought round to the front, sir?"

Anthony sighed to himself. "Not needed. It was such a lovely morning I decided to walk across the course via the back gate … That's why I bought the old Rectory in the first place; it's the perfect location for a devoted golfer."

Slipping him a handsome tip he thanked Alfred and adjusting his designer sunglasses he wandered off home across the greens reminding himself that he needed to feed Scargill before meeting the returning Greenham rabble rousers.

It was late afternoon when Mr Morgan's minibus drew up outside the Lugworth Arms, it was no longer green and white. Apart from the mud-splashed wheels, the bodywork had been artistically painted with deep purple patches and the rear windows sported a selection of anti-nuclear slogans.

It was also a bit of a mess inside the vehicle. Stale food, paper bags, toys and books littered the floor; the smell of damp tents and clothing invaded the nostrils and lingered for most of the journey home. Despite more than the usual comfort stops, the last 100 miles or so was very tiring but thankfully the children had managed to sleep and most of the passengers had dozed for the last couple of hours. Exhausted after the long drive, Mr Morgan praised the Lord for the safe journey home and for finding him a comfortable bed and breakfast run by a kindly soul in nearby Newbury. She had sympathised with his difficult situation over a late night cup of hot cocoa and gave him a full English breakfast to send him on his way.

Sliding the doors open a weary Mr Morgan announced.

"Wakey, wakey one and all, we're home. Everyone out of the bus please and calmly make your way to the WC." Words fell on stony ground. If he had not been on the offside of his vehicle he would have been brushed aside by the instant awakening of large and small bladders heading towards the public toilets behind the British Legion. Desperate for a pee, little Ronnie Logan couldn't wait; casting aside his prep school upbringing and smiling with relief, he widdled against the letter box outside the post office. Ever the local snob, his proud mother smiled as she pointedly announced to her travelling companions.

"You see. That's what you pay for when you give your children a top, private education. If they need to pee outside, let them do so discreetly in the right places." Making a quick dash for safety, she was bombarded with stale buns and apple cores as she headed for the safety of her double fronted Georgian house beside the church.

Inside the Lugworth Arms, Anthony was enjoying a quiet drink and making polite conversation with an anxious Lady Llewellyn-Llewellyn. Unbeknown to Anthony, she had given up her seat on the bus in favour of her sister's camping kit and was half explaining that Daphne had been arrested and was up before the Newbury beak on Monday. Angela, Janet and Dee had stayed on to see fair play. Tony all but exploded.

"What! Arrested, bloody arrested. All of them, my wife included. What the hell for?"

"It appears my eccentric sister along with a few other women, defied top security to climb the wire fence surrounding the United States Air Force base to stage a 'sit in' on the nuclear bunkers said – and I repeat said – Tony, to be armed with nuclear rockets."

Anthony was frantic. "Please God, not my wife. I'll be finished if it is; any hopes for political ambitions at Westminster will be blown sky-high."

"Not an appropriate phrase under the circumstances, Tony, and you haven't the decency to ask if they are okay. Now pull yourself together and have another large scotch on me."

She waved to George behind the bar.

"A double malt for the Chief and a large gin and tonic."

"For whom, your Ladyship?"

"For me you old fool and double quick time if you please. He's in shock. Now, now Tony stop shaking, get a grip and behave as a caring husband, and I choose that term lightly; now listen to me. I have been in touch with the family solicitor and he has asked an associate in Newbury to represent my sister in court; he has since contacted me to explain the situation first hand. As I understand it, she was arrested with others and bundled into the paddy wagon – I do love that term, don't you – by over-enthusiastic members of the MOD, Ministry of Defence, police."

Anthony sighed. "Yes, yes I do know what MOD is. Just get on with it. Is my wife in jail or not?"

"Not at the moment. It is likely that the local force may have overstepped the mark by making arrests on American soil which, according to military regulations, is not on. Well, that's his proposed defence; he is checking it out with Foreign Office and the US Embassy. We won't know much more until they arrive home so be patient until then, there's a good chap. As soon as the hearing is over with, they can pick up a train at Oxford and you can collect them from Newport."

Before Anthony could think up a suitable excuse Lady Ann warned him.

"I know it's a good hour away but you can forget about defence exercises, Council meetings, golf and Mrs Tremlett and find out when the train is due. Oh yes, and you would be wise to remember that Hugh Tremlett is back on the patch and if he discovers your little peccadilloes with the lady wife, official secret act or not – if Ms Donnington gets the slightest a whisper – Ruth's political expectations are up in smoke and your Knighthood will disappear into the mists of time. So check the time tables and get on with it."

Head in hands, Anthony pondered the situation but not for long. Outside in the street the Lugworth campaigners tumbled out of the mini-bus to be noisily greeted by friends and family.

Spotting the dishevelled passengers, George went on the defensive.

"Keep 'em out of here, Ted. Keep 'em out; the great unwashed are not coming in this bar covered in mud and certainly not smelling of roses – at least not until they are scrubbed up. Thank God the bargain-breakers have left for the station. Otherwise trade would fly out of the window."

"Trade down, George! You get more than enough trade from us most days of the week to cover your bargain- breakers. They only come in the summer, we keep you going all year round so keep your hair on otherwise we're off to the British Legion for a cheap pint."

Lady Ann laughed. "See what I mean, Tony, I'm not stopping much longer either, not with this rabble in full throttle. Believe me, I can't tell you how glad I am I didn't go with them. God knows how poor old Mo Morgan survived the ride. It would be worth an arrest just to come home on the train. Best warn Ruth you could both be blown out of the water."

Just as Tony took a swift gulp of his whiskey, she slapped him between the shoulder blades, it went down the wrong way and he almost choked.

Three days later the Greenham Three plus one ex-prisoner arrived home in a chauffeur driven limousine piled high with well-used camping kit. Not too sure of dates, times and Anthony's reliability, she had called in a favour from one of her cronies in the House of Lords. Keen to oblige his socialist adversary, she insisted her chauffer, who had family in the area, drive them home to Wales. Unloading his passengers he saluted and set off for Builth Wells to visit his sister for an overnight stay. Relieved to see her own sister safe and well, Lady Ann clamped an arm around her and after suitable goodbyes took her home.

Watching the two of them walk away, Angela shrugged her shoulders and sighed.

"Well, girls, it's been great but tiring. I can see my husband's prized car and I will at least get a ride home before the inquest begins."

Delighted her kindly old godmother was in the safe hands of her sister, she hugged her two chums, climbed up the steps leading to the lounge bar and assured of large Gin and Tonic prepared to meet her doom. To avoid a difficult drive home in the dark, Janet offered Dee her spare room for the night in readiness for the final meeting of the Nuclear Defence Committee next day. As they approached the front door of her cottage, Pankers was waiting on the front step, her cat-like questioning stare suggesting she was not happy with the extended homecoming.

Next morning the two women woke up in the same bed with Pankers grudgingly stretched out in a dip in the duvet end at the end of the bed. Realising they had overslept Jan tossed aside the covers and the cat which made a fast exit to the landing and down the stairs. Dee peered through one eye, looked about her and said. "How did I end up in here, Jan, or is it simply my lucky day?"

Dragging on her silk kimono she yelled back. "For God's sake, Dee, we've overslept. How you ended up in my bed we can leave until later. Now grab the first shower and I'll make the coffee, my mouth tastes like sheep dip."

Chapter Fifteen

The final meeting of the Nuclear Defence Committee with the full Council was, to say the least, a shambles. The growing 'ban the bomb brigade' outside the Council Chamber was kept behind a makeshift barrier constructed from spare cattle pens from the cattle market. Time had prevented the usual after-sale hose down and arrived by van covered in dry cow shit, which, thanks to an unexpected bout of very warm sunshine infiltrated through the town causing a run on paper hanky's at the local chemist. Aware her future prospects depended on how she would cope during Operation Fall Out, Acting Police Inspector Patti Lloyd ignored well-meaning advice from the local copper, s and took the safest route to policing crowds by calling for reinforcements from over the border well in advance of likely trouble. Baton extended, she forced a gangway up the steps of the building before realising all parties, apart from Crispin Davenport-Jones MP, were already seated in the Council chamber. By the time he arrived most of the demonstrators had drifted away leaving Inspector Lloyd and fifteen subordinates from the lower ranks to escort him into the building. Overcome by enthusiasm she announced, "Stand aside, VIP approaching."

Anxious to get him safely inside the building she accidently caught his rear end with her baton. Surprised at the unexpected touch up, he skipped a step or two, smiled at her and sauntered through the swing doors. Inside the Council chamber all appeared well; light-hearted banter between Councillors and officials improved the usual solemn proceedings nevertheless Anthony Anderson-Shelta was determined to get on with the meeting. Keen to avoid spending time with Ruth, he had been promised an afternoon's golf on the links at Borth with his opposite number from West Wales and he needed time on his side. Encouraging the Chairman to start procedures before the mood changed, compulsory prayers had just about ended when the Member of Parliament stumbled through the swing doors still smiling. In her usual place on the front bench Janet Bodmin turned to Ben Neal.

"Oh my God. It's here then. Late as usual and smelling of roses."

"Makes a change from the cattle shit invading the nostrils," Ben replied, loud enough for Ruth Tremlett to bring out the ever-ready lemon handkerchief to cover her nose. Already irritated by the late arrival of his parliamentary chum, Tony sarcastically welcomed him to the meeting.

"So glad you could make it, Crispin. We all are. You have missed prayers and it's now time for the business of the day. Are you ready with your note book, Mrs Tremlett, it is vital we have detailed minutes."

"Every letter, word, comma and dot, my liege," she replied, wagging her pencils over his head.

"It will be 'once more unto the breach' next he if he can't get a grip on her." Janet whispered to Dee seated behind her in the press box.

Hand over mouth Dee stifled a giggle before muttering.

"He's been at the breach more times than she cares to remember but unable to break through," she replied without looking up.

Picking up on the welcome speech the Chairman heaved himself onto his feet, farted and addressed the meeting.

"Ladies and gentlemen, once our MP has settled in, we must concentrate on the job in hand. We have heard much about preparations for the defence exercise from the sub-committee chairman, but what we need to know today is; the start, finish and matters in-between plus the amount of government grant available. We already know who will be in charge of day-to-day operations, the emergency services and the walking wounded, however the purpose of this exercise is based on a nuclear device dropping on Birmingham. Thus it is assumed that depending on the weather forecast it is highly likely that deadly radiation could drift west towards Wales bringing in hordes of escaping refugees. Who will be responsible for them?"

Interrupting him, Bill Jones pleaded. "Get on with it otherwise it will be all over before we get started. Anyway, we have been through all this at sub-committee stage.

"Yes I know that, but I'm not the one responsible for policing the English border and Offa's Dyke if refugees and ruffians leave the West Midlands to avoid the fallout. What we also need to know is how many of us will have a place of safety to fall back on for family and friends."

Turning to a surprised Anthony he added, "Can we rely on your expertise Chief Executive to see us all through safely without fear or favour."

The long silence ended when Crispin laughed and announced. "I'm afraid to say it will not be 'women and children first' as on Titanic, or even lower the lifeboats."

The mystery voice from the public gallery could stand it no longer "Who the hell will it be then? I tell you who, Mr Member of Parliament, not us the stupid ratepayers and voters who chuck our cash into the kitty to keep you lot in perks and pensions. No room in the bunker for plebs like us, you can bet your life on that. Go hang your heads in shame."

A ripple of unexpected applause echoed around the Council Chamber causing chaos in the press box and forcing Councillors to their feet. Pompously ignoring appeals for order Crispin dug his already shallow hole deeper still. Red faced he addressed the press and public gallery.

"Whoever it is making these uncalled for speeches clearly has no idea of Government and Council procedure at this level. Thus I shall enlighten you all. Standing orders clearly confirm that Members of Parliament can over-rule the Chair and Chief Executive at all times on matters affecting their constituency, I'm afraid."

Confused and concerned over protocol everyone present looked towards the Chief Executive and his legal officer for confirmation of the ruling. Before they could reply Bill Jones drew in his breath and retorted.

"Then be afraid, be very afraid, Crispin, old boy. Get your head out of your arse and read the minutes of our first meeting some months ago, when all this information was sorted out. The Welsh Office memorandum irrevocably states that every aspect of the nuclear exercise remains in the safe hands of the Chief Executive of the administering local authority. He is and will remain the lead officer at all times."

Pausing only to nudge Janet Bodmin and grin, he added, "If, however, it's the real thing; then it will be every man – and woman for themselves when the bomb drops."

His final comment came as a bolt from the blue for Tomo; heart racing and head spinning at the realisation that, despite his position, he could be excluded from the bunker.

"Are we talking about the real thing again or what. If so, I trust the UK early warning systems are at the ready just in case; if not will there be room for all of us, and our families."

Bewildered, Anderson-Shelta looked at his confused officers and raised his arms heavenwards; Ruth took the chance to grip his knee which did little to help his immediate thoughts. Calming his flustered brain he announced.

"This has gone far enough. It is a practice, a game, not a war; we must keep it in perspective and stick to the rules. Since the directives from Central Government, via the Welsh Office of course, week in and week out we have been through this charade and the matter of bunker space has already been settled and approved at the highest level. Today we are here to finalise the program and timings for Fall Out Day and make contingency plans for the PM after the event. Councillor Neal kindly press on with any last minute arrangements and we can be on our way."

"To Borth to play golf," Janet whispered to Dee. "Angie mentioned something about it yesterday when she suggested we meet up for lunch after this waste of time meeting." Nevertheless Crispin interrupted again.

"Should all go well on the day can one hope for an after show party so to speak, contingency plans and all that?"

For the first time in the meeting Arthur Yorkshire, looked at his Chief and then at his account sheets before sardonically adding. "I'm sorry, Chief Executive, PM or not the contingency fund allows for the consumption of food and drink for officials during the working day, but not for after event jollies I'm afraid, sir, otherwise it's packed lunches for all and sundry."

Before he could continue the unknown member of the public was at it again, this time aiming his comments at Crispin.

"Yeah! We've heard it all before. I'll bet a penny to a pound food and drink will be on tap at the Lugworth for the nobs but not for ordinary folk like us. It will be WI sandwiches, crisps and urns of tea in the Methodist Hall for everyone else. Anyway, what's the PM got to do with it?"

Crispin winked at Anthony, tapped his nose and replied, "Bit of a secret isn't Chief Executive. No names no pack drill as they say."

Janet was about to burst. Catching Dee's eye, she paused for breath, giggled and proclaimed.

"Oh please, Chairman, can we nip this one in the bud and get on with the business of the morning, otherwise nuclear war will have passed unnoticed. Thanks to my colleague Councillor Neal, whom I might add, has taken the brunt of organising this stupid idea from the Welsh Office, appears to have everything under control, Our duties are listed, the town is papered with instructions, the border with England will be shut, emergency stations on standby and the fallout shelter open for business the moment the hooter blasts off. In my humble opinion this crazy happening has become a Whitehall farce of Brian Rix proportions and to be quite frank, every damned meeting we have had has been more of a fallout. The sooner it is over and done with the better we shall all be, however I somehow fear the aftermath should it all go wrong."

That said, and despite a query from Ruth Tremlett as to recording Janet's comments in the minutes, the meeting wound down well before lunch leaving the officers and some Councillors disappointed at a missed opportunity to claim extra allowances and overtime payments. Anderson-Shelta headed for the links at Borth, before leaving he asked his secretary to send a round robin to all involved in the defence exercise. It read:

Good Luck on D Day and be well prepared for the Fallout.'

Ten years on from that fatal day, Angela, by now comfortable with her new life in Villafranca, had emotionally accepted that escaping to Spain when Anthony's mid-life crisis kicked in, was, all things considered, the right thing to do. It was punishment enough living under the same roof with him at any time, but following the catastrophic cock-up on Nuclear Defence Day his unending recriminations had reached tipping point and she needed to wipe her husband from her past. Relaxing on the terrace at sunset she was well into a good bottle of vino, the fiery red sky was reminding her how Anthony's nuclear chaos brought him to his political downfall, all credit to his beloved golf club.

Chapter Fifteen

The unexpected emergency meeting of the Mid Border District Council sent shock waves through the Chamber. Rumours that the dispute with Lugworth golf club over the use of a dilapidated WW2 air raid shelter in a the small wooded area adjacent to the practice green, would, subject to refurbishment and planning permission, be suitable as a civil defence nuclear bunker, were about to be confirmed. However, for many years the concrete building used to store mechanical equipment and vehicles used by the green-keepers was no longer available. Ownership was in dispute and talks ended in deadlock.

On the advice of her boss and at short notice, Ruth Tremlett quickly organised a 'closed' meeting of the Council to discuss ways forward and most members turned up; public and press (apart from Dee Donnington) were excluded.

Janet and Dee arrived together. "Any idea what it's all about, Jan?" Dee asked.

"Not in detail. According to Bill the golf club have claimed squatters rights to the old wartime shelter behind the practice green and until all the legals have been sorted we don't have a nuclear underground bunker for the civil defence exercise."

"Bit bloody late in the day for that," Dee exclaimed. "We are under starters orders for blast off in less than ten weeks."

"I know, but the Defence Committee has been looking at alternative sites and some genius has come up with a plan."

"I'm not surprised the club has backed off. When Anderson-Shelta told the Greens Committee about the defence exercise, wires got crossed leaving councillors believing that the green would have to be dug out, voted against."

Dee laughed. "Silly sods, so we have to find a new venue for falling out in. This should be fun."

"Fun! Dee. It's a bloody calamity. Nobody seems to know who owns the place. God help Lugworth when all this gets out. I expect Tomo will tell all when he finally takes the Chair."

Taking her place in the empty press gallery Dee waved to Bill and Jan and pointed to the unsteady figure of the Chairman of Council.

"He looks bad, Bill," Jan said. "He must have been up all night to look like that in the morning." "So would I with his problems. Anderson-Shelta has some explaining to do and his pal from Westminster. Listen up he's on his feet."

Breathing hard and looking very shaky, Tomo Thomas apologised for the short notice and in the interests of speedy consultation immediately passed the buck.

"Gentlemen, thank you for coming at such short notice but it is vital we get this through today. I call on the Chief Executive to explain fully what has happened."

Watched by his unusually attentive officers and encouraged by the good and faithful Mrs. Tremlett, Anthony quietly announced:

"Gentlemen and Ladies, too, we have a small technical hitch re Operation Fall Out."

"Small technical hitch, it's catastrophic and it's down to him and that idiot MP that we are well and truly in the mire." Bill muttered. "Wait for the rest of it to come out, Jan, and you will see what the Defence Committee has been landed with."

Aiming his comments at Bill, Anthony continued, "What I mean is. With only a few weeks to go, we no longer have a nuclear fallout shelter, pretend or otherwise. However our planning officer and his team have come up with a near perfect solution."

You could hear the smallest pin drop, apart that is, from Ned Tonkin's practised fart for all occasions and for once Ruth Tremlett had no lemon-scented hanky to cover her nose. It was too long a silence before Anthony spoke again. Clearing his throat he could not ease the nervous twitch under his left eye. Clearing his throat and speaking less positively than usual he rose to the occasion.

"Due to unforeseen circumstances, 'tempus fugit' – time flies – and we must get on quickly. By the by, for those who failed the eleven plus and missed out on a Grammar School education, this is Latin for time has caught us on the hop. Thus a decision has been made to convert the former Victorian Pump Rooms and Mineral Baths in our once tropical gardens, into a temporary nuclear bunker for the duration of Operation Fall Out which of course, must be ratified by full Council. That is why we are here."

Slipping from his chair, Tomo was saved from hitting the floor by the strong arm of Dick Doby. Staggering to his feet he demanded.

"Pray tell me, Chief Executive just who, when and why authorised this decision without first notifying full Council and under what standing order?"

"An ad hoc sub-committee of Councillors Ben Neal, Bill Jones and I as Defence Exercise Commander plus, of course, my personal assistant Mrs Tremlett to take the minutes. This was set up some years ago should an emergency event arise."

Shock waves reverberated through the Council chamber forcing the Chairman to call for a fifteen-minute adjournment to enable the reality of the situation to sink in. In the stillness of the moment it was proposed, seconded and carried on the nod.

Dispersing to the Chairman's Parlour for light refreshments and thinking time, Jan spoke first.

"Hell's teeth, Bill, as my granny would say. I thought the old Pump Rooms are grade one listed and virtually untouchable. If this gets out before the big day there'll be TV cameras and reporters on every street corner in Lugworth. The Barratt Boys will play to the gallery for cash and half the town will be filmed taking to the waters again. My God, Dee will have her work cut out keeping this under wraps."

Bill sighed, "I always thought the Pump Rooms were sacrosanct regarding use but I suppose needs must when it comes to defence of the realm."

Janet shook her head in mock despair. Patting Bill on the shoulder she advised.

"Think again old boy. Anderson-Shelta can pull more strings than a puppet master. If a Lugworth landmark is about to be abused rather than used we must fight the good fight for Lugworth's heritage, otherwise it will be nodded through without a by your leave. It's a damned shame."

"So it is, Jan. I can remember the days when people flocked to Lugworth from all over the country by bus and train believing the minerals could cure most ailments. In the twenties and thirties it was fashionable to be seen 'taking the waters' and famous celebrities were photographed taking a healthy dip in the warm water spa for magazines. My late mother would swear that a weekly dip in the pool was a remedy for her aches and pains."

Built in the late eighteen hundreds the listed building sited in the botanic gardens had not been used for many years and befitting its former status as a popular health spa it had always been subject to a Welsh Heritage site preservation order. Owned and maintained by the Lugworth and District Water Company, health and safety inspectors insisted that the boiler house below the disused open-air mineral water pool must be boarded up. Nevertheless the substantial multi-roomed red brick building was in reasonable condition and before the preservation order was enforced, it was considered a suitable development zone for affordable and sheltered housing. Amid rumours that a number of 'get rich quick' local worthy's were keen to push the project through to outline planning the scheme was dropped. Eventually, to prevent sulphuric smells escaping into the air during the summer months the mineral pool was cleaned out, sanitized, covered by a large tarpaulin and fenced off. This did not deter the Barratt Boys from peeing into it on their way home from the Memorial Hall dances leaving a distinct odour of gentlemen's urinals to linger in the park until the next rainfall. The idea of it becoming a nuclear fallout shelter, however temporary, was, to say the least a big mistake and proved to be so.

Such was the effect of shock, the short break lasted more like an hour or so, due perhaps to Tomo opening up the Chairman's drinks locker. This caused a few raised voices to drift out of the window alarming passers-by and the bemused bunch of reporters, including Dee, seated outside the Lazy Poacher.

"Something's up, chaps; I'll pop over and find out what's going on."

Attempting to follow the Councillors emerging from the Chairman's Parlour, she was stopped in her tracks by a determined Ruth Tremlett who barred her from entering the Chamber. Officious as ever she declared loud enough to scatter the pigeons.

"No press allowed, kindly wait outside on the benches provided. Radio and television crew please remain in the car park. A press release will be issued later."

Rarely gobsmacked, Dee said, "Am I not the press adviser for the Council?

"Not this time, dear," Ruth replied and trotted back to her duties, leaving a bemused Dee to shrug her shoulders and re-join her colleagues in the Lazy Poacher.

"Well boys all I can say is something is definitely going in there. Something we are barred from knowing but I will before the day is out. I thought I had seen and heard everything about the madness of the Mid Border District Council but this beats it all."

Keen to get more information, Johnno from the Usk Courier pleaded.

"Give us a clue, Dee. We're all in this together. If something tasty is brewing we need to know before the deadline. So give it up please."

Head in hands she replied, "Ruth Tremlett has finally lost it. She barred me, us, from the building and, wait for it, warned radio and TV crews to remain in the car park. TV crews! The one and only time a TV crew made an appearance was in Lugworth when 38 residents swore they saw a space ship hovering above the town lowering little green men onto the golf course. Cameras, microphones and dotty UFO spotters camped out for weeks just in case it returned. After a local enquiry by the UFO Society it turned out that they had all been to the picture palace on a mini bus to see *Close Encounters of the Third Kind* stopped off for cider and swore blind they were about to be kidnapped and taken to another planet."

Shock over and done with and full Council reconvened to discuss alternative plans for fall out Day, the reporters telephoned their editors. Later Dee, Jan and Bill met up with Sandy, the Scottish deputy manager of the Lugworth and District Water Company, for a bit of advice on the future of the Pump Rooms, knowing full well that after a couple of hours on double malts they would have full knowledge of any plans for the boarded up swimming pool and it's part in the defence exercise. It was clear Sandy was keen for an opportunity to obstruct in any way possible, Anderson-Shelta in revenge for an unfortunate incident at a NALGO conference five years before. It was a chance he had been relishing since then and thanks to the bunker situation his time had come. His drunken reminiscences provided the three conspirators with enough information to pre-empt chaos from day one of the exercise.

Apart from the late arrival by train of the lieder hosen clad Bavarian town band, from an administrative point of view the day began well, that was until the unexpected lift off from inside the bunker. The rushed through refurbishment of the Pump Rooms into a base for the emergency services, police, military and the like had proved a reasonable success and the exercise was running smoothly until an anonymous tip-off to the national press – said to be from a disgruntled employee from the water company – the shit hit the fan. The caller warned that the boiler house below the spa pool and steam room was more than a bit dodgy and the area should have been cordoned off years ago. Panic wasn't the word; within twenty-four hours a press release from the Welsh Office assured the township that the bunker was built in case Russia got the hump with the West and shot off a rocket thus the civil defence exercise was only pretend. It took some convincing, most people believing it was the same bunch of crooks keen to demolish the Pump Rooms and build posh homes for Londoners.

Overseen by Dee Donnington, TV crews, presenters and press reporters from across the Wales and the West Midlands were staked out in the Methodist Church Hall in return for a large donation to the church roof fund. The local WI provided tea, coffee and bacon baps at reasonable prices and the memorial hall became the refugee centre for the unsuspecting walkers straying across Offa's Dyke into Wales. Health and safety refused to sanction the 'drive thro' car wash as a suitable decontamination centre and allowed eager fire crews to hose down unworthy locals. Other than the untimely concert by the Bavarian oompah band, (supposedly cancelled by the normally perfectionist Ruth Tremlett), most of the community chose to ignore the warning and road signs crudely over written by the Barratt Boys and carried on as normal.

The arrival of the mythical rocket, represented by ten rings on the curfew bell, had little response. Most thinking it was the funeral toll, they carried on shopping in the market square, propping up the bar in the Lugworth Arms or walking the dog on the playing field. The only visible response was the shocked bargain-breakers keen for a quiet weekend in the country, didn't have a clue that nuclear war was on the horizon.

However, war almost broke out when members of the dramatic society overdid their role as refugees from the Black Country and refused to retreat from the Barratt Boys looking for a fight.

Meanwhile job just about done, feet up and comfortably ensconced in the recently decorated and stylishly furnished war offices in the former Pump Rooms the defence committee and their chosen few enjoyed a last lunch on expenses and quietly praised each other for insisting the temporary bunker had flush toilets. Congratulating Anthony on a jolly good show Crispin assured him his name would be on the New Year Honours list for a possible Knighthood. Unable to take much more Janet and Bill walked out into an imaginary radiation cloud.

Sweating it out in the empty spa pool above the dodgy boiler room, emergency personnel expensively kitted out in oversized protective clothing, played with brand new rescue equipment and wore gas masks while chatting on under charged walkie-talkie phones to pay as you go journalists after a good story. Always on the lookout for a nice little earner, PC Dai Davis had beaten them to it and was telling a good tale or two in the Methodist chapel where Dee Donnington was already doing her stuff direct to camera.

Mainly because the cellars in the Pump Rooms were more or less soundproofed, particularly the boiler house, it was all quiet on the Lugworth front. But it didn't last long, at about 2.30 p.m. on that fateful day the balloon went up. Unbeknown to Anderson-Shelta and his political chums resting up in the makeshift bunker, Sandy, the former water company engineer, had quietly oiled and adjusted the wheel valve on the old steam pump. Previously used to filter the muscle easing warm water into the spa pool, a simple touch was all that was needed to activate steam, but well-oiled himself, he overdid it muttering.

"One day I'll wring his bloody neck," and gave it the full works. Freshly cleaned and thoroughly sanitised, a top of the range military marquee had been erected over the pool and lashed to all the sides of the baths with guy ropes; that is except the four corners which had been slackened off. Housed beneath the marquee a large camp kitchen with matching camp chefs, a communal dining area and a resting place with camp beds offered respite for the emergency teams and their volunteer 'ladies'. Behind a row of linked hospital type screens six male and six female toilets with washing facilities had been positioned over the old wastewater outlet at the bottom of the empty pool. Very slowly at first, steam began to rise hence the sweating personnel awaiting the call to arms.

By now halfway to the Methodist hall press centre to meet up with Dee, Janet and Bill felt the blast before they heard it and spun round.

"What the hell was that, Jan, I thought this a basic civil defence exercise not the real thing?" and fearing the worst ran for cover in the church porch.

Under the increasing pressure of escaping steam and suspiciously loosened guy ropes, it was up, up and away as if in slow motion leaving the emergency services below and a hearty couple copulating in the toilet tent, exposed to the elements.

Guy ropes dangling it drifted across the town followed below by a steady trial of sight seekers keen to be at touchdown. They need not have worried. After grappling with the church tower it eventually broke free from the cross and sailed westwards towards the county golf club near Brecon. Unaware of the blow out in

Lugworth, Anderson-Shelta and co had moved on for afternoon tea with the club captain in the conservatory tea room.

Further complimenting Tony and once more raising hopes of a Knighthood, Crispin assured him.

"As I said earlier, your more than competent display of man-management deserves a 'K' in the New Year's Honours list or perhaps even the House of Lords. Well done old boy."

Panting profusely and clasping Tony's hand between her knees Ruth joyously acclaimed. "At last, at last together. Lord and Lady Anderson – Shelta. What a glorious climax to our working relationship."

As if by magic the dream was over. The room descended into darkness except for a hint of the sun through a window broken by the church weather vane hanging from a tangled guy rope ...

Meanwhile back in Lugworth the clearing up operation was well underway and by opening time the town was declared safe and all clear by anxious Health and Safety officials. In the market square the Bavarian band and the Lugworth Handicapped Morris Dancers entertained the locals and tourists alike with a display of English Country dancing openly mocked by the Barratt Boys, heavy on cider.

The same evening, Sandy from the Water Company held court with his personal explanation for the unexpected calamity at the Pump Rooms.

"As I mentioned some time ago, Bill, the steam pipes in the boiler house might have rusted and seized up over the years were it not for my close interest in mechanical engineering. I always loved dabbling with pipes and boilers, it is my unofficial hobby. A touch of oil here and there on rusted up steam valves during the recent refurbishing easily did the trick and bob's yer uncle."

"Plus a few untied guy ropes and Fanny's your Aunt I suppose!" Bill said.

"I understand revenge can also be taken with a large whiskey or two, so make mine doubles," Bill suggested.

"Hear, hear," Janet responded. What a day this has been" and called for another round.

Chapter Seventeen

It took Angela more than two years to dump the emotional baggage Tony had left her with. The inevitable break came with the damaging report from the Welsh Office blaming him for the whole nuclear debacle. The aftermath from fall out was unending; buck passing was rife, press and public alike were clamouring for his head and an acting Chief Executive Officer was despatched from Cardiff to keep the District Council running. As expected, the Council's officers agreed to early retirement on full pay for the first year, resettlement expenses if they moved from the area within two years and a comfortable pension pot. Full Council immediately stepped down, Janet Bodmin retired gracefully with little fuss and an acting Council co-opted until elections could be held.

Crispin Davenport-Jones's hopes for the Welsh Office were shattered when he lost his seat at the next general election. Following reports of 'ill health' Anthony was awarded the MBE for Services to Local Government in Wales and a substantial retirement package rewarded his silence. It was said Ruth Tremlett was offered a year's gardening leave and two years on the sick with full pay. For her silence she was given a comfortable pension package with BUPA for the rest of her days. Anthony's farewell gift from the Lodge, colleagues and friends was a lifetime subscription to

Borth Golf Club where, to Angela's delight and encouraged by the now widowed Ruth, he re-discovered his game. When Ruth's husband died of a fever in some remote corner of South America, Tony asked his wife for a divorce.

With Anthony finally out of her life Angela was more than happy with her new one. She was welcomed into the family at Villafranca and surrounded by beautiful countryside and memories of her dear old Aunt and godmother to keep her amused life was good and enjoyable. The Spanish lifestyle suited her well and she chose not to make too many changes to the property preferring to keep the semi Moroccan style and her Aunts bits and pieces. She had also transported paintings and furniture from her family homes in Farnborough and the Old Rectory in mid-Wales. Inheriting a housekeeper, gardener and a few local cats, she was never short of visitors. Before her death in 1990, Lady Ann, accompanied by the Rev. Clive Makepeace, came for their holidays, bringing news and gossip from the valleys.

Janet and Dee had been regular visitors to the guest suite but the situation changed when Dee became the UK TV presenter for Sport Euro based in Madrid. Not wanting to be apart from Jan for too long, she agreed to commute from Cardiff four days a week until her employers pressured her into a permanent move if she wanted to present the 1992 summer Olympics. It was all she had ever wanted but so was Jan; they had become very close since Angela had moved to Spain and it was 'make your mind up' time for both of them. Janet was the older of the three friends and Dee, a good few years younger, was conscious of her friend's growing aches and pains brought on by the damp, winter conditions of rural living. Her little cottage wasn't the warmest place in town and needed some refurbishment if she was to end her days in reasonable comfort. Angie had left a gap in both their lives and despite regular visits to Villafranca they missed her more than ever and they both agreed that since Pankers, her companion cat, had died after 17 years, perhaps it was time to move on.

When Angela came to London for the memorial service for Lady Anne at Westminster Abbey, she hinted that the Spanish sun would soon put a spring in Janet's step and if they should ever consider moving to warmer climes, she had some good contacts in the property investment business. After weeks of discussion Janet took the plunge and put her cottage on the market; Dee agreed to sell her Cardiff apartment, pool resources and ask Angie to find a largish property with sunny outlook not too far from the sea.

Angela did more than that; she snapped up a disused winery on Castillo estate with plenty of space for conversion and set in acres of Cava grape vines and wild flowers. Just a short stroll from Angela's home and an hour or so from Sitges, considered by some to be the St. Tropez of Spain, its film, arts and music festival's promised a cultural outlet for Janet's creative writing. Keen to have Angela's English friends in residence on their estate, it didn't take long for the popular and powerful de la Barca family to arrange for special planning permission. A very fair price was agreed and the family architect and building company were contracted to make good the basic structure before refurbishment was started. Thanks to the family solicitor Senor Cabot, the deal was done in record time and without the usual hitch or two. Anxious to be in residence before the Welsh winter set in, Janet eventually sold her little cottage at a handsome profit to a retired wildlife warden from West Wales. He was later advised that the only wildlife he would see in Lugworth was on Saturday nights at the Memorial Hall when the Barratt boys kicked off if the town lost a cup match.

Under Angela's watchful eye, building and refurbishment work on Jan and Dee's villa progressed at a steady pace and after a number of weekend visits to discuss interior décor, furnishings and fittings, their soon to be shared Spanish style home was accomplished. After a farewell party at the Lugworth Arms the town turned out to wave them off; the Barratt Boys pulling Mr Morgan's new taxicab to the edge of the town with ropes. Clive Makepeace went with them to Cardiff airport and could not hold back the tears as they boarded the flight to Barcelona. No longer a man of the cloth as such, he was working at a mission station teaching English to adults in Central Africa. He had leave to see them off and promised to visit them next time round.

Clothes personal items of furniture and family memorabilia were on the way to Spain in Mr Morgan's removal van driven by his eldest sons Jona and Josh – Mr Morgan had by now being semi-retired – leaving the donkey work to his strong boys. They had never been to Europe before, except on a trip to the Menin Gate at Ypres to find his grandfather's name on the war memorial, so he went along for the ride. The Red Dagon of Wales emblazoned on the back of van, the Morgan trio headed for Plymouth for the overnight ferry to Santander followed by a four hundred and fifty mile drive to Villafranca. Dee had agreed removal expenses with her employers, TV Sporting Euro, ensuring Mr Morgan and sons were well provided for on the long journey to Spain. Marvelling at the splendour of the surroundings, they arrived tired but happy to see their old friends again. Janet and Dee organised the unloading and after a comfortable night in a nearby hostelry the

Morgan trio left for Lugworth loaded up with fruit, wine and goodies and a safe pass through customs, courtesy of Senor Cabot. Five days later Dee left for her rented apartment in Madrid and a full-scale debriefing for the Olympic Games with the Head of Sport Euro and a final technical rehearsal with her team from London.

It was a month to the start of the Barcelona games but apart from the arrival of King Juan and Queen Sophia at the opening celebrations, much had been kept under wraps from the general public and the media. Despite discussions over budgets the Olympic Village was finally built on a derelict site close to the sea. Rumours of performance related drugs used by some athletes made the headlines and the official mascot Cobi, a Catalan Sheep Dog in Cubist style was popping up everywhere but the main event was still under wraps until opening night. It came dramatically on July 25. Janet and Angela were invited to view the opening ceremony with the de la Barca family from their sponsored VIP box but after few days watching games where Great Britain had a chance of medals they decided to go home to Villafranca, promising to return for the closing ceremony. Keen to complete the unpacking and finish the final touches to the refurbished winery, they wanted to see the nameplate up before Dee returned from the debrief in Madrid.

The Olympics over and done with and despite the UK low medal count Dee returned from Madrid happy to be back with the family, so to speak. Nevertheless, she needed plenty of time to wind-down; being waited on hand and foot by such good friends was such a joy.

It was early September when Dee finally returned from Madrid to her half of the substantial residence. Delighted with the colourful surroundings, countryside views and the grape harvest festival, the prospect of a closer friendship with Jan made her smile. Knowing she had a place and friends again – including a ginger tabby cat, she was more than keen to stay around – which added to her peace of mind. So much so, she took a mug of tea into Janet, promised to make breakfast and telephoned Angie to come and join them. While she was waiting she sat down and read her fan mail. Breakfasting on the terrace was like old times again. Much had happened since Angela's divorce and her move to Spain five years ago she and her friends had a lot to catching up to do. "Is it true Anthony and Ruth married at Graceland in Memphis?" Janet asked.

Dee laughed, "You bet he did. It was the talk of the county. Believe it or not they walked down the aisle to Elvis singing 'The Wonder of You'. Thanks to yours truly, the press had a field day and I arranged for a photo of the happy couple dressed as Sue Ellen and JR to be sent down the wire; the Western Mail gave it half a front page. Surely you heard about it, Angie?"

Angela dropped her head onto the table. "I did and can we gloss over this please? It's bloody embarrassing to say the least. More coffee anyone?"

Two weeks later, a seriously bored Dee dropped by the local office of the Catalonian News, a weekly regional newspaper printed in Spanish and English. She had been easily persuade by the editor, to write the occasional feature aimed at English residents and tourists and she was keen to keep her hand in.

Paulo had spent most of his early career training in Fleet Street before moving on to become Press Officer for the Spanish Consulate in London. He returned to Villafranca to marry and settle down with his sister's best friend from Barcelona had three children and now lived in a traditional Spanish villa on the coast outside Sitges. A family man through and through, he had struck up a friendship with Dee during the Olympic Games when he turned up in a Barcelona football shirt and asked him why.

"I have season ticket to Camp Nou for many years. For Catalonians it is 'Me's que un club' (more than a club) and I will take you to a match and show you best team in the world."

Explaining she was a Spurs fan they had a friendly discussion on the merits of Terry Venables (El Tel) when he managed the club and before long they became good pals exchanging football gossip from the UK whenever they met up. However, this morning Dee called in to remind Paulo to bring his family to the wine festival at the De Barca estate over the weekend. Travelling grape pickers arrive in batches to help the estate owners and workers bring in the harvest; tradition has it that all invited guests must remove footwear, climb into huge wooden vats and dance away until sunset until the harvest is in. The first crop crushed is passed around and the singing and dancing continues all weekend and later the vats are delivered to the bottling plant and laid up in racks until the wine has matured. It is a great family occasion and a highlight of the year across the wine-growing areas in Spain; competition between local estates for the finest wine goes on and on.

Dee was finishing off her Cappuccino when Paulo sat up and passed her the latest copy of *The Guardian*; it had arrived via courier from Barcelona the previous day and he was casually reading through it for possible stories that may interest the English community – the Women's pages always catching his eye.

"Take a look at this, Dee. It's right up your street. You might be able to do something with it!"

"Err. What? Let me finish the coffee and I'll take a look. What's it about?

"Something about a peace camp full of women based at some USA airfield in England who tried to stop nuclear missiles being stored there. Sounds a bit crazy to me but perhaps you could do something with it?"

"Up in flash, Dee snatched the paper from him, scanned the page headline and shouted. "Do something about it, Paulo? I was bloody there. So were my mates Janet and Angie, I need to get home now and go through all this with them. Can't think why this is happening now, it's not been in our subscription copies of *The Guardian*, mind you we are usually a couple of days behind. What date is this? Where's the front page?"

"On the floor where you dropped half the paper," Paulo said. It should be yesterday's copy. UK papers are flown into Barcelona on the early morning plane from Heathrow, collected by Head Office and distributed via currier to outlying editors. I took the afternoon off yesterday, shopping for Jose's birthday and must have left before it arrived on my desk. Look, take it with you and we'll catch up with the story later."

In her haste to get back to Jan; she phoned ahead from her mobile and suggested she asked Angie to be there when she got home. By the time she found her car parked in a nearby Super Store, it took about forty minutes to drive home. She was overly excited and needed to calm down and drive carefully to avoid yet another speeding ticket on the dual carriageway out of town. Recklessly skidding to a halt alongside the front door, she stumbled into the hallway, almost tripping over the elderly cat, to be greeted by her bewildered friends on standby with a large Chivas Regal. Tossing the part read newspaper at them, she breathlessly announced.

"Sit down and get your head round this girls, I need a pee before I believe it," and dashed for the bath room.

Bewildered, Jan and Angie had no idea of what they were supposed to be looking for; some pages were scattered across the table and needed to put together in some sort of orders.

"Have you found the date," Dee yelled.

"We haven't found the bloody front page yet. It's in a hell of a muddle." Angie replied.

Dee came back into the room, sorted through the pages and held the front page over her head. "Got it. Tuesday 15th September, yesterday in fact. Now listen to this, it's all over the page."

Angela tried to calm her friend down, "Sit down and take a deep breath Dee. Unless it's the end of the world finish your whisky and take your time."

"I can't believe it. It seems that after almost twenty years, the Greenham women have finally left the peace camp and the last few caravans moved out a couple of days ago. They are organising a day long picnic before they go."

"It had to happen one day, Dee." Jan said. "Once the missiles and aircraft went in ninety-two, the battle against the base was over although a good many stayed on to make sure the land was handed back to the local Council."

"What will happen to it now?" Dee asked. "There are so many memories and so many people to share them with. It can't be allowed to slip away."

"That won't happen, not while Greenham peacemakers and their families are still alive and kicking. Gosh it's great to think we were around when history was made and never forget it."

Angie who had been quietly studying the rest of the page, clapped her for attention.

"It says here that the airfield is to be changed into a retail park with a Sainsbury super store leading the way."

"That's a laugh, Dee said. "Bit late for that now the women have left the site. After all, the local traders made a bomb, if you'll pardon the expression, on food and drink when thirty thousand peace women joined hands to 'Embrace the Base'.

Don't you remember we circled the perimeter fence and the yanks thought we were bonkers but didn't rough us up like the Ministry of Defence police did."

"Yes and twelve months later they were all evicted by Newbury District Council but there was no giving up and a new camp was set up within days," Jan reminded.

"And stayed put through all the negotiations over who owned what land and what to do with it." Angie claimed. "It was a long wait until the United States Air Force agreed to pass it back to the Royal Air Force."

"Very true" Jan responded. "Yet it took another year or two before the Secretary of State for Defence declared the base surplus to requirements and gave it to Newbury District Council for re-development – plus a very big headache to go with it."

"Agreed but not before the yanks stripped the base of the $250,000 worth of facilities the put in and then demolished and removed most of the buildings."

"Bit mean that. They could have handed a couple of small buildings and other stuff over to the peace camp," Dee said.

"I suppose so, but none of us had any idea how long it would be there and what the base could be used for, despite reports of new housing, a business park and believe it or not a new airport for London or returning it to common land for the people. That's what I would go for if I lived nearby. More aircraft noise over Hampshire and Berkshire; wow! Janet suggested.

"People won't be too bothered about that. After all, screeching military aircraft have dogged the UK skies for many years and most people are already immune to the smell and noise. And lest we forget, helicopters hovered over the peace camp at night to prevent sleep, particularly the kids. It was shameful"

Looking over Angela's shoulder Dee pointed out. "According to this report, if and it's a big if, the Commemorative Appeal can raise enough funds local planners are thinking about a Greenham Common Memorial area with a visitor centre in the old wartime control tower."

Pausing for a moment, Jan quietly added. "Well we need something on the site to remind the world that Greenham Common will always be respected for resistance against nuclear weapons, otherwise it would have been for nothing."

Angela, too, was in thoughtful mode, "If there is going to be an appeal for memorial funds I'm up for it. How about you two? I know we were only camped out a few couple times but we were always there in spirit, the same spirit which brought us together in the first place. Looking back now it was that historical, or should I say, hysterical trip to Greenham years ago with Aunt Daphne in tow that still links us and thousands of women to an emotional journey of discovery about ourselves. It must not be allowed to fade away. So, how about it, shall we dusk down the cheque books and send a donation and I can chip in with what's left from the Daphne Oxbridge estate; it's still in the bank in Farnborough."

For a brief moment Angie's touching words caught Janet off guard, forcing her to clear her throat. Nodding to Dee she quietly suggested.

"We're with you, Angie, aren't we, Dee? Life has been good to us one way or another. Anyway you can't take it with you."

Three years later it was announced in *The Guardian* and a few other nationals that the Women's Peace Camp at Greenham Common was to finally close after 19 years of continuous campaigning. Declared a Commemorative and Historic site the Greenham Common Park Trust will feature memorial sculptures, memorability and pictorial history of the women' of the formidable campaigns and once. Eventually, plans were approved the park opened to the public again. It was the opportunity the three devoted old friends had been waiting for and had been toying with the idea of a personal pilgrimage to the site for some time. Ignoring ageing limbs, a return trip was about to begin.

The day was pleasant enough for travelling; a comfortable limo with driver was on standby to whisk them off to Barcelona for the first class return flight to Heathrow and the best rooms at The Queens Hotel, Farnborough Park already reserved in advance for the two day stop over.

Angela was feeling apprehensive; she had not been back to her roots for many years, not even to visit the family grave in Ship Lane cemetery. When she finally decided to settle in Spain, she changed her married name, Anderson-Shelta, back to her family name, Plunkett-Brown and was hoping that she would not be recognised in Farnborough Park. It took just over the hour to reach Barcelona. The airport at El Prat Llobregat 14km from the city centre, had been enlarged and refurbished for the Olympic Games. The stainless steel glass walls and walkways reminiscent of the first time Jan and Dee arrived in Spain, reminded them of the day they arrived to see and hear of Angela's unexpected inheritance years before. Angie sighed.

"It feels quite strange coming here again after all these years. It's as if Aunt Daphne is still around. The mirrored walls no longer reflect the countless flights she must have made between Cardiff and Villafranca, just to see her beloved Consquela. Today they reflect, at least for me, so many good memories to hang on to."

"It took us all by surprise when you told us she had a secret lesbian lover and never breathed a word," Dee said.

"You couldn't back then, it wasn't socially acceptable like it is now. But for all that, she was a game for anything old girl and certainly lived life to the full. I've still got the photo I took of her kitted out in her Greenham gear, tent, and long wave radio for the Ashes series in her backpack as we climbed on board Mr Morgan's mini bus. All we can do this weekend is mark her place in Greenham Park, plant a few bushes and trees for her and hope she can see them wherever she is." Janet confirmed as they waited to be called for the flight.

The three friends were unusually quiet as the Iberia Airbus crossed the channel on the way to Heathrow. The flight was not to long but the sight of the White Cliffs and the stunning English coast brought a touch of nostalgia as the aircraft circled the south London stack to await landing instructions. As they finally approached Heathrow, they nervously played 'spot the famous buildings' until the wheels touched down.

"Thank God for that," Jan said. "I have never been a fan of heights at the best of times and I'm really not happy up in the clouds."

"Yes we can see that but we're on terra firma now so let's go through the formalities, get our bags, declare the extra bottle of Chivas Regal and head for the exit. What say you, Ange?"

"Not a lot, Dee. Going back to Farnborough Park won't be easy on the memory I suppose; the parents are long gone and come to that so is Anthony, still, God willing, living the life of Riley in Florida with the missus she so long wanted to be."

Jan tried to lighten the situation. "At least you've got a memory, these day's mine's on the slippery slope to losing the keys and forgetting names. Anyway we are here for the Greenham girls, not for reminders of your posh upbringing, best we find the hire car and get onto the hectic whirl they call the M3 before the rush hour.

Parking the hired car at the rear of the Queens Hotel was a bit of a shock for Angela.

"Gosh! It's a long time since I have been here, it may be the same frontage but now it's a Holiday Inn with all the trimmings. Who would have thought it? Daddy and Mummy would be turning in the family grave."

"Are you planning to drop by the cemetery?" Dee asked.

"I would like to. They rest in the military section and I don't suppose I will be passing this way again. The plan was that I join them when I pop the clogs, so to speak but I doubt it. From time to time I have visited the cemetery, more so after Mummy died six years after Daddy but Anthony's attitude didn't help. By then we had bought the Old Rectory and with no kids on the horizon he joined the Masons and divided his time between the district Council and the golf club and we rarely left Wales. Now and again I contact the chap in charge of the cemetery; he takes care of the upkeep, the head stone and seasonal planting. He is a jolly nice chap with a friendly black dog called Ben but I doubt he's still there."

Dee changed the subject. "Enough of all that, Angie' let's check in and freshen up before dinner. There's a spa and pool downstairs, it's been a long journey and we have a busy day tomorrow."

Angela looked around the foyer with all its light wood, soft furnishing and modern lighting and shook her head in disbelief. "This is typical Holiday Inn and I bet all bars are named after supersonic pilots; Neville Duke, John Derry and even Bill Beaumont. These were the sonic boom flying aces at the Farnborough Air Shows when I was growing up. "

"Did you see many?" Dee asked.

"See many? The main approach to the runway was over our house and when they eventually flew faster than the speed of sound, we listened for the double boom. When it came it was goodbye to the windows and green houses in the vicinity. It was an exciting time, though, and I wouldn't have missed it. Now up to our rooms and then dinner."

After a good night's sleep and an enjoyable English breakfast it was off to Greenham to plant shrubs and trees in memory of Daphne and the many friends she made there.

Still in nostalgic mood Angie suggested her friends might like to see the Garrison Church where she made the unfortunate mistake of marrying Anthony. Pointing out that the once Victorian barracks and parade grounds along the Queens Avenue had been replaced by buildings befitting today's modern army. Passing the thirty foot high statue of the first Duke of Wellington, victor of the Battle of Waterloo, astride his favourite charger, Copenhagen, took her back to her father's stories of Aldershot's historic past.

"You know it all then, Angie?"

"Well, just about, Dee. That's what being a Brigadier's daughter does for you. Although if I was a son … it would have been very different. For me it was Hillside Convent School for Girls and finishing school in Switzerland; we have to pass my old school and Ship Lane cemetery on the way to the M3 at Frimley."

"If you want to, Angie, we could make a slight detour on our way to Greenham," Janet touchingly suggested.

It took longer than expected to reach the former Peace Camp, new roundabouts on the A339 Newbury to Basingstoke road had brought easy access for visitors to Greenham Park. At first sight the three friends gasped at wide open spaces, sitting back to admire the distant view of natural heath land, Janet spoke first.

"Where has it gone? No concrete silos to sit on, no cruise missiles below or the high barbed perimeter fences thousands of women tried to tear down. Only the wartime Control Tower lives on to honour the past."

"It may not be the only memory left. The information blurb shows that Yellow Gate camp is here somewhere and we must find it." Dee said.

Tempted out of the car by the warm September sun, it was an emotional moment for Angie, Jan and Dee. Stretching stiff legs and gathering up guide books and maps, they headed for the visitor centre housed inside the control tower and after a longish tour of the park they admired the accommodation centre for small workshops and offices.

After a short break for tea, they walked back to the car to collect the shrubs and bushes to plant in Daphne's name and silently read the words on the memorial sculpture. The most recent 'changes' created from recycled materials found on the former airfield comprised nine pieces of folded steel representing the creation and dismantling of a fighter aircraft. Each piece sitting on a concrete plinth reinforced with recycled concrete dug from the airfield's former runway. Another the 'Flame' is surrounded by a circle of seven standing stones to represent a campfire always a familiar at the old Greenham Common.

"Makes you want to weep and then smile when you see it altogether like this." Jan said. "Dear old Daphne, Lady Ann, Mr Morgan and the rest of the Lugworth brigade who came with us nineteen years ago would be so proud today."

"And I suspect the bar of the Lugworth Arms will forever remember the banter about the local women who fought to ban cruise missiles from England's green and pleasant land," Dee added.

It was towards the end of the day when the Lugworth Three finished planting the shrubs and small trees; the sun slowly dipping below the western horizon cast shady shadows over the fields of wild flowers planted so many years ago by families, friends and supporters of those determined Peace Women.

Turning to look back at a sight they might never see again. Janet dug deep into the saddle-bag draped across her shoulder and momentarily lingered in the long grass and wild flowers.

Dee shouted. "What's the problem, Jan? Are you okay?"

"Nothing. I want to drop something off for Daphne and this is the right time and place to do it. Remember, I spotted it in the clematis hedge on the patio fencing at your place in Spain," Jan explained. "It was during our first visit We had just finished enjoying supper on the terrace and after a bottle or two of good local wine, we mulled over Daphne's unexpected secret and were astonished at the outcome. The brew seemed to go to my head and needing to clear it I went walkabout in the garden and there it was; I have kept it ever since."

"What for?" Dee asked.

"The right moment to return it to its owner. Come over here and I'll show you."

Launching a small crumpled purple, green and white knitted doll, the fading colours representing women's suffrage, she reminded them.

"On that glorious day years ago, fifty thousand peace women circled the air base in protest against nuclear weapons; thousands of these little dolls were handed out and later attached to the perimeter fence. The MOD attempted but failed to remove all of them and I suspect many disappeared when the fencing was pulled down and the site demolished. Your Aunt was there, Angela, in all her eccentric glory and if she was here today she would do the same. All things considered that day was the beginning and eventually the end of the cruise missiles in the UK and I want her to have it back,"

"And you've kept it all this time, Jan, when you could have come here and laid it to rest, anytime. Why so long?"

"It kept my own memories of her warm, her shining spirit alive and still reminds me of the fun and laughter we shared in the Lugworth years ago. This maybe our final visit to Greenham and what better place to lay down shared memories; here the sense of sisterhood is all around us. You can feel it in the heath land, the fields of wildflowers, the memorials and in the everlasting history of women. More than ever, in the hearts and minds of the women at the wire who stood firm in the name of peace, their sons, daughters and grandchildren."

After what seemed an overly long silence, Janet walked into the long grass, tossed the little woolly doll as far as possible into the air it landed amongst the wildflowers. Turning to face her chums she quietly said.

"Job done girls, it's time to move. Who's driving us back to the hotel? After today, we all need a large ones."

Dee took the wheel for the drive back to Farnborough. Passing the Ship Inn, Angela suggested a quick one.

"Daddy used to drink here. It was his favourite watering hole on the way back from the Military Academy at Sandhurst; when he got home his usual excuse was always – 'It's been a piddle of a day and I needed to wind down'.

Daddy liked the old pub; it had a picture on the wall of a famous bare-knuckle boxing match in the late eighteen hundreds which started outside the pub and ended up over the border in Surrey. Mr Ford was the landlord; he had an old collie dog called Bosun pottering about the place and if it was early evening Jack, the superintendent from the cemetery dropped in and three of them would put the world to rights over pint or two. Mummy always thought it was his wish to be buried as near as possible to the Ship Inn and he is."

After a few drinks, Dee excluded, Angie and Janet giggled their way back to the Queens Hotel for an early dinner. To the surprise of her friends and after some discussion, Angie suggested.

"Why not move on from here tomorrow and head up the M4 to Lugworth while we still can?"

Dee was astonished at the suggestion. "What! A farewell trip to Lugworth? Good God. What next, a wet weekend in Borth? Have you been encouraging her to do this, Jan, and if so what about flights home, the cats and my feature deadline?"

"Well, I think it's up to Angie. If she wants final closure on the past, we must support her. For her there is still much to erase, perhaps us, too. Let's give it a go, it could be fun spotting old faces in the Luggie Arms, but about the arrangements."

Encouraged by the sudden change plan Angie explained.

"Look you two, it's no problem changing flights or booking a good hotel. We can ask reception to rearrange things and find us accommodation near to Lugworth. Our flights are open ended and we can telephone Iberia Airlines and book return flights from Cardiff International and leave the hire car to be up picked there. I will cover all the cost; after all we have had a memorable time and ending up in Lugworth could be the icing on a very enjoyable cake."

Transferring arrangements was easy. Rooms had been booked at a luxury Country House Hotel and Spa near Builth Wells, about an hour or so's gentle drive through the upper Wye Valley to Lugworth. Over dinner that night they made plans for a last drive and lunch in Brecon.

Jan laughed. "That means another nostalgic moment for you, Dee"

"Why?"

"Apart from your old apartment near the river, what about the doctors daughter from Cardiff, wasn't she a regular visitor on cold winter nights?"

"Yes she was. So!"

"So indeed. Didn't she work at the Welsh Office and tip you off, if that's the right word about the Nuclear Defence Exercise well in advance?"

"You mean bloody 'Fallout'," Angie said. "Gosh you knew before Anthony did. Wow you kept that secret, even from you, Jan. How did you get the information?"

"Don't ask," Dee said. Just remember the fun games we had."

"Maybe for you and Janet, but he and that idiot MP Crispin, drove me mad for days and days over Aunt Daphne on the peace march."

Dee chuckled. "Well someone had to start the ball rolling otherwise it would have been cut and dried with any loose ends tied up tight by Anthony and his band of useless officers at the first meeting."

Jan laughed with her. "And we know what happened then, Dee. It all kicked off when Bill Jones went to the gents. When Crispin showed up after a few gin and tonics in his usual pathetic state, all hell let loose in the Council Chamber."

"And what happened next? Angie asked. "Was Anthony up on his usual high horse?"

"At the gallop with the Tremlett saddled up behind him. He would have lost it but for Ruth calming him down. It's no wonder he called the defence exercise Operation Fall Out, it almost came apart before it started. There's book in there somewhere if I ever get time to write it."

Dee teased her. "Why not? It's something you enjoy and it will to keep you up to scratch in your dotage, old girl. You need to think Mary Wesley for creative stamina; she started writing at seventy and during the last twenty years of her life she wrote ten best-selling novels. She was born not far from here at Englefield Green.

"Come on, Dee. Don't tease her. Angie confidently suggested. "She still has time. In fact all the time and space she needs back home in Villafranca, even if we have to lock her away with her laptop and a bottle or two. Now who's for another night cap before we go up, it's early breakfast in the morning then we hit the M4 and head for Wales."

After a brief stopover for lunch at Membury Services, it was agreed Dee would take over the driving. More familiar with the route, she suggested the old Severn Crossing and the scenic drive through the Wye Valley to Monmouth. From there she headed for Mid Wales and then Builth.

In the distance, the red and orange sky gave notice that Borth was in for another brilliant sunset and a bright weather forecast for the following day. Next morning after a comfortable night and a relaxing breakfast they discussed their next move. Spreading the travel arrangements across the table Angela said.

"Our options are open until our flight leaves at 15.30 on Monday, check-in is about an hour before. Our original plan, lunch in Brecon and on to Lugworth for the memory tour; depends on how it goes from there. ."

"Sounds good to us, Angie, I'm keen to see St. David's Hall." Jan suggested.

"And I'm keen to see the Millennium Stadium if we can fit it in." Dee added.

"If that's what you two want, fine. You can park me in the biggest and best department store and leave me to shop 'til I drop; to hell with the luggage allowance. Are you ready to hit the road again, Dee."

For the next mile or two Janet stayed quiet; it was as if she was reminded of some event or other from way back. Laughing at her own thoughts she mused.

"I bet you two didn't know that during WW2 the vicars from churches along the Welsh border, were told to immediately report any unusual military activity in their parishes to the war office,"

"Bit like spies I suppose and not a bad idea in the circumstances," Dee suggested.

"After all, the clergy are good at local gossip and well aware of the goings and comings in the parish. But why, nothing much happened in mid Wales during the war, did it, Jan?"

"I don't know a lot about it really except that according to some war records I turned up, when the Americans eventually came on board they were billeted around here to await orders to move to the South Coast for the final push into Europe. It was reported that German agents were landed on the Welsh coast to report back troop movements to the generals back home."

"Blimey. Never heard that one, Jan. What happened next?" Dee asked.

"It all went pear-shaped when a local vicar invited the Yanks to church on Easter Sunday morning. Thinking it could be their last, the Commanding Officer ordered his troops to turn out for hymns and prayers leaving little room for the regular worshipers. Gossip and rumour gave the game away, the military commanders withdrew the troops and it was all over bar the shouting."

"Well no surprise there. We can only thank the good Lord that Anthony wasn't in control. It would have been a bigger cock up than the Lugworth exercise."

The weary travellers arrived in Lugworth during the afternoon. Turning left into the hotel car park Dee parked up between an elderly white mini bus and a stone wall. Getting out of the car Dee looked around her and said.

"Is that Mr Morgan's old mini bus, surely not? It should have been pensioned off by now."

"I would have thought so," Angie replied with a smile. Perhaps he's waiting for us inside."

"I doubt it" Jan replied." I expect his son uses it to ferry his six kids around.

Dee nodded. "We will soon see for ourselves if we ever get inside. I need refreshment to cope with all this nostalgia."

With legs stiff from the long journey they eased their way to the rear entrance. Pausing on the top step, Angie gasped and declared. "I don't believe it. I don't bloody believe it. I'm sure that's Anthony's precious classic car just inside the old garage."

An unbelieving Dee trotted across the cobbled yard to inspect it. Touching the polished paintwork she quickly responded. "I very much doubt it, Angela, it's in really good nick but not taxed."

"Of course it isn't taxed, classic cars are exempt from road tax. Be that as it may, Anthony always kept the paintwork as clean as a whistle, Dee, as well you know. It was his pride and joy and he loved it more than me. If it's British Racing Green and has a personal number plate ANT 100, which, by the way, cost him a small fortune, it most definitely is the prized Armstrong Siddeley and he vowed never to part with it."

"Then why is it parked up in Lugworth when he is supposed to be in a posh retirement village somewhere in Florida with the missus?" Jan questioned.

"Good question, Janet. I suspect the answer lies in the lounge bar. Shall we go in?"

Chapter Eighteen

No longer the Trust House Inn of old, the Lugworth Arms was currently owned by a chain of respected Welsh hostelries catering mainly for bargain break holidaymakers and casual tourists. Well used and supported by the local community and despite the passing years, the five hundred year old, black and white Elizabethan exterior had weathered gracefully. Inside, it was much the same; the wood panelled walls, oak beams, high ceilings and wide wooden staircases rising to the upper floors had escaped the fashion for modernisation. Since merging with the Offa Hotels Group, the main lounge had been extended into a large traditional conservatory with patio access for family dining. In the gardens at the rear of the main building, stone built, open plan chalets await the bargain break weekenders from the West Midlands. The comfortable snug bar, set aside for the locals, faithfully recorded Lugworth's social and community history. Framed photographs from the past times cluttered the walls and precariously fixed to the oak beam above the inglenook fire place, a collection of aging newspaper headlines and photograph's framed under yellow stained glass lightly covered in dust, highlighted the town's more bizarre and for some, remarkable twentieth century 'nuclear' disaster. When the unexpected arrivals strolled into the main lounge bar, it was more a stranger's gallery than the once popular watering hole of days gone by. Insisting local customers generally preferred the snug across the hall, the porter led the way. It too had been extended by converting an adjacent games room to create more space needed to meet the new non-smoking regulations. . It was now more a clubroom separating the bargain-breakers from the old Lugworthians.

Directed to an empty table in the far corner the three women sort out a familiar face or two. There were a good many but older now. The usual regulars were at the cribbage table and propping up the bar the elders of Lugworth's farming community were heatedly discussing the rising price of beef and lamb at last week's cattle sales at Penybont.

"No change here then, same weathered faces, same old bar chat, same old card table and same old pictures on the walls. Bit creepy," Dee hinted. "If we are staying overnight, I could do with a drink."

"I'll get the round in, Dee" Angela offered. "You're off the hook for driving. Jan will drive us to Cardiff later. I'm undecided at the moment. Seeing Anthony's car has left me feeling uneasy. Let's see what happens and leave it at that. Usual malt for you Dee. What about you Jan?"

"I might be driving later so its tomato juice for me please."

"Good one, old girl. I'll have Chivas if they have it, Ange. Nuts or crisps anyone?"

An hour later the clatter of spiked boots announced the arrival of a mixed group of cricketers neatly turned out for a special game. Today Club President of Lugworth CC, former club captain Sir Tim Taplow, Member of Parliament for the Mid-Border Constituency had arranged to umpire a charity match to raise funds for the family of former 'demon' bowler Rick Richards.

Rick suffered a fatal heart attack on the pitch when delivering the last over of the day against bitter rivals Arrowtown. The match, watched by his wife and five children was abandoned and the shocked town persuaded Sir Tim to organise a sponsored celebrity fund raising match. Out of respect for their former adversary, three Barratt boys agreed to play and so far £5000 had been raised to cover outstanding funeral expenses.

Collecting box in hand, Sir Tim wandered through the room urging donations for the Rick Richard fund. Unexpectedly confronted by Angela, he adjusted his designer spectacles and closed in on her.

"Good heavens, it can't be the first Mrs Anderson-Shelta, as lovely as ever, too. What are you doing in this part of the woods?"

"Not expecting to see you." Looking him up and down she nudged Jan. "He seems to have developed a middle-aged paunch since entering the House; must be all the "freebie" lunches and dinners you are invited to!"

Dee laughed when Janet suggested, "You were always so fit when you captained the cricket team what went wrong?"

"Rushed into marriage, a condition required if I wanted to take over poor old Crispin's patch. I wasn't quite ready for domestic life but needs must and found myself proposing to Rhoda Gilligan-Forbes an old flame. She was Head Girl at Roedean and I was at Eaton where she was nicknamed Rodeo because we all tried to ride her but always managed to slipped off before we got stated. Anyway she was up for marriage and as it turned out she is a very good wife and mother to our four lovely children. "

"Good for you, Tim. Now and again I pick up on your political career on the BBC World Service and sometimes the Guardian if you have made a mess of something. What you are doing for Rick's family is great, he was quite a character at times and a good all round cricketer. I only wish I could umpire with you."

"Come and umpire a session this afternoon, his eldest son, Ricky junior will be following in his father's footsteps and tossing down few overs. Why don't the three of you come, all the locals will be there and will be really pleased to see you all again."

Meanwhile Angela was scrabbling around for her chequebook. "We might do that. We are flying back to Spain tomorrow evening and have reserved rooms at the airport hotel for tonight. It will be great fun seeing everyone again and then drive to Cardiff later on. It will be a happy end to a good week. Meanwhile, add this to Rick's fund."

Seeing the sum of £2500 Tim asked. "Are you sure about this, Angela, it's a lot of money?"

"I've got a lot of money so why not help a worthy Lugworth family. Play your cards right and Jan and Dee between them might double it."

"No sooner said than done," Jan said as she passed on another £2500. Now find me a white coat, a straw hat and Angela will bring on the drinks and Dee can take the photograph."

"Not before I announce your generous donations."

"No need for that, Tim, but if you must perhaps this is the right time."

Reading from the hand written note Angela had passed to him Tim announced. "Ladies and Gentlemen the three women seated beside me have generously donated a cheque for £5000 to the Rick Richard Fund. More known for their exploits at Greenham Common and I might add the calamitous Fall Out in the early 1980s they would like to promote and sponsor an Annual Single Wicket competition for men and women cricketers playing within the Mid Border Cricket League. Rules to be set by a committee of former Lugworth and Arrowtown players, matches played alternatively between the townships and for goodwill, the now respectable Barratt Boys (laughter) to see fair play. Monies raised will be added to the Rick Richards fund and the winning club will receive The Daphne Oxford Silver Plate suitably engraved to keep for one year, the best player will be presented with a small replica. If it can be agreed, the Member of Parliament will take on the Presidency whatever the party of Government."

The earlier trickle of applause broke into cheers of joy; the Richards family broke down in tears.

Swept up by the emotional atmosphere in the clubroom, customers and visitors from the main lounges eagerly donated cash into passing buckets. Fazed by the unexpected announcement Jan, Dee and Tim Taplow waited for the room to calm down.

"Where did that come from, Angie. It's a great idea."

"Well it wasn't out of the blue. I have been thinking for a way to commemorate Daphne's extraordinary life for some time. I know we planted trees and shrubs in the wild flower fields at Greenham, but for me and perhaps for us I wanted a more personal reminder of something she truly loved and enjoyed."

In unison they agreed, "Cricket."

"Yes cricket," Angela said. "Whether or not she was playing, umpiring, watching or on tea duty she lived, loved and I believe prepared to die for fair play in a game. I can see her now, sitting in her garden listening to Test Match Special and wearing her prized Combined Women's' Services pullover and matching pull on wide brimmed hat. I do so miss her.

"But why this, Angie," Tim quietly asked. "It's a lovely idea."

"And she would have approved of it, too," Jan said.

"Of course she would. Anyway Lords or The Oval was out of the question although she spent a fortune on test match seats. Anyway she always said she had more pleasure watching Lugworth on the village green. She paid for her own bench on the pavilion veranda and for repairs when needed. She always wanted to ride the heavy roller but health and safety said not on your life."

"Well, Jan, if you are umpiring this afternoon best be on our way; that's if you are still keen." Tim asked.

"Keener than ever old boy, now where are my specs otherwise I shan't have clue about LBW decisions. It's been a long time since I stood at the wicket."

The match was a huge success, Janet played umpire until tea when Mr. Morgan was due to take over. Angie and Dee joined them for Mrs Morgan's traditional cricket tea in the pavilion and for the regulation thirty-five minutes they chatted as if they had never been away.

"It's so good to see you all again, it really is. Life in Lugworth has been so much quieter since the nuclear mess up. It will never be the same again. Even the Barratt boys say that; they have all settled down with families to take care of but manage to have a drink or two on the anniversary of the event."

"Back in Spain we usually do the same, after all despite everything that has happened in-between, good and sad we shared so much fun."

Just as the bell went for start of the final session Mrs Morgan interrupted.

"Best tell them about the posh car in the back garage. They must have seen it when they were parking."

Mr Morgan lowered his aging eyes. "Not now, mother, it might be a little upsetting for Mrs Anderson-Shelta, what with the divorce and that."

Angela reminded him. "That was a long time ago, Mr Morgan, and best forgotten. These days I'm Angela Plunkett-Brown and happy to be so. Now what's this about Anthony's classic car; surely it was shipped to Florida when he remarried?"

Ma Morgan proudly answered for him. "No Missus. He trusted my husband, like he always did, to keep it ticking over until 'err finally conked out."

"And it's running well, Mr. Morgan? "

"Smooth as ever. We take the family to classic car shows and send him photos. Hope you don't mind?"

"Not at all. I'm so pleased he passed it on to you. After all he refused to trust anyone else when it came to servicing his beloved old Armstrong. Sweet as a nut he always muttered after you had tuned it up."

"He had tears in his eyes when he handed me the keys and the paper work. So did we when he told us it was worth rather a lot of money and that I should accept it as a well-earned pension, not a gift."

Turning to her friends Angela said. "Well, who would have thought it? He did the right thing for once."

"He knew it would always have a good home with the Morgans," Dee said and patted him on the back.

The match turned out to be a draw and after celebrating with champagne and a promise that they may come back next year for the return match the Greenham Three were given a rousing send off from the Lugworth Arms.

Emotions were on a knife edge as they headed for Cardiff airport. Thanks to the Green Park Memorial site the past few days had become an unexpected and memorable never to be forgotten trip. Angie, Jan and

Dee remained very quiet for most of the journey home each keeping a few feelings to themselves.

Flying over the channel they relaxed, ordered a few drinks and toasted the peace Greenham Women fought so hard for.

As ever Dee broke the mood. "We need to toast another great step forward. After more than twenty years, we have discovered in one short day that the Barratt boys are no longer at war and playing happy families, for the very first time in his non-political life Anthony became Mr Nice Guy, the cricket match against rivals Arrowtown ended in a gentlemanly draw and the Lugworth Arms is still standing. Whatever happened to falling out! Cheers."

THE END